The Amish Mother's Secret

Amish Adoption Series

Book 1

DIANE CRAVER

Vinspire Publishing, LLC
www.VinspirePublishing.com

For my amazing children, Sara, Christina, April,
Bartholomew, Emily, and Amanda

He heals the brokenhearted and binds up their wounds.
(Psalm 147:3, NIV)

I can do all things through Christ which strengtheneth me.
(Philippians 4:13, NIV)

Pennsylvania Dutch Glossary

ach	oh
aenti	aunt
appeditlich	delicious
boppli	baby
bruder	brother
The Budget	a weekly newspaper serving Amish and Mennonite communities everywhere
daadi	grandfather
daed	dad
danki	thank you
ehemann	husband
English, Englisher	non-Amish
fraa	wife
froh	happy
gut	good
gut nacht	good night
kaffi	coffee
kapp	prayer covering or cap
kind, kinner	child, children
mamm	mom
mammi	grandmother
nee	no
Ordnung	the set of rules by which the Amish live
Pennsylvania Deutsch	The language most commonly used by the Amish. Although widely known as Pennsylvania Dutch, the language is actually a form of German (Deutsch).
Plain	the Amish way of life
rumspringa	running-around time and is before an Amish young person officially joins the church
schee	pretty
schweschder	sister
wunderbaar	wonderful
ya	yes

Prologue

Columbus, Ohio

Lindsay enjoyed watching Phoebe get a group picture with her high school friends. They just received their diplomas, so they now had the proud honor of being called graduates. Huge smiles were pasted on their faces as they posed. Lindsay wanted to get a photo with her daughter while she still had her white graduation robe on, but it looked like it would take several minutes for the photos to be taken. Phoebe looked beautiful with her big, brown eyes and long, black hair. Lindsay briefly reflected on how her daughter resembled Harris, Phoebe's father, a great deal.

When some of the graduates were taking pictures with their relatives, her friend Roberta Sterling invited her and Phoebe to join her family for a photo. That wasn't a surprise since Roberta's daughter, Haley, had been Phoebe's best friend since grade school. Lindsay and Phoebe had been invited throughout the years to their house for holidays and birthdays. Even though Roberta had invited them to their graduation party, Lindsay would've enjoyed going to dinner alone with Phoebe to celebrate. Of course, she knew it would be more fun to join Haley's exuberant family.

For the photo, Phoebe put her arm around her shoulders. From the corner of her eye, Lindsay saw her friend Roberta, an attractive woman with auburn hair, touch her daughter's arm. "You did an outstanding job on your valedictory speech. You made me feel so many emotions. I laughed, and I cried."

"Thank you. Mom helped me write it."

"I only helped you a little, and your delivery was awesome." Lindsay smiled at her daughter.

"Nicholas, get over here for our picture before we all blow away!" Roberta smoothed her hair into place. "It's a beautiful day except for the wind."

A good-looking boy left his group of friends to join them. "Sorry, I thought we were done with pictures."

Haley rolled her eyes at her brother. "I think you enjoy making us wait on you."

Nicholas grinned. He had blond hair like Haley and their dad. The other two Sterling boys had auburn hair like their mom. "Not true, but I appreciate you waiting on me."

Several minutes later, Lindsay and Phoebe were in the car waiting for several vehicles in the line ahead of them to leave the parking lot. She noticed Phoebe seemed subdued. "Are you feeling okay?"

Phoebe frowned. "I'm a little sad. Kari reminded me I don't have a dad and that I don't have anyone except you. She said I go to Haley's house all the time but they aren't my family."

"Honey, Kari's probably jealous you were valedictorian and wanted to take a jab at you." The competition had been fierce between the girls, and Kari had gotten second place.

Her brown eyes widened. "Mom, most of the time it's been great being an only child, but it's weird for me to not have a father or any living relatives. I enjoy spending time with the Sterling family, but it'd be nice to have others in our life."

"I understand how you feel. I was an only child as well."

"If Dad hadn't died before I was born, I might have had a younger sibling. Kari's not the only one who's made comments to me about not having a dad." Phoebe sighed. "I wish Dad had been in the audience to hear my speech today."

"I'm sorry he wasn't." Lindsay's heart thudded at Phoebe's mention of her father. She'd kept a secret from Phoebe. Paul Prescott wasn't her father. He knew she was pregnant with another man's baby but had still married her. Lindsay wished with her whole heart that he hadn't died in an automobile accident.

"I don't even have grandparents."

It wasn't any great loss to Lindsay that her mother had died. She hadn't been there for her for years. After Lindsay's beloved father passed away, her mother hadn't been the same. She had turned to alcohol to cope. Paul's parents knew their son wasn't Phoebe's father. They'd refused to accept her and considered Lindsay to be lower class. She'd hoped their attitude would change so Phoebe could have grandparents, but it never did. They had passed away when Phoebe was a young child.

She hated to see Phoebe sad and wanted to cheer her up. "If you want to stay on campus instead of living at home, that's fine. Your scholarship covers your tuition for all four years. I can pay for your room and board."

Phoebe grinned at her. "Hey, are you trying to kick me out of the house? Ohio State is, like, ten minutes away from us. It'd be silly to pay for a dorm room."

"I wasn't trying to kick you out, but if you decide later you want to live on campus, I'll understand."

Phoebe squeezed her hand. "There are many students commuting to OSU. I look forward to staying at home. I love you, and really, it's okay that I'm an only child. It means I don't have to share you with a brother or a sister." She laughed. "And Haley's brothers treat me like a sister, anyway."

Phoebe was not, in fact, an only child. Lindsay couldn't tell her she had been born with two sisters. Why had she ever promised to keep the adoption a secret? It seemed like the right thing to do when she'd given Phoebe's sisters, Amy and Jenna, to Katie and Roman to adopt. Family was so important to the Amish, and Katie yearned to have children. As a teenager, Lindsay couldn't raise triplets without support from anyone. Seeing her triplets graduate together today would have been wonderful, but it wasn't meant to be.

She smiled at her daughter. "The traffic is disappearing. Let's get to the party and start celebrating."

"I'm hungry. I couldn't eat a lot at breakfast. I was nervous about giving the speech." Phoebe giggled. "Kari should be glad she got to go first. I had to wait forever to give my speech."

As Lindsay pulled out of the parking lot, she decided to tease her daughter. "I'm sure you won't have to do a speech at Ohio State. I mean there are *thousands* of students in each class."

"Haley's in the other lane." Phoebe raised her hand and waved. "That's good you're not expecting me to be valedictorian again. That means I can slack off at college. I'll just need to keep my grades up enough to keep my scholarship."

"Very funny. I can't see you slacking off. Besides, I was kidding you."

A serious expression took over Phoebe's face. "Let's go do something together before we go to the party."

Lindsay stopped at the traffic light and turned to stare at Phoebe. "I'd love to. What do you have in mind?"

"I'm hungry for pancakes. We missed getting our pancakes this morning. I'll text Haley and tell her we'll be a little late."

Getting pancakes and bacon was something they did together on Saturday mornings. Happiness flooded her heart at getting to enjoy time with her sweet Phoebe before attending Haley's party.

Shipshewana, Indiana

"The breeze feels *gut*," Katie Yoder said. She loved having the windows open in their farmhouse. Her mother, Naomi Gingerich, and sister, Lizzy, came to her house to visit. Her niece, Jane, was fast asleep on Lizzy's lap. When her sister and brother-in-law adopted one-year-old Jane, they'd already been blessed with four *kinner*. It'd been a big surprise. No one had expected them to adopt. Everyone adored Jane, and she was such a blessing to the family. "Would you like another piece of cake, *Mamm*?"

"*Nee, danki*. It was *appeditlich*," Naomi Gingerich smiled. "I want to save some for Seth. I know how much he loves cake."

"*Ya*, he does. He really can put away the food." Katie laughed and sipped her coffee. "He reminds me all the time that he's still a growing boy."

Naomi nodded. "He does have a healthy appetite."

"Did you want me to put Jane in the crib?" Katie asked. Lizzie's oak chair was shoved away from the table, so she couldn't finish her coffee.

"*Nee*, I love holding her." Lizzie pushed her glasses up her nose. "It's nice having this time with Jane while the other *kinner* are in school. Jenna's such a *gut* teacher."

Katie nodded. "She loves teaching."

"I remember you said Lindsay became a teacher. That's something Jenna has in common with her birth mother."

Why was her sister on this topic again? Ever since Lizzie adopted Jane, she'd urged her and Roman to tell their daughters they were adopted. She wished Lizzie would drop the topic. "I know what you're going to say next, and I don't want to tell Amy and Jenna about Lindsay. God blessed us with them." A lump formed in her throat. "I'm their mother, and it'll confuse them to know about Lindsay."

Naomi reached her hand across the table to squeeze Katie's hand. "*Ya*, you're their mother and always will be, but they are eighteen now and can handle learning the truth. Lizzie's right. You should tell them."

"Lindsay agreed to keep our secret. I'm sure she means to keep it from Phoebe too." Katie stared into her cup and thought about how adopting the girls brought meaning to her life. For years, she watched her younger siblings have *kinner* while she remained barren. Then a miracle happened, and she became a mother to Amy and Jenna. A short time later, she became pregnant with Seth.

"We're going to tell Jane she's adopted."

"I'm sure she'll figure it out anyhow. Jane will realize at some point she looks different from us." Jane was an adorable Asian baby. Katie drew a deep breath. "Phoebe hasn't been around to see her sisters, so I know Lindsay hasn't told her the truth."

Lizzie leaned down and brushed a kiss on Jane's forehead. "Even if she weren't Asian, I'd still tell her the truth. You should pray about it."

Naomi traced the rim of her cup with her finger and looked at Katie. "I wonder how Lindsay is these days. She did a wonderful thing giving her babies to you and Roman, but it broke her heart. I think you should contact her and see how she feels about revealing the truth to the triplets. It'll be a shock, but I think all three of them can handle knowing the truth."

I can't call. What if Lindsay agrees with them? I've been a good Amish mother, but what if Amy and Jenna come to love Lindsay more and want to live with her in her secular world? I can't risk that happening.

A mixture of guilt and determination filled Katie's heart. She hated being at odds with her family, but her *mamm* and *schweschder* were wrong. Amy and Jenna must never know about Lindsay and Phoebe.

Chapter One

Four Years Later, Columbus, Ohio

Lindsay Prescott sat in her hospital bed, knowing she couldn't keep the truth from her daughter Phoebe any longer. Guilt and anxiety filled her soul as she remembered what she'd done twenty-two years ago. As a single mother without the means to make enough money to support her family, she had to make a hard choice. Giving away her daughters broke her heart, but keeping Phoebe had helped ease the pain throughout the years. Lindsay felt sick to her stomach at the thought of revealing the truth to Phoebe. Would her daughter understand how impossible it would have been to have kept Jenna and Amy?

Maybe this was why cancer had invaded her body. God wanted her to finally confess what she'd done. She'd promised to never see her beautiful daughters again, but her situation was different now. She needed to see them before she died. It was the right time for Phoebe to know the truth. Lindsay didn't want Phoebe to be alone when she was gone.

But where are Amy and Jenna now?

Lindsay looked at the envelope sitting on top of her blanket. Before going to the treatment center, Phoebe had grabbed the mail. Her daughter must've only glanced at the top one because she surely would have questioned a returned letter from Indiana. When Lindsay gave her daughters to Roman and Katie Yoder, they were living in Shipshewana, a lovely town where many Amish lived. It seemed unlikely that they'd moved from their white clapboard farmhouse situated among beautiful, rolling hills.

When Katie had made her promise to never contact Amy and Jenna, Lindsay had requested to receive a letter each year on their birthday. She was sad Katie had only agreed to send her an annual letter during the girls' childhood. Once they had graduated from eighth grade at the age of fourteen, there were no additional letters from Katie. Fingering the envelope, Lindsay remembered reading in the last letter in which Katie said her obligation was finished. Although Lindsay appreciated the letters, she wished they could have continued exchanging correspondence. At age twenty-two, Amy and Jenna could be married now. They may have even given birth to their own children. Amish women were sometimes married in their early twenties or younger.

Tears fell onto the envelope as Lindsay thought about how much she had missed by giving her children away. If Harris had known she was pregnant, would he have married her? Well, as a single mother, she'd done the best she could and never regretted for a minute that she'd kept one of her daughters.

Lindsay used her sleeve to wipe her face. After being in the ER room for hours, she'd been admitted to a hospital room earlier in the afternoon. Her first chemo treatment hadn't gone well. Phoebe had been with her during the IV infusion when many things went wrong. With sudden chest pains, low blood pressure, and low hemoglobin, Lindsay was put on oxygen. When it was decided she needed to go to the ER, a nurse pushed Lindsay in a wheelchair quickly to the hospital wing.

Rachel, the same nurse from the ER, stood next to Lindsay's bed. "I'm sorry we don't have the blood for your transfusion yet. It takes time to get blood with the type of antibodies your body needs, but I know you'll feel better after you get it."

Lindsay saw the concern in Rachel's eyes and appreciated having the kind nurse taking care of her. "I'm okay. I'm surprised a letter I sent to friends was returned to me today. I can't believe they moved."

"When I moved, the post office forwarded my mail for six months."

She nodded, noticing Rachel looking at the envelope. "It's been some time since I wrote to them. I wish they had sent me their new address."

"I see they lived where a lot of the Amish are located. Shipshewana is a lovely place. I visited there with my grandmother, and we stayed at a place called Blue Gate Inn. We wanted to go for a buggy ride, but it rained the whole time we were there. They canceled the rides."

"That's too bad. I went for a ride and enjoyed the gentle sway of the buggy. The rhythm of the horse's hooves against the pavement was soothing."

While Rachel took Lindsay's vitals, she said, "I hope you can learn your friends' new address."

"I do too," Lindsay murmured, feeling relief at the sight of her daughter returning to her room. Thank goodness she wouldn't have to continue talking about Katie. Saying she was a friend had been stretching the truth. Well, she once been a wonderful friend, but she was not close enough to share her new address.

"I called Vickie and Michelle," Phoebe said. "They're praying for you."

"Thank you."

"Would you like me to contact Drew too?" Phoebe winked at her.

She laughed. "No. There isn't any reason to tell him anything."

Phoebe tapped her finger against her bed. "Really? I think you should tell him you're in the hospital."

"Stop. We only went out a few times. Besides, he's in Germany for his job." Drew Morrow was their widowed next-door neighbor. Phoebe was such a tease and often liked to throw his name out in conversation. Drew was nice, but it'd been hard to go out the few times they had because he traveled for his job. Plus, he had an eight-year-old son, Matthew.

After quietly recording Lindsay's blood pressure and other measurements, Rachel walked over to Lindsay's IV and looked at the fluid level. Her movements were quick and competent.

"Do you think I'll be discharged tomorrow?" Lindsay asked, squeezing the blanket with her fingers. If she were still able to receive her transfusion this evening, she should be able to leave.

"It's up to the doctor, but I think it's possible. I'll go see if the blood is on the way here."

After Rachel left her room, Phoebe glanced at the envelope. "Who are Katie and Roman Yoder?"

Her stomach tightened at Phoebe's question. *Should she blurt out the truth now? No, it isn't the right time to explain everything. It would be better to wait until they were no longer in the hospital.* "I knew them a long time ago."

Phoebe laughed. "It *must* have been a long time ago because I've never heard you mention them. Were you close in the old days?"

"We spent time together."

"Were they Dad's friends too?" Phoebe tossed the envelope on the bed and pulled a chair close to her bed.

"No. He never knew them." *Well, that was the truth.* Her husband, Paul, had died in a car accident before the triplets were born. He'd only been her spouse for a month. Once he knew about the pregnancy, Paul wanted to marry her. Her high school boyfriend had been there for her. Harris never gave her a chance to tell him about the pregnancy before he dumped her. In spite of a broken heart, she'd married Paul. It wasn't fair for him to have been burdened with her pregnancy, because in the end, he'd died at the young age of eighteen.

"Good news, ladies. I have the blood." Rachel rushed into the room.

"That's wonderful." She watched the nurse hang the bag on the IV pole next to her bed. Meanwhile, Lindsay was relieved Rachel's appearance had interrupted Phoebe's questions.

Phoebe ran her fingers through her black hair. "I can stay here with you tonight. I don't have to go home."

Lindsay saw the dark circles under her daughter's brown eyes. "I'll be fine. It's been a long day for both of us. You should go home. I love you."

"Okay, I'll leave so you can rest. I'll be back early tomorrow morning. I love you too."

In the quiet hospital room, Lindsay closed her eyes, wishing she hadn't dismissed her cancer symptoms two years earlier. She'd had severe abdominal pain, night sweats, and bloating. Touching her stomach, she groaned at the memory. Each time she had become ill, CT scans at the ER had shown an enlarged spleen. She'd gotten an appointment to see a GI physician. The doctor had thought she had liver cancer, but she didn't. Then a referral was made to see an oncologist. According to her blood work, there was no cancer.

Recently, her night sweats had started becoming worse, and a loss of weight occurred. Lindsay thought she was going through early menopause. What was the point in seeing either the GI doctor or oncologist again when nothing had been accomplished?

As she rubbed her collarbone, Lindsay felt the lumps that had scared Phoebe. "They're cysts. Nothing to worry about," she'd told her daughter. "Besides, I have a lot to do at school."

"Geez, Mom, you need to see your doctor and not worry about your students."

At the continued insistence of Phoebe, she'd finally gone to the doctor to see why she felt so lousy and told her family physician about the other symptoms she'd experienced. He feared lymphoma cancer. After the CT scan showed enlarged lymph nodes in the abdomen, spleen, armpits, shoulder, and collarbone, a biopsy was ordered to confirm cancer. It was devastating to hear she was in stage four of lymphoma cancer. Once again, she'd messed up her life by putting off her own health. If she'd gone right away, her chances of sur-vival would have been almost one hundred percent, instead of the sixty-five percent survival rate she was now facing.

She sucked in her breath, realizing Harris needed to learn the truth. A cynical laugh escaped her mouth. Not about her cancer but about their daughters. It would be difficult to face him after all these years, but what else could she do? Once she told Phoebe, she'd summon the courage to tell him. She couldn't imagine he'd be thrilled to learn this secret now.

Harris's love for her hadn't been enough or real. It seemed she'd been a summer fling because he went on to marry Callie. Once Lindsay was out of his sight, Harris decided to forget about her. If only she'd known about her pregnancy before he left. It might have made a difference. Or probably not. She was sure his parents hadn't wanted her as a daughter-in-law when they could have Callie, the perfect woman for their son with an impeccable background. Cal-lie's mother wasn't an alcoholic, and her parents were suc-cessful.

If her dad hadn't died young, she might have grown up in a stable home. Turning to alcohol had been her mom's way of coping after his death. *Why couldn't she have loved me enough to fight her addiction?*

Leaning her head against the pillow, Lindsay felt exhausted. For years, she'd been a strong woman and mother. She hadn't shed a tear when the biopsy confirmed she had lymphoma cancer. Knowing what had caused her many symptoms and lumps had been a relief. Her hand flew to her abdomen remembering the horrible physical pain.

Today, a different kind of pain was suffocating her whole soul. Without being able to tolerate her first chemo treatment, she realized she could die. She must confess the adoption to her precious daughter.

If she got to go home tomorrow, she'd tell Phoebe everything. It would be difficult to explain how she had no choice in the decision that was made years ago. Hopefully, her daughter would eventually understand and still love her. *I will hate seeing the hurt in Phoebe's eyes that I kept this secret from her, but it has to be done.*

Once she found Amy and Jenna, they would want to know who their birth father was. She'd have to tell them how Harris never knew about them. The secret of the adoption was one thing, but revealing Harris to them and the truth to him would affect all of them. She pressed her hand against her chest, feeling the heaviness. Then the pain moved throughout her whole body. What had she done by keeping her daughters and Harris in the dark for years?

She'd soon find out because the search for Amy and Jenna needed to start soon. If the Yoder family left Shipshewana, where were they now?

～

Exhausted from the stress of seeing her mom admitted to the hospital, Phoebe tossed her bag beside her on the gray sofa. She exhaled a deep breath. It wasn't just that her mom hadn't tolerated the chemo, but everything had sapped her energy. It seemed like it'd taken too long to have the tests scheduled. Then they had to wait for the biopsy results to confirm whether or not it was cancer. The sadness she'd carried with her all these weeks seemed to multiply. Her mom had looked fragile and pale when she'd left her at the hospital. Why hadn't she gone to the doctor months ago? Now she couldn't even get the first treatment done.

Phoebe's eyes had filled with tears when the oncologist had explained the diagnosis. He'd said, "Non-Hodgkin's lymphoma is treatable, especially in the beginning stages. Even though you're in stage four, Mrs. Prescott, you can beat this disease."

Phoebe wondered if her mom could survive cancer. The trouble with her blood made her a patient at the hospital today. *I don't want to lose her. She's the most important person to me.*

The silence in their house disturbed Phoebe. She missed her mom's presence greatly and hoped she'd be discharged from the hospital tomorrow. Glancing around the living room, she didn't see anything that needed to be done. Since it was an open-concept floor plan, she could see the white cabinets with the black-and-white granite countertop from the sofa. The kitchen had been their last remodeling project. For the backsplash, her mother had chosen a soft gray subway tile, but Phoebe had gotten to pick out the stools for the island. She'd chosen ones with red seats to add a pop of color.

Phoebe turned her head to stare at a picture of them from their beach vacation over a year ago. She picked up the photo to look at it closely. The ocean water in the background looked blue and beautiful. She loved her mother's huge smile in the photo. They'd gone during their spring break. Fortunately, her college break and her mother's school spring break had been the same week. Whenever they went to the beach, it was fun to pack for their road trips. Her mom bought the pop, bottles of water and juice, fruit, and other snacks. Phoebe enjoyed their shopping trips to Kohl's to get some new things to wear on their vacations.

She couldn't believe how different her mom looked now. *On the beach, she was healthy, but now she's so thin. I should've realized something was wrong when she started losing weight.* Loss of weight was a symptom of lymphoma.

At the sound of her ringtone, Phoebe pulled her cell phone out of her bag. Seeing it was her close friend, she answered. "Hi, Haley. I'm glad you called. I'm feeling down."

"Did they get the transfusion started?"

"Yes. I left the hospital after that. Mom told me to go home."

"I'm sorry she didn't get to finish her treatment. I'm sure it'll go better next time."

"This illness has taken a lot out of her. I can't believe how much weight she has lost."

"Your mom is such a great, strong person. In time, she'll be a cancer survivor, and you two can take another beach vacation together," Haley said.

Phoebe and her mom had talked about taking their annual summer beach vacation before the diagnosis, but she wasn't feeling up to it. "I don't think we can. She has several months of chemo ahead. I might not be able to go to medical school this year."

"Don't decide now. Her treatments will go smoother next time."

"I think she cried when I was out of the room. She seems depressed and afraid she won't get better." Phoebe remembered how awful the abdominal pain and spleen attacks had been. Her mom could barely walk to the bathroom. Today, her face showed again how she suffered from pain. *I can't admit out loud to Haley that I want to be with her as much as possible because Mom might die.*

"Maybe you could work fewer hours this summer."

"They might fire me anyhow. I've missed a few shifts recently, and they know I'm not working when I start medical school. Instead of going full-time, I could just take fewer graduate courses. I want to give Mom as much support as I can."

"Lindsay's still young and has always been a fighter." Haley chuckled. "Look how she survived your childhood."

Phoebe laughed. "Hey, you were the troublemaker. I still can't believe we left school early to go to your house."

"It was not fun being grounded. That's for sure."

Before ending their conversation, they talked about other crazy memories from when they were in school. After saying goodbye a few minutes later, Phoebe leaned back against the couch cushion, feeling grateful for Haley's call.

"Lord, thank you that Haley made me laugh. It felt good after spending the day at the hospital. Please help my mom get well and win against this cancer invading her body. She's always been the best mother, and I'm thankful you picked her to be my parent. Bless her doctors daily as they administer to her. Give me the continued strength to take excellent care of Mom when she's home in between treatments. Thank you for all your blessings. In Jesus' name, I pray. Amen."

At ten o'clock, she decided to go to her mother's bedroom to read. She couldn't sleep yet. That was for sure. Her mother's room had light blue walls with a cozy chair next to her bed. Ever since she was a teenager, they'd read the Bible together before going to bed. Lifting the Bible from the nightstand, Phoebe turned quickly to sit. Her elbow hit a glass of water. Horror went through her body as she grabbed the tipped glass. Water seeped into the partially opened drawer. In a hurry, she ran to the bathroom and picked up the hand towel. She wiped up the water, then removed the bottle of hand lotion, small devotional books, and aspirin from the drawer. Wrapping them in the towel, she next lifted the shelf liner, noticing it was only damp. At another glance, she saw a large envelope. It looked like it had escaped water damage.

Confusion entered her mind. *Why is Mom hiding this in the bottom of the drawer?* She freed her hands from the towel to pick up the envelope. Should she open it to see what was in the envelope? Maybe it was a life insurance policy. The other day, her mom had talked about having a policy to use for expenses after her death. If that was it, then the document was a thick one.

I'll take a peek and see what it is. I have to make sure nothing is wet inside. Okay, I'm being nosy. It probably isn't damaged. After lifting the envelope flap, she pulled out letters that were tied loosely with a narrow pink ribbon. Sitting in the chair, she saw each envelope was addressed to Lindsay Prescott, and the sender was Katie Yoder in Shipshewana, Indiana.

Her throat tightened, and Phoebe blinked rapidly to look again at the envelopes. Untying the ribbon, she counted fourteen letters. The postmark on each envelope was the date of her birthday. The bedroom was warm, but a shiver coursed through her. *Why would this Katie person send letters every year on my birthday?*

Rubbing her forehead, Phoebe could not fathom the truth behind these letters, but it definitely had something to do with her. Her heart sank, and her stomach turned over. There was one thing she did realize—the person she'd trusted her whole life had lied to her.

Chapter Two

Millersburg, Ohio

The store was quiet. They hadn't put the Open sign on the front window. Katie Yoder glanced at the wall clock and was glad it wasn't opening time yet. Katie enjoyed these few minutes before opening their general store at eight o'clock because she could be alone with her husband, Roman. Their daughters helped out at the store, but they weren't there yet. Amy would do the bookkeeping and wait on customers when needed. Jenna loved talking with the customers. But lately, she seemed bored with working in their store.

Katie had just finished frosting the warm cinnamon rolls and two coffee cakes. Her freshly baked breakfast items would go fast. The *kaffi* drinkers liked something sweet. Jenna would bake muffins and cookies when she arrived. Customers liked buying groceries and getting a free cup of *kaffi*. Though, there was a blue canning jar by the coffeepot if a customer wanted to donate.

After she poured the coffee into the thermal carafe, Katie turned to watch Roman. As he refilled the display stand with brochures about the various Amish attractions tourists loved to visit, she silently admired his radiant green eyes and dark brown hair highlighted by several strands of gray. Her husband was a handsome man, but more importantly, he was a good Christian man. Their thirty-three years of marriage had been filled with ups and downs, but through it all, she had always been loved by God and Roman.

"Do you ever regret leaving Shipshewana?" A year ago, Roman's relatives wanted to sell their store to them, and they'd accepted.

Roman paused what he was doing and gave her a serious glance. "I know it was hard for you to leave Shipshewana. When my aunt and uncle told me they were retiring, we felt God answered our prayers. I love being a store owner. Our family has settled well into living in Millersburg."

She grinned. "And you get to spend more time with me."

He gave her a broad smile. "That too." He kissed her lightly on the forehead. "Being in the store with you is much better than factory work."

His factory job wasn't the ideal environment for an Amish man. It'd meant being away from home a good part of the day. The high production pressure had created stress for Roman. He had to work there when their farm couldn't produce enough to pay their bills.

"I hated your factory job too. I guess it's bittersweet for me because I grew up in Shipshewana, but it's nice you're back where your relatives live." A twinge of nostalgia tightened her throat. She needed to visit her parents and siblings sometime.

"God's been *gut* to us."

"*Ya*, especially with our *kinner*. They are blessings, for sure and certain."

After ten years of infertility, she'd been delighted to adopt Amy and Jenna. They'd met pregnant Lindsay when her car broke down, and they offered to help her. After giving birth to identical triplets, Lindsay reconnected with Katie and Roman. They'd adopted Amy and Jenna with the agreement that she wouldn't try to get her daughters back if her financial situation changed. Katie never forgot how Lindsay could have allowed the media to interview her and photograph her daughters for potential fame and fortune. Having identical triplets via natural birth was a one-in-a-million occurrence. She respected the young woman for not cashing in on such a unique opportunity. It wasn't just Lindsay that Katie feared would change her mind about the adoption, but she also feared their biological father would learn about them someday and would influence them to leave their simple life.

Getting pregnant after adopting their daughters had been a huge surprise, and she'd been thrilled to give birth to their son, Seth. He had the same lovely color of green eyes as Roman, but his hair was light brown like hers. She never told Lindsay about Seth in her annual birthday letters. If she learned about Seth being so close in age to Amy and Jenna, Lindsay might have decided to ask for her daughters back. She'd felt God had wanted her to give them to Katie and Roman because they'd been childless and knew they'd have a stable family life. Lindsay might have been glad to learn they had a *bruder,* but why take the chance? Then as years passed, she thought it'd be nice to have *grandkinner.* Her friend Miriam talked with her about the joys of being a *mammi.* All of her children, except for one of her adopted sons, had joined their faith. He'd left to join his English birth parents.

"I'm concerned about Jenna and Amy. I thought the Lord guided us here for them to meet their future husbands. Then they would decide to take their kneeling vows."

Roman narrowed his eyes. "It's better they wait. They need to make sure it's right for them. If they join and then change their mind, shunning will happen. I know you don't want that."

She pressed her lips together to keep from saying anything. How could Roman say it was better for them to wait to join their Amish church? They were twenty-two years old.

It was upsetting because young women usually joined the faith earlier than the young men. It happened in the late teens or early twenties. Instead of taking their baptism classes and proceeding to their kneeling vows, Jenna and Amy were determined to do something in the medical field. In their new, small town, they were looking for Amish individuals to become emergency medical technicians. If they had remained in Shipshewana, this never would've happened. She didn't know of any Amish becoming involved in this career. Male Amish firefighters were one thing, but goodness, women EMTs seemed inappropriate and unnecessary. She'd been proud of Jenna teaching in their Amish school in Shipshewana and Amy working in a fabric store.

Katie shrugged. "I like working together as a family in the store. Seth isn't here much, but he does help us whenever he can." Once they moved from Shipshewana, Seth started working for a construction company.

"He seems to like his job a lot."

"I hoped Amy and Jenna would go to the singings and other youth activities here so they could meet young men." The singings in Millersburg were like the ones held in Shipshewana. Every other Sunday, the Amish families would meet for church at someone's house or barn. Then, in the evening, the youth attended the singings to socialize and meet their life partner. At times, the youth played volleyball before the singings. Katie recalled her singings fondly, so she didn't understand why the evening Sunday gatherings were not a priority to her daughters. It was a time for fun and joking as the youth gathered in the farmhouse. A removable wall extended the open space in the kitchen so there was room for over a hundred people. She liked how the adults sat at opposite ends of the room. After a couple of hours of singing songs in German, snacks were served.

Katie shrugged. "I'm relieved they have never been interested in experiencing English things, like driving a car, drinking, or wearing English clothes during *rumspringa* as some young adults in our communities have done. Seth has a cell phone, but he only uses it for work. It's nice they never did any running around, but still, I'm not *froh*. They think they're too old for singings. At least Seth is attending the youth get-togethers. I know Miriam's daughter, Veronica, has her eye on him."

He tucked a lock of her hair under her *kapp*. "I know you want them settled with husbands because of their English background. But they might never learn about Lindsay and Phoebe."

Katie hoped not. To their ambitious daughters, Lindsay's and Phoebe's college degrees might give Amy and Jenna a reason to want more education in their lives. Leaving their community would not be *gut*. Their Amish lifestyle was a source of strength within their safety net of loving friends and relatives to surround them when disasters hit. She loved how they helped one another whenever needed. They didn't need insurance if their barns burned or if people had huge medical expenses. They joined together for barn raisings and had fundraisers to raise money for hurting families.

"Would you like a cup of *kaffi*?" Katie asked. At Roman's nod, she poured it. "I wish Lindsay would've agreed to us taking all three of them. They should've been kept together."

He squeezed her shoulder gently before taking the cup from her. "It was hard enough for her to give us two."

She nodded. "I know it was difficult for Lindsay, but she didn't have a husband or family to help her. She was so young . . ." Her voice trailed off, remembering how young Lindsay was when they'd met her.

"Katie, do you remember her reaction when we tried to adopt all three? She couldn't do it."

She knew what Roman referred to. When they had suggested taking the triplets and not splitting them up, Lindsay had become hysterical. After that, they'd agreed to take two instead of three. Katie and Roman were anxious to add children to the family. They'd been married for a long time and hadn't been blessed with children. Having *kinner* was an important part of an Amish marriage.

"I can't imagine our life without the twins. I hope they never learn about Phoebe. What if they decide to jump the fence and leave us to be with Lindsay? Lindsay's and Phoebe's life might appeal to them. Amy complained constantly about the lack of science at school and wanting more education." Katie exhaled a deep breath and continued. "It will break our hearts, and Seth's, if they decide not to become Amish."

Roman grinned. "Or Phoebe might decide to join the Amish church. That would be something, wouldn't it?"

She laughed. "*Ya*, I'm sure that will happen, you silly man."

He put his cup beside the coffeepot. "How about a quick kiss before we open the store?"

"You never have to ask to kiss me."

Clasping her face between his hands, he sealed a kiss on her lips. Roman's kiss was as tender and light as a summer breeze. Out of the corner of her eye, Katie saw Jenna entering the store.

"I wondered why the Closed sign was still on the door. I should've realized you two were smooching again." Jenna laughed. "You two can go in the back room while I take care of the customers."

Roman kept his arm around Katie's midriff. "*Ya*, we should. It's hard for me to keep my hands off your *schee* mother."

～

Later in the morning, Jenna touched Roman's arm when Katie left the store to go to the bank. "*Daed*, Amy and I need to talk to you. Or I do." Jenna smiled at Amy. "I seem to be the voice for both of us."

Amy rolled her eyes. "Geez, you never let me forget I used to be shy."

"Was shy? Just the other day you told me to order our food for lunch."

Amy grinned. "You do a better job than I do. The last time I ordered, they got it wrong."

"And I'm the one with divine direction, so I should explain." Jenna's expression became serious.

Roman had a feeling it had to be about their training. He would be caught in the middle if he agreed to them becoming paramedics because there was no way Katie would give her approval. "Is it about becoming EMTs?"

Jenna nodded. "I haven't mentioned this before, but God definitely wants me to become a paramedic. Remember a few weeks ago when an ambulance went by our store?"

"*Ya*, we prayed for the injured person," Roman said.

"I heard God's voice telling me to become an EMT." Jenna's brown eyes widened. "Do you think that will convince *Mamm* to allow me to start classes?"

He shrugged. "Maybe, but don't count on it. I'll tell her."

Amy edged closer to him. "I've always wanted to do something in the medical field. If I go to EMT school with Jenna, that would be a good opportunity to get my foot into eventually doing what I want."

Roman sighed, knowing Amy had a higher ambition to become a nurse. "For sure, Amy, your mother won't want you to become a paramedic if your plan is to do more education later. I'm not crazy about you becoming a nurse either. That would mean several years of college. How will you join our church then?"

"I still can. I'll get permission from Henry. As our bishop, he might realize that an Amish nurse would be great for our district." Amy twisted the end of her *kapp* strand.

"Bishop Henry told us we could start the classes," Jenna said. "I don't see how *Mamm* can still say we can't become EMTs."

He ran his fingers through his hair. Roman hated to burst Amy's plan to become a nurse, but he didn't think Henry would approve of it. He'd never heard of any bishop approving such a thing, but Bishop Henry did like for the Amish to contribute to the community. Several of their young men had become firefighters. If Katie thought this was Amy's long-term plan, she would never go for any of her medical plans. Truthfully, Amy might stop trying to be a nurse and remain with Jenna.

"I'll talk to her soon. I'll tell her God is calling you to become EMTs." Roman grinned at both of his daughters. "It seems he's planted the idea in your minds."

Amy hugged him. "*Danki, Daed.*"

"*Ya, danki,*" Jenna said. She turned her head at the sound of the front door opening. "We have a customer."

Amy chuckled. "Not just any customer, but someone Jenna seems to be especially interested in. She met him the other week at the bank."

The young man's eyes lit up as soon as Jenna reached his side.

"What's his name?" Roman asked.

"His name is Eli Zimmerman. He's an EMT." Amy grinned. "I'm not saying this is the reason Jenna's so interested in taking the classes, but it definitely is a plus for her. Eli loves his work. He said it helps to be Plain when they go to an Amish home."

He nodded. "I can see why that would be helpful. It has to be reassuring to have an Amish EMT to assist them."

Amy tapped his arm. "I do want to get started soon on learning to be an EMT. I'm twenty-two and feel like I've lost too much time getting started on my dream."

Roman knew where his daughters got their medical interests from. Their biological father had planned to go to medical school. He supposed Harris Manning went forward with his plan, especially since his parents were doctors. Lindsay could've handled him being in medical school, but Harris Manning never gave her a chance to be part of his world. Did Phoebe end up going to college? Was she attending school to become a doctor or to do something in the medical field? At times, he wished Katie hadn't stopped writing Lindsay. It'd been interesting to hear how Phoebe was like their daughters in so many ways.

Except there was one big, crucial difference. Phoebe had been raised by a single mother in the English world. Amy and Jenna being interested in becoming EMTs instead of choosing something related to their upbringing seemed peculiar in a way. When he thought about how their biological father and grandparents were doctors, it made sense. Roman wondered if God had given them a nudge to tell their daughters about Lindsay and Phoebe because of their possible career choices.

Wouldn't it be better for us to tell our daughters about their biological mother and sister? I need to convince Katie that Amy and Jenna should be allowed to start EMT classes. More importantly, Katie needs to understand it is time to tell the girls the truth about how Lindsay loved them enough to give them up.

Her friend, Miriam, had tried to convince Katie it was better to tell them the truth. After all, she had told her adopted sons about their biological parents. Sure, one left the Amish faith, but he was still close to Miriam and her husband, Pete. The other adopted son had taken baptism classes and joined their faith.

Sometimes Katie worried too much instead of trusting God. She missed seeing the whole picture of what was right. *Ach*, but he loved this frustrating woman with his whole heart.

Chapter Three

"Breakfast was delicious," Lindsay said, holding a mug of tea. "It's great to be home. I slept better last night in my own bed."

Phoebe glanced at her mother, thinking how she definitely hadn't slept well the last two nights. How could she sleep after seeing the fourteen letters sent to her mom? Her life wasn't what she'd thought it had been. Obviously, her mother had cherished the letters, yet hadn't shared any content with her. Confronting her mother might destroy the closeness they'd shared. When dishonesty existed in a family, pain was inevitable. Her mom might have a serious reason to keep the truth from her, but it still hurt a lot. Had she wanted to protect her from something that had involved Katie Yoder?

As much as she'd wanted to ask about the correspondence immediately, she had decided to wait until her mother was back home. Her insides ached from an emotional soreness that had started the same night she'd found the hidden envelope. Phoebe supposed other daughters would've read the letters. She'd thought about it, but it felt like a betrayal of her mother's secret. It was hers to tell.

She should be able to ask about the letters soon because her mom had eaten a tiny amount of scrambled eggs, toast, and bacon. Even though her hemoglobin had gone up enough for her to be discharged from the hospital yesterday afternoon, Phoebe reminded herself how her mother was not well. But how could she wait another day to learn the truth?

As she put their dishes into the dishwasher, Phoebe said, "Would you like more tea?" Her mother looked tiny on the sofa. Her mother had always been thin and petite, but these days, she was too thin.

"No, thank you." Her mother patted a spot next to her on the sofa. "We need to talk."

"Yes, we do." *Does Mom know that I found the letters?* Putting her hands on her hips, she remained standing. "I need to tell you what I found after I left the hospital."

Her mother gave her a puzzled look. "I don't understand. What is it?"

"I accidentally knocked over your glass of water in your bedroom. Water dripped into your drawer." Phoebe lifted the envelope from a spot behind their stand mixer and waved it at her mom. "Fortunately, your letters didn't get wet."

Her eyebrows shot up. "Did you read them?"

Phoebe shook her head and joined her mother on the sofa. "No, I didn't read them because I want to hear the truth from you. Why did Katie send you letters on my birthday? Is she a relative?"

"Katie isn't a relative. She's a lovely Amish woman I met years ago when I was pregnant. When my car broke down in Shipshewana, she and her husband, Roman, helped me. I know this will be hard to believe, but I planned on telling you today what happened a long time ago. I even thought about telling you at the hospital, but it didn't seem like the right time."

"Obviously, the letters from Katie have been important to you, so it's hurtful you never shared them. I've been trying to imagine what else you've kept hidden from me. Why haven't I ever met this woman? Is it because she's Amish and it's hard for Katie to leave her family?" Her stomach turned at her attempts to stay calm.

"I made a promise to Katie to keep our secret. I decided to break my promise recently because of my health." Her mom rubbed her forehead, looking troubled.

Phoebe's patience was wearing thin as she tapped her foot. Maybe she should have read the letters herself. She wasn't surprised her mom would take her time. It seemed to be her way whenever she explained anything. Maybe it was because she was a math teacher and her mind followed a logical course.

"If I hadn't found the letters, were you really going to tell me about them today?"

"Yes, I planned on revealing the truth to you because of having lymphoma and ending up in the hospital, but it has always bothered me to keep this secret from you. I can't honor Katie's wish any longer. You need to know about everything." She gave Phoebe a weak smile and placed her cup on the coffee table.

"I'll start with how I met Katie and Roman. One Sunday, when I was five months along with my pregnancy, I drove to Indiana to see my girlfriend, Deana. I was feeling confused and desperate and decided that talking to her might help clear my mind about what I should do. My obstetrician told me I needed to stop working. I stopped in Shipshewana to use the restroom and get something to eat. When I went back to the car, it wouldn't start."

"Did you call your friend?" Phoebe wondered why she had never heard any mention of this Deana person before. They must not have been close in later years.

"No, because I was still a couple of hours away from Deana's apartment. Roman and Katie saw my condition and how upset I was that my car wouldn't start. They took me to their house while my car was towed to an auto repair shop."

"You had quite the experience. What was their house like? Did they have an outhouse? I heard the Amish are pretty backward and don't even have indoor plumbing."

Her mom exhaled a deep breath. "They had indoor plumbing and two bathrooms. Katie and Roman Yoder's house was lovely. They were wonderful to me. I met Katie's parents and siblings. I loved how important their family was to them."

"That's nice, but why did Katie send letters to you on my birthday? And why did she stop?"

"I asked her to send me letters. I wish with my whole heart she hadn't stopped. I have something to show you. Please forgive me for the secret I've kept from you."

Phoebe's heart quickened as she stared at her mother's pleading eyes. "I don't know what to say since I can't imagine the kind of secret you could have that would need forgiveness." She squeezed her mother's hand, hoping to give her encouragement to spill whatever had happened.

Her mother cleared her throat. "My bag is on the end table by you. Hand it to me, please. I have something to show you."

Phoebe gave her the purse and watched as her mom removed a small-framed photo.

Glancing at the picture, her mother's eyes filled with tears. "I gave birth to identical girl triplets. This is a picture of you with your sisters, Amy and Jenna. I gave them to Katie and Roman to raise."

Phoebe heard her mother's words, but her brain wouldn't let her process them. It couldn't be. How could her mom have kept such a secret from her all this time? It seemed unreal to think she had two sisters and was just now hearing about them. "What?"

She handed her the photo. "The letters you found were sent every year on your birthday because I asked Katie to do this for me. That way I could still have a connection with Amy and Jenna. I mailed letters to Katie and Roman about you. Katie stopped sending me letters after the girls finished eighth grade."

Phoebe held the frame tightly as she stared at the three babies. Her head spun as she took several deep breaths. It was hard to comprehend her mother had given birth to triplets. Pain exploded in her chest and betrayal sliced through her heart. How could her mother have kept the secret about her sisters from her? They had such a close relationship.

Her mom pointed to the baby on the right end of the photo. "You're the one in pink, Amy is in lavender, and Jenna is in yellow. When you and your sisters were three months old, I had this picture taken."

Phoebe stared at the photo of her and her identical sisters. As a young child, she'd had strange feelings of missing something from her life. Now it made sense. She'd shared a womb with her siblings. And for the first few months of life, they were together.

She couldn't breathe, but she managed to ask her mother an important question. "Do Amy and Jenna know about me?" Phoebe glanced away from the picture to look at her mother, realizing that saying their names seemed weird. It wasn't every day a person learned they were not an only child. If Amy and Jenna knew about her, why had they never reached out to her?

"No. Katie didn't want them to know they were adopted. She wanted you too, but I couldn't give all three of my babies away." Clutching a throw pillow against her chest, she continued. "It was difficult enough to give Amy and Jenna to the Yoders. I stayed with them for six weeks—"

"Why would you give my sisters to an Amish family?" Phoebe's voice grew louder with each word.

"I knew they'd have a stable family life. I was on welfare. I tried to work from home, but I couldn't handle it with three babies. I knew I couldn't give all of you the life you deserved. Katie and Roman had been married for ten years and were childless. They yearned to have a family."

Staring again at the photo, Phoebe couldn't wrap her head around the fact that she had two sisters who looked exactly like her and her mother had lied to her for years. "I can understand a little why you couldn't raise three babies on your own, but I still don't get why you didn't give them to non-Amish parents. There had to be lots of other couples you could've chosen." Phoebe couldn't keep the accusatory tone out of her voice. It seemed wrong that her siblings were raised in a place without the benefits she had enjoyed.

"Amish seldom divorce, and I felt they would be raised in a loving, Christian home. I'd heard the Amish make exceptional parents. Amy and Jenna wouldn't lack food and clothing like I did when growing up. I grew up with an alcoholic mother, and I felt God put the Yoders in my path at the right time for a reason," her mother said in a firm voice.

Phoebe placed the photo on the coffee table and briefly touched her mom's arm. "I'm glad you kept me. I've heard how the Amish only go to school through the eighth grade. I can't imagine having such a limited education. And you became a teacher. It seems like you would want them to be educated."

Her mother frowned. "The Amish never stop learning. They have many options to continue learning for their careers. If they have a business, they need certain skills to make a living."

"Where are Amy and Jenna now? Still in Shipshewana, I guess?"

"That's a great question. I don't know. They lived in Shipshewana, but you saw the returned letter. They must have moved. I'm surprised because they lived on a beautiful farm." Tears welled in her mother's eyes. "I'm going to find them. I've missed them so much. I wrote Katie to tell her I have cancer and that I need to see Amy and Jenna. I told her you should have a chance to connect with them because I could die."

Phoebe hugged her. "Don't worry. You aren't going to die. We'll locate them."

She laughed a little. "They won't be on Facebook."

"That's true."

"I'm not sure I want to announce on social media that I gave my babies up for adoption. I'll go to Indiana soon. I'm praying it might be a little easier for them to learn the truth since they're both adults now."

At the sight of more tears, Phoebe stood. "I'll get you a tissue." *How in the world did Mom decide which baby to keep when we were all identical?* With a box of tissues in her hand, she walked back to the sofa. "Why did you keep me? Was there something special about me?"

Softly, her mom said, "You were the last one born and the smallest one. You needed me a lot and took the longest to nurse."

Phoebe sniffed and grabbed a tissue. "I'm glad you kept me."

Her mom squeezed her hand. "There's more. I stayed with Katie and Roman for six weeks. You cried when Katie tried to give you a bottle."

"How old were we when you left the Yoders' house?"

"You were seven months old. I had a difficult time but knew in my heart I couldn't keep all three of you. And Katie and Roman were happy to finally have children to love."

Phoebe still couldn't fully understand why her mother gave Amy and Jenna to an Amish family.

At the sound of a ringtone, her mother stood and walked to the kitchen counter to see who was calling. She glanced at her cell phone. "It's the oncologist's office."

Phoebe thought they must be calling to see how her mother felt. She was scheduled to have her chemo next week, and hopefully, she would tolerate it. Phoebe thought her mother's voice sounded strained as she spoke to the nurse, but it was no wonder after revealing the truth about her two sisters. What a burden her mother had carried. *I can't believe it. It seems like Amy and Jenna would've been interested in learning about their biological mother and have a desire to visit her.*

"Mary, a nurse from the oncologist's office, called to check on me since I'm home now." Lindsay sat on the couch. "How are you doing? I know I gave you a shock today."

Phoebe tucked a lock of her hair behind her ear. "Yes, you did, and it's hard for me to imagine I have two identical sisters. I want to find them, but since they had never contacted us, does that mean Amy and Jenna still don't know they are adopted?"

She cleared her throat. "I doubt they do. Katie never wanted them to ever know. I think she thought they might want to leave the Amish if they knew. She insisted on a clean break from me and didn't want any part of an open adoption."

"It seems like someone in their community would've told them the truth."

"Not necessarily. I suppose it helped they were adopted as babies, and the Amish might have felt it best to keep quiet." Her mom fingered the hem of her blue robe. "Amish adoptions occur frequently. I suppose some tell their adopted children about their birth parents and others choose not to. Katie told me someone in their district already had a large family, but she'd adopted a foster child. Amish will even adopt children of various races."

"That's nice." Phoebe curled her legs under her. "What did my dad think when he heard you were having triplets? Or did he even know before he died?"

"When we married, Paul and I didn't know we were having triplets. We were young, and I worried about him being in college with a baby on the way. We learned I was expecting triplets right before he died." Her mother buried her face in her hands. Her voice was husky with restrained emotion. "We'll talk more about your dad later. I'm going to take a shower and get dressed."

After seeing how upset her mom was, Phoebe assumed her dad had done something wrong. But it wasn't a good time to ask. A conversation break was good for both of them. Hearing about one huge secret had been overwhelming. She'd been under the perception for years that her mother hadn't liked talking about her husband because he'd died suddenly. Now it sounded like there was something her mom had kept hidden about her dad. Maybe he hadn't wanted triplets. Briefly, she thought about the father she never knew. It didn't seem like there could be anything big for her mom to talk about concerning her high school sweetheart. She already knew how her mom was pregnant with her before they got married.

"Will you be okay? Do you need any help?" Phoebe knew the answer before hearing it. Lindsay Prescott was an independent woman and hated having anyone fuss over her. But it seemed she should offer assistance seeing as how her mom had just been released from the hospital.

"I'm fine, honey, but thanks for asking." Her mom hugged her. "How did I get so lucky to have you?"

"I'm the lucky one. I love you, Mom." Her mind swirled with the knowledge that she had two sisters. She loved her mother, but Phoebe resented the fact she was just now learning about Amy and Jenna.

"I love you to the moon and back." She tucked a lock of her long hair behind her ear. "You should read Katie's letters. She shared many wonderful milestones, like when Amy and Jenna took their first steps. It's interesting how all three of you walked right before your first birthday. And I have a photo album I want you to see. I have more photos I took before I gave the girls away."

Once her mother left the room, Phoebe went to her bedroom to grab her laptop. She should start researching the Yoder name in Shipshewana. There could be a non-Amish relative to contact about her sisters' whereabouts. Phoebe's heart quickened, thinking about having two sisters. She wanted to meet them. And her mother needed to see Amy and Jenna. It seemed her mother wasn't the only one with secrets; Katie Yoder was also guilty of deceit.

Both mothers were Christians, but were their secrets really what was best for everyone?

Chapter Four

Millersburg, Ohio

As they went home from their store on Saturday, Roman thought about what he needed to do for Amy and Jenna. He glanced at his wife, noticing how happy she looked. Mentioning their daughters going for EMT training was not a topic he wanted to bring up to Katie. He loved her, but sometimes she could be difficult. She had a bit of a controlling personality. Katie had been the eldest child in her family. She'd been a great big sister to six siblings and had spent a lot of time helping her mother in the kitchen. Early in their marriage, when they hadn't yet been blessed with *kinner*, Katie wasn't too worried. She knew it would happen in God's time. As the years went by, she became bitter. She couldn't understand why God hadn't given them any *kinner*, especially when her younger married siblings were having babies.

Katie wanted to become a *mammi*, but Amy and Jenna hadn't seemed interested in finding their life partners. Seth didn't have a girlfriend, but he was a little younger and still went to the singings held by their district.

She touched his leg. "The weather is lovely."

Roman nodded. "It's a *wunderbaar-gut* day to spend with my best girl."

"A buggy ride is romantic." Katie grinned. "Well, maybe not as much in daylight. Or when we were young and you enjoyed kissing me during our night buggy rides."

He turned his head away from the road and planted a kiss on her cheek. "I love you."

"I love you too." Katie raised her eyebrows. "Okay, what's wrong? I can tell there is something you want to say. You have glanced at me several times like you're contemplating whether to speak now or later. You know I hate it when you bring something up in bed right before I go to sleep."

"You know me too well. Okay, it's about our daughters." He hesitated, wishing he'd told Amy and Jenna to talk to Katie. It seemed like too many times he was caught in the middle.

"It must be something I won't like."

He shook his head. "It's something positive. Jenna said God told her to become an EMT. It was the day an ambulance went by our store."

Katie frowned. "Why didn't Jenna tell me God told her to become an EMT?"

"It could be because you have said several times that you don't approve of them attending the classes. We should tell Amy and Jenna it's okay for them to start taking the classes. It's *gut* they want to do it together." Roman smiled. "Jenna has already met Eli, and he's a paramedic. He might become a boyfriend."

"Is he Amish?"

"*Ya*, he is."

"If Seth wanted to be an EMT, I'd understand it more. Amish men are volunteering at the fire station. It's important to be part of the community. I just have trouble seeing women going in ambulances at all hours and being around the English more."

He was glad their horse, Dan, knew the way home since he needed to concentrate on crafting a convincing argument. "One reason our daughters might be interested could be because they want to do something different with their lives. Working in the store isn't enough for them. Then, too, their grandparents are doctors, and their biological father might be as well. It's in their blood."

Katie was quiet for a moment, then she raised her hands in the air. "I give up. They can take the classes. I need to honor God because Jenna heard His voice to become an EMT."

"I'm glad you've changed your mind. We can tell them tonight."

Katie twisted her *kapp* tie around her finger. "I wonder what Phoebe has done with her life. That would be something if she has married and isn't interested in a career."

"I suppose Phoebe could've gotten married. I don't like keeping secrets. Lately, I've felt a stronger nudge from God."

Katie smiled. "*Ach*, so now you are getting nudges from God too."

"I think He wants us to tell our daughters about Phoebe. Telling them about their sister might bring blessings to them. I have this strong feeling that Phoebe needs to know about Amy and Jenna. As far as we know, Lindsay has never remarried and had more children."

"*Nee*, I don't agree, because then we have to tell them we adopted them. We raised them, and they don't need to know anything else. If God truly wanted our daughters to know about their biological mother, then it would've happened by now. Lindsay has never reached out to us to reveal the secret."

As their horse turned into their driveway, Roman said, "That's true, but we did move a year ago. Now that they are adults, she might want to see them."

Katie shrugged. "I suppose so, but Lindsay might not want Phoebe to know she gave away her siblings."

"I hope Phoebe would understand how she couldn't support three children."

"It doesn't matter. God gave us Amy and Jenna. We don't have any obligation to tell them about Lindsay."

Roman pulled on the reins. "Whoa." He stopped the buggy by the back door so Katie didn't have to walk from the barn to their house.

She frowned. "I wish you didn't want to tell them about Lindsay. I love that I'm their mother. Our agreement was to keep their adoption a secret. I don't want to share them with Lindsay. Besides, what if she has never told Phoebe anything about us or our daughters? *Nee*, I don't agree with you. Telling them would not help anyone."

Katie stepped out of the buggy, while Roman went to the barn to unhitch their horse. He was happy to see Seth had arrived home ahead of them. "How was work today?"

"*Gut.* I can unhitch Dan for you. I already brushed and fed Ace. I got home a little earlier today."

"*Danki,* but I can do it."

Katie had agreed to the EMT classes, but she definitely wasn't willing to tell the girls about their birth background. He had a strong feeling they should be honest. From the beginning, Roman had hated not being forthright about their births. It might be better to give his *fraa* several minutes to be alone with her thoughts. Maybe God would speak to her heart that it was time to tell Amy and Jenna about Lindsay and Phoebe. Or was Katie right that Lindsay had also kept Phoebe in the dark about having siblings? It'd be hard for Lindsay to tell her daughter that she'd given her sisters up for adoption.

Maybe I should call Lindsay. I can tell her how Jenna and Amy are going to take EMT classes this summer and ask her what Phoebe is doing with her life. Katie has Lindsay's phone number hidden somewhere. I'll ask her for it. Then I can ask Lindsay if Phoebe knows that she has sisters.

As he led Dan into the stall, Roman heard Seth chuckling. He turned around to look at his son. "What's so funny?"

"I've asked you twice if the store was busy today, and you haven't answered me. *Mamm* would say you have selective hearing."

Roman smiled. "Sorry. I was deep in thought about your sisters."

Seth leaned against the barn wall and snapped his suspenders. "I know. It's about the classes they want to take. That's all they talk about these days."

"We decided to tell them it's okay to take the EMT classes."

"The nice thing is they both will be doing it together and can help each other learn the material."

Roman put oats in the trough for Dan. "It's great the community wants to include Amish people in their EMT classes. It's hard on your mother, though. She had hopes Amy and Jenna would marry instead."

"I haven't met anyone I want to spend my life with either. You and *Mamm* fell in love when you were kids and knew you'd marry someday."

"You're young. It'll happen."

Seth gave him an unconvinced look. "I don't know. Maybe none of your *kinner* will marry."

"Pray about it. God has a young woman in mind for you. When the time is right, you'll meet her."

"How did I get such a wise father?"

Roman shrugged. "Many times, I don't have the answers, but I pray, and God helps me with everything." *I hope God will direct me to do the right thing concerning the adoption. It seems calling Lindsay might be the answer.*

Amy turned away from the pan on the stove. "Hi, *Mamm*. The chicken is done."

Jenna placed a vase of flowers from their garden on the table. "I'll get the iced tea and potato salad out. I'm glad you're home."

"This is nice not having to cook."

Amy and Jenna helped her with preparing meals and doing household chores. It was *wunderbaar* when they did the whole meal. Katie watched Jenna get a bowl of pickled red beets out of the refrigerator. Katie didn't want to lose the close mother-daughter bond she had with Amy and Jenna. Katie couldn't bear to lose any of their love or respect. *Yes, it's better to keep our secret.*

"Is *Daed* and Seth on their way in?" Amy asked, putting the fried chicken on a plate covered with a paper towel.

Before Katie could answer, Roman opened the screen door. "It smells great in here. I'll wash up and be right back."

Seth followed his father. Over his shoulder, he asked, "What's for dessert?"

Jenna said, "I thought you were in charge of the dessert."

"I can make my super cookie bars." Seth laughed. "I remember you loved those."

"*Nee*, don't ever make those again." Jenna rolled her eyes. "Whatever ingredients you used stuck to my teeth forever."

Once he was out of sight, Amy sighed. "Aren't you glad, *Mamm*, Seth isn't a twin? He would live on desserts if he could."

Jenna tucked a lock of black hair back under her *kapp*. "It's nice having only two siblings."

"I wouldn't have minded if Seth had a twin. I'll pour the iced tea. Looks like everything else is done," Katie said as she glanced at the table.

Jenna put her hands on her hips. "I knew it. Seth is your favorite. You'd like to clone him. He's the perfect son."

Seth entered the kitchen and pulled on Jenna's *kapp* tie. "Don't be jealous."

"I don't have a favorite child. I love you all the same." Katie started putting the filled glasses of tea next to each plate.

"But I'm definitely my *fraa's* favorite husband." Roman kissed Katie's cheek. "I'm hungry. Looks delicious, ladies."

Everyone took a seat and bowed their heads to silently pray. Once Roman finished, they passed the food around the table.

Katie picked up a breast from the plate of chicken, then glanced at Amy and Jenna. "Your *daed* and I decided it's okay for you to go to the EMT classes."

Jenna's fork clattered against the porcelain plate. She jumped up and hugged her *mamm* and *daed*. "*Danki*! I'm excited to get started. It's going to be hard to wait until September."

Amy gave a big smile and leaned forward. "This is the best news ever. *Danki, Mamm* and *Daed*. Jenna, it's going to be great to attend classes together."

"Hey, no cheating, you two." Seth took a bite of his chicken.

"We don't cheat, *bruder*." Amy glared at him.

"What about the spelling bee in seventh grade when you switched places with Jenna? She was still in the spelling bee, but you weren't. So the next day, you took her place because you wanted to win the spelling bee." Seth wiped his mouth with a napkin. "Wasn't that cheating?"

Jenna raised her eyebrows. "You're making that up. Besides, you can't tell us apart."

"*Ya*, I can." Seth waved his chicken leg at them. "I've been able to for years. I'm *froh* for you two. You both will make great EMTs."

Katie sighed. "I didn't realize giving permission for the classes would bring up childhood memories."

"Why don't you tell your sisters about the new house you're working on?" Roman said.

"*Ya*, you better tell us before you get fired," Amy said in a sweet voice.

Katie quickly said, "Seth isn't going to lose his job. He's one of their best workers."

～

As the porch swing moved back and forth slowly, Katie's hand was grasped in Roman's. "*Ach*, do you think we did the right thing? I worry about them being with mostly men in their classes and riding the ambulances with Englishers."

He squeezed her hand. "God will watch over them. It's going to be fine. Our daughters are bright, and they will be careful."

"One positive thing came out of telling Amy and Jenna that they can become EMTs."

"What's that?"

"They were so *froh* that Seth was able to convince them to go to a volleyball game with him. They never want to go to Sunday singings or any youth activities. It was nice seeing all three of them leave together to have a fun evening." Katie smiled, thinking how pretty the girls looked when they left. Amy wore a royal blue dress while Jenna's dress was lavender, her favorite color. With their beautiful faces, brown eyes, and black hair, they were bound to meet some young men.

Roman put his arm around her shoulders. "It's *wunderbaar* to have my best girl to myself."

Katie sighed. "I'm glad tomorrow is Sunday and the store is closed. I always look forward to having Sunday off."

"We can take a couple of days off soon and go on a mini-trip somewhere. Our daughters can run the store without us for two or three days. We should go before they start their classes."

"You're too good to me." She saw Roman's green eyes studying her. "Do you have any suggestions for where we should go?"

He shook his head. "I don't. Any place you want to go will be fine with me."

"How about Niagara Falls? We talked about going there before, but something always seemed to get in the way."

"That was fast thinking of where to go for our road trip. I like your idea. I'll get a driver when we decide on the dates." Roman gave her a thoughtful look. "I've heard the Canadian side is better. We need to get pass cards to go to Canada."

Katie hadn't thought of that, but she remembered a few Amish friends from their previous town had gone to see Niagara Falls on the Canadian side. They had mentioned it was possible to get the pass cards without having their photos taken. But still, it seemed like too much trouble. "Let's just go on the New York side. I don't see us using the pass cards again, and we can schedule our trip soon if we don't get them."

He nodded. "*Ya*, that sounds fine."

"Would you like a piece of apple pie now? We can talk more over our dessert." She laughed. "I couldn't believe Seth's face when he thought there wasn't going to be any dessert. He loves anything sweet."

Chapter Five

Columbus, Ohio

Lindsay removed a blue top from a hanger in her walk-in closet. Phoebe wore shorts and a sleeveless top while Lindsay decided to wear jeans. She definitely wasn't feeling it was warm enough for shorts. The weather seemed chilly for late May. Glancing at the full-length

mirror, it was strange to see her pale face and scrawny body. Cancer had altered her appearance, and feeling weak wasn't any fun either.

She felt free after unloading her burden and was relieved Phoebe took it as well as she had. Still, it was a lot for her to learn. She needed to keep an eye on how Phoebe handled it in the days ahead. She wasn't sure how Phoebe would feel when she learned the truth about Harris.

"Dear Father, I give you thanks for giving me the strength to finally tell Phoebe about her sisters. Help me to locate them soon. It'll be wonderful to have them all together again. And give me the right words to explain to Phoebe about her biological father. In your Son's Name, I pray. Amen."

Upon Lindsay entering the living room, Phoebe closed her laptop. "I started looking in Shipshewana, but I haven't found anything helpful to locate Amy and Jenna." Phoebe stared at her for a moment. "You look pretty in the top I bought you."

"You always spoil me. I told you not to get me anything for Mother's Day." Lindsay worried about the medical school expenses Phoebe would rack up as she studied to become a physician.

"I feel refreshed after taking a shower." Lindsay sat by Phoebe on the sofa. "I wish Katie's siblings or parents had a business in Shipshewana because that would help locate Amy and Jenna."

"Mom, after you graduated from college, did you consider asking Katie and Roman if you could have your daughters back to raise?" Phoebe pursed her lips and ran her fingers over her laptop. "It would've been an adjustment, but we were still children."

"I couldn't. I had promised Katie I wouldn't ask for them back, even if my financial situation changed." Lindsay paused for a moment. "Katie said she wouldn't raise them only for me to take them back. She said it wouldn't be fair to do that to them. At the time, I wasn't sure I would ever be able to support three children. By the time I could've, they already thought of Katie and Roman as their parents."

"It seems to me that Katie took advantage of your youth and your desperate situation. It might not have been right to take Amy and Jenna from their adopted parents, but I wish we had been raised together," Phoebe said, sadness brimming in her eyes.

"I'm sorry. I wish that too." Lindsay touched Phoebe's arm. "When the news reporters heard about me giving birth to identical triplets, they wanted to do a segment on us. Identical triplets are a one-in-a-million phenomenon. I didn't want them to film us because it was embarrassing that I was a single mom with no resources to raise children. I wasn't on welfare yet, but I knew I would be soon unless some miracle happened. While I had all three babies, I used thirty diapers a day. The people I worked with at McDonald's gave me a supply of diapers for the first month. I saved money by breastfeeding, but I still needed baby formula to supplement the feedings."

Phoebe propped a cheek on her fist. "I wish Dad hadn't died before we were born."

Lindsay thought for a moment on how to begin talking about her romance with Harris. "Paul's parents considered me lower class."

"Sorry, Mom."

Lindsay bit her lip. "Well, that's not the only reason they couldn't accept me as their daughter-in-law. Paul wasn't your father."

Phoebe's brown eyes widened, and her hand dropped to her lap. "What? I don't understand. Are you telling me I have a father who is alive?"

"Yes, your father is very much alive. His name is Harris Manning. Deana and I decided to get beach jobs after our high school graduation. While I was working as a hotel maid in Myrtle Beach, I met Harris and—"

"Wait. I can't believe this. I actually have a *father*." Phoebe's bottom lip trembled.

She nodded, feeling queasy at upsetting her daughter. "After he'd graduated from college, Harris decided to rent a beach house with his friends. I fell in love with him, and he said how he loved me. Harris promised me we would get married."

"I can't believe I've been lied to for years about my father. I wished so many times my father had lived. I thought Paul Prescott was my father. I don't understand why you didn't tell me the truth about my father years ago. I could've handled it."

"I should have, but I was afraid you wouldn't be accepted in his world. I found out he had a girlfriend the whole time we were seeing each other. I was just a summer fling."

With tears pouring down her cheeks, Phoebe walked to the counter, grabbed a tissue, and wiped her eyes. "That's awful you went through that. I don't think much of my father. He used you. I don't want to know him, but I do want to find Amy and Jenna."

"I'm so sorry I lied to you all these years. I know it was wrong not to tell you." Hiding the truth had hurt Phoebe. How could she ever make it up to her? All she could do now was try to explain more why she'd made the decision to keep Harris a secret. A distance existed between them when all she wanted to do was draw closer to her daughter.

As Lindsay slowly moved toward the counter, Phoebe said, "I understand a little bit why you never told me about Harris."

Lindsay continued with her explanation as she stood across her daughter. "When Paul learned I was pregnant, he offered to marry me. It seemed like the right thing to do. I cared deeply about him. His parents refused to help him with living expenses. His scholarship was only for tuition. Knowing the babies were not Paul's made them even more disgusted with me."

As Phoebe twisted her birthstone ring on her finger, Lindsay remembered how she'd given it to her when she was a teenager. The purple stone for February was surrounded by tiny diamonds. Lindsay had told Phoebe the ring would help to remind her to stay pure until marriage.

"Did you tell Harris you were pregnant?" Phoebe asked in an accusing tone. "It seems like he should've taken some responsibility and given you financial support."

"I didn't know I was pregnant until Harris returned home to Cincinnati. As soon as I realized it, I tried to call him. I left several voicemails, telling him it was important I talked to him, but Harris never returned my calls. Then I swallowed my pride. I went to his parents' house to confront him." Lindsay walked to the sofa and sat down.

Telling her daughter about going to the Mannings' house had brought back an agonizing memory, but she needed to tell the rest. "There were a lot of cars around this mansion. Even though I realized there was a party, I was determined to tell him about my pregnancy. At the time, I didn't know I was pregnant with triplets. A woman came to the door, and it was Harris's fiancé, Callie. She showed me her engagement ring and told me Harris didn't want to see me. Callie said I needed to stop calling him."

"That's why you looked uncomfortable whenever I asked you about my dad." A flash of irritation crossed Phoebe's face as she sat on a stool by the counter. "I wish I had known the truth about my father, but Harris Manning lied to you. You had to raise me by yourself. It wasn't right you had to be alone."

"I wasn't alone. I had you. You have brightened my life in countless ways."

"But my father took advantage of you," Phoebe complained. "I hate men who take advantage of women. And you were young. It sounds like he was a rich and spoiled person."

Lindsay shook her head. "Maybe he did love me while we were together, but Callie came from the same type of affluent background as he did. His parents were successful physicians."

"Oh my gosh, are you kidding me?" Phoebe wrapped her long, black hair around her finger. "Being in the medical field runs in the family, then."

"Harris is also a doctor."

Phoebe frowned. "How do you know he became a doctor?"

"I'm sure he did. That was his plan." Lindsay gave Phoebe a small grin. "You happen to have other characteristics from your father."

"I'm guessing you're referring to my black hair and brown eyes."

Lindsay nodded and stood. "I have a picture of us together on the beach somewhere. I'll get it."

Chapter Six

Bitterness clouded her thoughts as Phoebe did stretches while waiting on Haley. They planned to run along the Olentangy River. She was hurt her mother had lied to her for years about her siblings and her father. *Mom never should've waited this long to tell me. If she didn't have cancer, she might have kept it from me forever.*

Phoebe wanted to tell her mother it wasn't fair that Amy and Jenna were kept together. She couldn't imagine being raised in an Amish home, but it would have been wonderful to have been with her sisters. *Or Mom should've insisted that we be allowed to visit Jenna and Amy while we were all growing up. I could've spent a week or two with them at their house in the summer.*

If having sisters wasn't enough to absorb, the news about her father was overwhelming. She had wished for years that Paul Prescott hadn't been killed in an accident. If he'd lived, Phoebe felt sure he would've kept all three of them. Sure, it'd been hard when he and her mother were only eighteen, but together they could've made it. Instead, her biological father was a rich and selfish physician. Harris made promises to a beautiful teenager, but he never meant to marry her. At the time Phoebe was conceived, her father was engaged to another woman. He'd used her mom and then forgot about her.

Her mom was right that he felt she wouldn't fit into his privileged world. His attraction had been superficial, and he'd lacked morals. Her resemblance to him must have been hard on her mom.

Her old boyfriend, Jared, hadn't been engaged to someone, but he ended their relationship when she wouldn't sleep with him. Phoebe stopped stretching, remembering how she'd met Jared at church. It'd hurt a lot when he'd broken up with her. She hadn't dated anyone since their breakup. She'd gone to the usual college parties, but the guys were immature. Were there any decent men around?

"Hi. Sorry, I'm running late," Haley said breathlessly.

"It's okay. I didn't even notice you were late." Phoebe saw Haley was dressed similar to her, wearing leggings and a tank top. Haley's blonde hair touched her shoulders.

"Did you get any sleep last night? I shouldn't have listened to you and went to your house anyway."

Phoebe saw the concern in Haley's gray eyes. Yesterday, when she'd called Haley to tell her she had two sisters, her best friend had offered to be with her. "I haven't slept much since learning I have sisters and a father who's alive."

"Why don't we walk first?" Haley touched her arm. "I can tell you're upset."

Phoebe nodded. "I do need to unload. I can't believe I have two identical sisters. When I was little, I felt like part of me was missing. Now I understand why I had these feelings."

As they walked along the river, Haley gave her a warm smile. "I'm glad your mom kept you. It had to be awful for her to give Amy and Jenna away."

"I wish she would've stayed on welfare. Maybe then she could've raised all of us. When we were a little older, she could've gotten a job."

Haley shook her head. "I can't see your mom staying on welfare. She's an independent woman. As only a high school graduate, any job she could have gotten would've been a low-paying one, and childcare would have been expensive for three little kids."

Phoebe nodded. "That's true. Mom was only seventeen when she graduated from high school. I can't imagine being young and pregnant. It's unfair she didn't have any family to support her."

"I've admired Lindsay for years, but I do even more now. She found herself in such a difficult situation and made a hard decision by herself."

Phoebe shrugged. "I guess, but I wish her decision could've been a different one."

Haley tucked several strands of blonde hair behind her ear. "You two have always been so close. I'm surprised Lindsay didn't tell you a long time ago about your sisters and father. It must've been hard to have kept it all bottled up."

Phoebe thought about how her real father could've made a difference in her life. All her life she had missed not having a dad to do things with. The father-daughter dances had been hard because she'd never had a dad to take her to them. There wasn't even a close relative to step in on his behalf.

A rock was in her path, and she kicked it hard. "I would love to meet my father and tell him what I think of him. He was a jerk and should've returned my mom's calls. With all his money, he could've easily supported us."

"If your father had known about you, maybe his wealthy family would've gotten custody of you and your sisters. It doesn't sound like your father wanted Lindsay in his life."

As a few joggers went around them, Phoebe and Haley mumbled greetings to them.

Would my father have wanted us if he'd known? Phoebe wondered. "When I found Harris Manning on the internet, I read he's a gastroenterology doctor. It's unbelievable that I've always wanted to become a doctor. Now I'm not sure I want to. I feel sick thinking I'd be following in my father's footsteps."

Haley shook her head in bewilderment. "You can't give up your dream because of him. You need to contact him. He should know he has daughters. Does he have other children?"

Phoebe's heart lurched, and she drew in a deep breath. "Oh my gosh. I could have other siblings . . . well, half-siblings. I don't know anything about his family. I just saw information about his practice. I searched on Facebook, but I didn't find him there. I guess I could've looked under his wife's name. Maybe she's on social media."

"We can look on Instagram and Facebook."

Phoebe gave a weak laugh. "I looked for my sisters even though I know the Amish aren't on the internet. Some have websites for their businesses, but they wouldn't be on social media."

"Your mom should contact your dad," Haley said eagerly. "He could hire a private eye to search for them."

She thought for a moment and appreciated Haley's positive take on her unbelievable situation. "I don't know. Mom wants to find Amy and Jenna, but she seems weak and worried."

"That's why you should get your dad involved."

"Geez, he doesn't even know about us." A lump formed in her throat thinking how her mother had cancer. "What if Mom dies without seeing them? I'm disappointed I grew up without my sisters, but I love my mom. I know she always put me first and did the best she could. How can I live without her?" Tears welled in her eyes at the realization she could be alone. "I have to find my sisters for us."

～

Lindsay was thrilled Phoebe decided to run by the river. It got her out of the house to do something she loves. I don't suppose Amy and Jenna enjoy running. I don't know of any Amish runners.

As she poured a cup of coffee, she thought of how little she knew about Amy and Jenna as adults. Her heart skipped a beat remembering how the letters had stopped after the girls graduated from the eighth grade. It'd been awful being cut off from their lives, and it had broken her heart. Katie's letters had filled a void. She'd sent a letter to Shipshewana each year on their birthdays until Phoebe graduated from high school. Those letters were never returned. Katie and Roman must have moved sometime within the last four years.

Lindsay went to her home office where she did some of her schoolwork. She'd write a letter to Harris even though Phoebe wasn't anxious to meet him. Her daughter needed to connect with her father. Where should she send the letter? Maybe she could use the address of his practice.

She sat at her desk and removed several sheets of paper with her name printed on them. After taking a deep breath, Lindsay started writing a letter that should've been written a long time ago.

Dear Harris,

I'm sure I'm the last person you ever expected to hear from. In case you don't remember, I was the hotel maid you met and promised to marry. After you left, I learned I was pregnant. I left you several voicemails, but you never returned any of them. I went to your parents' house to tell you in person that I was pregnant with your child. Callie came to the door and showed me her engagement ring.

I didn't have any family to help me, but my high school boyfriend, Paul, had always been in love with me. He married me even though Paul knew the baby was not his.

Her eyes misted, and she attempted to blink away the on-coming tears. How could she continue to write about the secret she'd kept from Harris? But she needed to continue to tell him about their daughters. She grasped the pen tightly and resumed writing.

Soon after, I learned I was pregnant with triplets. Then Paul was in a fatal car accident.

I turned to God after Paul's death. I became a Christian and knew God would help me. I gave birth to three beautiful, identical baby girls. They have your black hair and brown eyes. Their names are Amy, Jenna, and Phoebe. I worked at McDonald's before they arrived, then I had to go on welfare. With only a high school education and no family support, I felt God wanted me to give our babies away. During my pregnancy, I met a wonderful Amish couple who had been married for ten years. Katie and Roman hadn't been blessed with children.

When the girls were almost five months old, I went back to visit them. Katie and Roman wanted to adopt all three of them. I stayed with them for several weeks to see how my babies adjusted to Katie. Since Phoebe refused to take a bottle from Katie, I felt like she needed me more than the other two. I decided to keep her, and she has been the greatest joy in my life. She has graduated from college and plans to start medical school.

Did you and Callie have children? It would be nice for Phoebe, Amy, and Jenna to have half-siblings. I'm sure Katie and Roman never had other children. I'm sorry this might disrupt your family life.

Katie agreed to write me one letter a year about Amy and Jenna until they finished eighth grade. She didn't want them to know about me and Phoebe. Katie wasn't interested in an open adoption.

She stopped writing and took a deep breath. Writing a letter revealing everything to Harris was breaking her heart. She glanced out the window at the sunny day and thought it was a shame to have to write news that would affect many. Hopefully, once the numbness wore off, her daughters and their father could develop a meaningful relationship with each other. She resumed writing.

I wouldn't bother you now, but it's time for the truth to be known. I don't need your financial help. I have a college degree, and I have a career as a teacher. Phoebe and I live in a lovely house. The problem is that I have non-Hodgkin's lymphoma cancer, and I'm in stage four.

This past school year, I ignored my cancer symptoms, which worsened my condition. I might survive, but if not, I don't want Phoebe to be alone in this world and without family as I never remarried after Paul's death.

I told her the truth yesterday. She now knows you are her father. We have always been close, and I know it has hurt her that I have lied to her for years. She thought Paul was her father. Harris, she needs you in her life. I know she has missed so much by not having a father. Phoebe was also shocked when I told her that she has two sisters.

I wrote a letter to Katie a couple of weeks ago, and it was returned to me. I can't believe Katie and Roman moved and never gave me their new address. I am going to look for them. I can't imagine why they moved. They lived on a farm in a lovely house in Shipshewana, Indiana.

I am sending this to your office. I found your address online.

God blessed me with three healthy babies. I don't regret having them. I just wish I could have kept them together. I'm enclosing a picture of them. I went to JCPenney and had their picture taken when they were three months old.

I'll include my business card with my phone number and email address. I can understand if you need time to process this news of having three daughters.

In Christ's Love,
Lindsay Johnson Prescott

As she finished the letter, an unsettled feeling arose in her heart. Maybe this wasn't the time to send Harris a letter. She wanted Phoebe to have him in her life, but was this the best way to tell him? It'd be good for her to have a father, but would it be destructive for Harris, Callie, and their family?

Chapter Seven

"How was your run?" Lindsay poured a second cup of coffee before glancing at Phoebe. *Please, dear Lord, help Phoebe forgive me for separating her from her sisters.* She had heard Phoebe moving around the last two nights, so she knew she hadn't slept well. Maybe meeting Haley by the river helped. The two girls had always been close friends.

"Haley and I decided to walk, so we could talk about everything." Phoebe walked to the kitchen and removed a glass from the cabinet.

Lindsay smiled. "I thought I felt my ears burning."

"Haley thinks you did the best you could under the circumstances." Phoebe put the glass under the water dispenser on the refrigerator. After she took a big drink of water, Phoebe continued. "I forgot to take any water with me this morning."

Lindsay shrugged, sitting on a stool by the counter. "I tried to do the best I could. It seemed like I never got a break. My mother had hurt me my whole life. It seemed she never could love me. Then Harris broke my heart. I believed he loved me, but he never meant any of it. When I became a Christian, I felt truly loved. Unconditionally. Jesus became my best friend. It was a huge turning point in my life, and I turned to Him for guidance."

Phoebe gave Lindsay a hug. "I have always felt loved. Now that everything is starting to sink in, I believe you when you said God directed you to let Katie and Roman adopt my sisters. I don't know how you did it after we were born. You were recovering from having a C-section."

At Phoebe's words, the sadness Lindsay had carried with her the last couple of days seemed to slide off her back. She pressed a palm to her heart. "I feel blessed that you've just learned the most incredible secret and you're giving me your support."

"Did you have anyone to help you after giving birth? I mean after you left the hospital." Phoebe leaned against the counter.

"No, but I had some time to recover because you three stayed in a children's hospital until you weighed enough to go home."

"I know you dressed us in different colors, but did you have other ways to tell us apart?"

"I didn't always dress you in different colors. Sometimes I painted each of your toenails a different color." Lindsay smiled. "Also, all three of you have the same birthmark, but each one is in a different spot."

At the sound of the doorbell, Phoebe said, "I'll get it."

Sighing, she hoped it wasn't a visitor because she needed to talk with Phoebe more.

Phoebe returned with a vase of white roses, blue delphinium, and other flowers. She set the vase in front of her and grinned. "Looks like you have an admirer."

"They're beautiful." She leaned closer and breathed in the sweet fragrance before removing the small card. After reading the message, Lindsay said, "They're from Drew. I can't believe he sent me flowers. What a thoughtful man."

"Does he know you were in the hospital?"

She shook her head. "No. I haven't talked to him since he left for Germany, but he knew I was scheduled for chemo this week. I'll send him a text later and thank him." She waved her hand, gesturing to the outside. "It's too nice to be inside. Let's go sit on the patio." *I need to tell Phoebe I wrote a letter to Harris. If he calls, she should be prepared for him to reach out to her. I've managed fine on my own, but I have to reveal the secret I've kept from Harris.*

Phoebe opened the glass sliding door to the patio, and they sat on the chairs by the table.

"This is a gorgeous day." Lindsay sipped her coffee and looked around the yard. "I love the petunias you planted. The hanging baskets look great too."

"You can never have too many flowers, and now you have a bouquet of them from Drew. He likes you. When does he come back from Germany?"

"I'm not sure. Maybe in a couple of weeks. He took Matthew with him. Drew's mother was glad to go see her sister in Germany, so she'll be watching her grandson while Drew's at work."

Phoebe took a drink of her water. "I want to find Amy and Jenna, but I've started wondering what their reactions will be when they learn the truth. They might resent me because I was the one you kept."

"I hope not. With having both a father and a mother, they should be happy. They also had a wonderful extended family with aunts, uncles, cousins, and grandparents on both sides."

"There's another thing I thought of." Phoebe leaned closer to the table. "You and I both have college degrees. They might feel like they were shortchanged with less education because they were raised in an Amish home."

"Even though the Amish stop education at the eighth grade, they do continue to study and read. Some need to take classes to learn more for their businesses." Lindsay put her cup on the table. "Amy and Jenna could even be married.

Amish women marry younger than English. Oh, they call us English because we are outsiders and not Amish."

Phoebe gave her a puzzled glance. "I didn't know they call us English. That seems weird to me. I guess I better learn about their faith and rules before I meet Amy and Jenna. Just think . . . If they are married, they might have children. I could be an aunt, and you might be a grandmother."

Reaching her arm across the table, Lindsay grasped Phoebe's hand in hers, giving it a squeeze. "When I was in the hospital, it occurred to me they might have children. I cried at how much I've missed of their lives. But you missed it too. I'm so sorry."

"If you hadn't gotten sick, would you have ever told me the truth?"

Lindsay noticed the slight movement of the tabletop from Phoebe tapping the metal leg with her foot. Her fidgeting made Lindsay lose her concentration, and she hesitated in answering. "Probably. Many times, I wanted to tell you everything, especially about your sisters. I should've told you when you graduated from high school."

"I wish you had told me and given me Katie's letters." Phoebe raised her eyebrows. "I guess Katie and Roman must've kept my sisters in the dark about us too. I wonder, though, how Katie managed to keep your letters a secret. It seems like Amy and Jenna would've asked about you when they saw your letters. They must've gone to the mailbox at times. Or maybe not since I never saw Katie's letters until now."

"Amish women do have English pen pals. Katie might have told them I was a pen pal. Or maybe she managed to get to the mailbox before the girls did. It was only one letter from me each year."

Phoebe looked surprised. "I never thought of the Amish having pen pals."

"Well, they don't have phones in their houses. They might have a phone in a barn, or what they call a phone shanty. Katie and Roman had a shanty some distance from their house. I've heard Amish women can vent in their letters to their English friends. They wouldn't complain about their children or other personal things to Amish women, but they feel free to express their feelings to an Englisher."

"I wish Katie would've continued letting you know what Amy and Jenna did after they were done with their school." Phoebe gave her a frustrated look. "And I wish she would've told you where they moved to."

Lindsay sighed, understanding Phoebe's annoyance. "It wasn't an open adoption, so Katie wasn't obligated to give me her new address. We had agreed on her sending me a letter while the girls were in school. And as you know, she did that. I'd hoped she'd continue writing to me because I sent her a letter each year around your birthday until you graduated from high school."

"We could go to Shipshewana if you feel up to it and ask around. Someone has to realize where they moved to." Phoebe sipped her water.

"I don't have the energy to go right now, and I have my chemo this week on Wednesday and Thursday." Lindsay ran her finger over the rim of her cup. "While you were out, I wrote a letter to Harris." She stared at Phoebe, afraid of her reaction.

Phoebe closed her eyes for a second. "I guess you can't hold off for a little time before telling him."

She shook her head. "In my letter, I told him about you, Amy, and Jenna. I put his office's address on the envelope. I don't know his home address, but I think Harris will get the letter at his office."

Phoebe frowned. "It might be better to contact him after we find Amy and Jenna."

"I think it's best to let him know the secret I've kept from him for years instead of waiting. It shouldn't take long to find them."

"Today is Monday, so he should get the letter tomorrow or by Wednesday. Cincinnati is only a couple of hours from here." Phoebe bit her lower lip. "Mom, I'm scared. Life is changing so quickly. What if Amy and Jenna don't like me?"

"Your sisters will love you. I'm sure they have grown into lovely and sweet young women. Just like you have." Lindsay leaned her chin on her hands, remembering how sweet Amy and Jenna were when she'd secretly visited them at their school. She'd gone because of a mother's desire to see how they were. She'd even had a conversation with young Jenna on the playground. Heartbreak entered her soul at missing her two daughters' childhood, but she blinked away her tears.

Sounding cautious, Phoebe said, "I'm not crazy about meeting Harris."

Lindsay extended her arm across the table and grasped Phoebe's hand. "I'm worried too, but sending a letter is the right thing to do."

"I guess."

"Calling would be painful for me and a shock to Harris. A letter he can reread so that the secret I've kept will sink in. I don't know what will happen. I hope we hear from him, but if we don't, I'll call his office," Lindsay said in a deliberate voice.

"Are you still in love with Harris?"

Immediately, she shook her head. He'd hurt her deeply when he left her to return to his life. Besides that, she was no longer a young girl in love with him. "No, I'm not."

"I'm sorry he treated you so poorly."

"Me too." Lindsay tossed her long hair across her shoulders. "We could've made it and raised our babies together, but he never cared enough to contact me. He knew Callie for a long time, so it makes sense he married her."

"I can't imagine what I'll have in common with my sisters." Phoebe pursed her lips and exhaled a deep breath. "Our lives have been so different."

"That's true, but it'll be fun to learn about them."

"It'd help if they weren't Amish," Phoebe said in an irritated tone. "Their form of transportation is a horse and buggy. I love being able to drive a car."

"All three of you have the same biological parents, so you have that in common." Lindsay smiled at Phoebe. "And you love to bake. They might enjoy giving you some of their Amish recipes."

"Why do the Amish dress the way they do? It makes them stand out."

A sense of strength and hope came to her at Phoebe's question because it gave her a chance to educate her about the Amish. "There are several reasons. One reason is that women must cover themselves and keep their hair hidden under prayer caps. This modesty in dress is also important in keeping their hearts and bodies pure. The Amish believe God has called them to be completely separate from the world, so it's another reason they choose to wear clothing that sets them apart from us. Yet, the plain clothing is a way to keep them all the same in their community, so no one person will stand out with fancy clothing." Lindsay laughed. "I remember how surprised I was when I saw Katie use straight pins when she got dressed instead of having buttons in her clothing."

"That's interesting about their clothing." Phoebe glanced at her watch. "I need to take a shower and get ready for work. If you still want to send the letter, I can drop it off at the post office on my way to work."

"Thanks. The letter is on the coffee table."

Before Phoebe left, she bent down and gave Lindsay a kiss on her cheek. "I'm glad you told me the truth. I hope Amy and Jenna will be happy to learn about us."

Lindsay stayed on the patio, thinking how the letter might change their lives.

Hopefully, Harris will be anxious to meet our daughters. I'm afraid Katie won't be happy to have Amy and Jenna know the truth, but with all my heart, I know it's the right time. God's timing is perfect.

But I'm nervous to hear from Harris. What if he doesn't believe they are his daughters? That's silly. They resemble him with their black hair and brown eyes.

⌒

"Hi, Lindsay. I received your letter today."

When Harris's name appeared on her cell phone screen, she felt like she was on a roller coaster with many explosive emotions churning inside her. "Hi." Holding her breath, Lindsay waited for the questions Harris would surely have for her.

"I read your letter several times. When I read you'd given birth to identical triplets, I was in shock. It's the most incredible news I've ever received."

With her heart thumping, she sat on a chair in the living room. Hearing Harris's deep voice made her nervous, but it was nice at the same time. "It was a huge surprise when I learned I was carrying three babies." She gave a little laugh. "I was lucky I didn't pass out. I couldn't speak for several minutes."

"I can't imagine what you had to go through to make such hard decisions. I'd like to visit you and Phoebe tomorrow morning." His voice was laced with emotion as he continued. "I wish I had known you were pregnant. I have *daughters.* I feel like I've won the lottery or something. I have to admit it's hard wrapping my head around the fact that I'm a father of three twenty-two-year-old daughters."

"I guess you and Callie don't have children."

"We weren't blessed with any. Callie had two miscarriages, and she didn't want to try again."

"I'm so sorry that happened." *That meant no half-siblings for their triplets,* Lindsay thought.

"Is it okay if I visit you and Phoebe tomorrow?"

"I have chemo treatments tomorrow and on Thursday." She blew out a breath, wondering how she'd do with her treatments. It was hard to predict since she'd ended up in the hospital after the first infusion last week. Should she ask him to wait until next week so she could have more time to find Jenna and Amy and recover from treatments? "You could come next week."

"I'm not thinking straight. I meant to tell you how sorry I am you have cancer. If there is anything I can do, let me know."

"Okay, I will, and thanks."

"I'd rather come this Friday or Saturday," Harris said with a sense of urgency in his voice. "I'm anxious to see Phoebe, and of course, I want to see Amy and Jenna soon."

Was she ready to see Harris? And maybe Callie. Her stomach turned at the thought of seeing Callie, but she tried to keep her voice normal. "Friday should work. Will you be coming alone?"

"Yes, it'll be just me. I haven't told my parents that they're grandparents. They're in Europe, and I decided to wait until we find Amy and Jenna." He paused for a moment. "Callie and I are divorced. It seems we both lost our spouses."

Harris's divorce both stunned and saddened her. From the beginning, it had seemed Callie and Harris had a lot going for them. It wasn't enough to have a lasting marriage. "I'm sorry about Callie."

"I keep staring at the photo of our triplets. They were beautiful babies. I have tons of questions to ask, but I can wait until we see each other."

"Our babies couldn't have been any cuter." She cleared her throat, wanting to end the conversation. She realized how different their lives had been, and it was painful to her. He never had a child to love and raise. "I'll see you soon."

"Hey, don't hang up." Then, in a softer voice, he said, "I want to see you too, Lindsay."

Her eyes instantly filled with tears. "See you on Friday."

Chapter Eight

Nervousness rushed through Lindsay's body at the sight of Harris. The father of her daughters and the man she had freely given her love to was in the same room with her once again. Growing older hadn't diminished his good looks. His black hair didn't have any gray in it. His face seemed thinner than she remembered from when they had their summer together. There was no ring on his finger, so he hadn't remarried after Callie divorced him. He filled out his jeans nicely and wore a gray striped shirt with short sleeves. He looked too handsome for a forty-four-year-old. Why was it some men seemed to grow even better looking as they aged?

Lindsay wasn't a vain woman, but she wished her looks hadn't changed. She was no longer the young girl Harris had kissed and pledged his love to, but she was now a forty-year-old woman. But even though her body had been through a lot with cancer, she felt attractive wearing a new bright blue sundress with a white sweater.

"Would you like coffee or anything to drink?" Lindsay asked.

"No, thank you." Harris's brown eyes studied her. "I'm sorry about your cancer. I want to talk to your doctor soon about your treatment."

"That's not necessary, but thank you." Lindsay pointed to the sofa.

After Harris sat on the sofa, Lindsay went to sit on a chair across from him. His eyes pored into her blue ones. "I didn't like learning you had cancer. I know stage four means it's spread to four organs."

"It was a surprise when I learned I had cancer."

"I rented a room at Holiday Inn because I'm staying here for the weekend."

"Thank you for making the trip."

"When can I see Phoebe? Will she be here soon?"

"Phoebe has a job at a restaurant. She'll be here after her shift ends later today."

Harris ran his fingers through his black hair. "I still can't absorb all this. I was in total shock when I read your letter. I'm unhappy that I didn't know you were pregnant but thankful I have a chance now to meet our daughters. I'm glad you kept Phoebe. Maybe we can see her at the restaurant where she works," he said eagerly.

"We can do that, but it might be less awkward for you to meet her at my house." Lindsay didn't think Phoebe would appreciate meeting Harris for the first time while she waited on customers.

"It's hard to wait now that I know I'm a father." His expression sharpened as he got to his feet. "I'm anxious to see pictures of Phoebe. I notice you have several here on the wall." Harris walked to a nearby wall covered with pictures. He stared at each one carefully. "Phoebe and you look happy. She's beautiful like you."

"I think she looks like *you*." She fidgeted nervously at his compliment.

"Phoebe's features are yours, but she does have my hair and eyes." He turned away from the photos to look at Lindsay.

"I don't have any pictures of Amy and Jenna except the ones I took when they were babies." She pointed to the photo album on the coffee table. "Amish don't take pictures, but I did take a couple of the girls with Katie and Roman. It's better not to ask the Amish if you can take a photo. That way they aren't posing for it, and they are okay with it then."

"I missed out so much by not knowing about our triplets." He remained standing as he looked at the photos. "We made beautiful babies. I can't believe how they are identical too. That must have been fun."

"It was. I did different things to help me know which one I held in my arms."

After a few minutes, he picked up the album from the table and sat on the sofa. He kept the album on his lap and stared at her with a thoughtful expression. "What made you give them to an Amish couple?"

"Phoebe asked the same thing." Lindsay explained her many reasons to Harris, but she could tell he wasn't convinced an Amish family was the best.

"I have to admit it's hard for me to imagine having two daughters being adopted by an Amish couple."

Her eyes flew to his, and in them, she saw compassion.

"I can see why you felt compelled to give them to a loving and stable family. An Amish couple would seem a good choice." Harris raised his eyebrows. "I hope Amy and Jenna will be open to getting to know us. They have probably lived a sheltered life."

"I felt God wanted me to give the girls to them. Phoebe had jaundice in the hospital and was the smallest. She needed me more and wouldn't take a bottle from Katie. I'm glad I kept her. I couldn't bear to give all three away."

He looked at another page in the photo album. "How much did they weigh at birth?"

Lindsay moved closer to Harris and pointed to the first baby in the photo. "All weighed three pounds plus some ounces. Amy is in lavender, Jenna's in the middle, and Phoebe is in pink. They were born at thirty-three weeks. I had a cesarean delivery because of having multiples."

"Do you feel up to seeing the private investigator this morning? I know you just had your chemo infusions. The appointment is at eleven o'clock. We can have lunch afterward." Harris squinted his brown eyes at her.

Harris had called her on Wednesday to see how her treatment had gone. She'd actually felt sick to her stomach, but when he asked her for permission to make an appointment with an investigator, she'd agreed to it. He canceled his Friday appointments with his patients so they could get busy finding their daughters. "Yes, I can go. I've tried to find them, but nothing has turned up. I called stores in Shipshewana. Some of the owners didn't know Katie and Roman Yoder. Others heard they'd moved to somewhere in Ohio."

Harris glanced at the clock. "We still have time to talk more. I think I'll have a cup of coffee." He stood. "I'll get it. Do you want a cup?"

"Yes, please."

"Do you still like it black?"

She nodded, surprised he remembered. Walking to the refrigerator, she grinned. "I hope you still don't put a ton of sugar and cream in yours. I don't have sugar, but I do have a creamer that is sweet. Phoebe uses it."

"I'll try it."

After they got their cups of coffee, they sat on stools by the counter. Harris took a sip of coffee. "I don't need sugar with this creamer." He turned his head and glanced at the sliding doors. "You have a lovely view. Your house is nice. I'm impressed by how well you have done."

"Thank you. We like it, but the house needed a lot of remodeling."

He studied her for a moment. "I need to tell you something. I thought about you a lot before I married Callie. I decided to look for you once, which wasn't a good way to treat my fiancé. I remembered you said you grew up in Granville. I was surprised you had married Paul. When I saw you with him, I wasn't aware you were pregnant."

Shock went through her heart. "We were only married for a month before he died. Who told you I was married?"

"I stopped in a diner that had a fifties theme. I went in to see if anyone could give me your address. When we were briefly together, I gave you my home address, but you never gave me yours. I saw you and Paul in a cozy booth in the restaurant. You looked happy." Harris cleared his throat. "An older waitress saw me staring at you. She commented on how sweet it was that you and Paul had gotten married and had been high school sweethearts."

"Was she short with gray hair?"

He nodded. "Her name was Pam."

Growing up, Pam had always been there for her. Whenever her mother went through a rage, Lindsay went to the diner to see Pam. Frequently, the kind waitress gave her a hamburger and fries. *How unfair life was that Harris came to see me when I had just married Paul.* "We did marry in a hurry. I was scared because I was pregnant. If we'd known I was going to have triplets, I'm not sure Paul would've married me."

In a defeated voice, Harris said, "I think one of the reasons my marriage failed is because I never loved Callie enough. As soon as I read your letter, I drove to Callie's house. She had deleted your phone messages because she thought you were after my money. She admitted you came to my parents' house when we had our engagement party. I lost my temper with her and told her how she never should've interfered in my life—and yours."

"It hurt me deeply when you didn't return my calls." Lindsay left out a frustrated sigh. "But I was happy Paul wanted to raise the baby as ours. Then, when I went in for my eight-week ultrasound, my doctor told me I was having triplets, and she thought they were identical, which was so rare. I felt sheer panic, and I almost fell off the table."

"I wish I had been there when you heard the triplet news." Harris smiled. "I might have fainted, but after the shock wore off, I would have been thrilled."

"It would've been wonderful if you had been with me, but we were young. Three babies at once would've meant you couldn't go to medical school, and your parents wouldn't have been happy."

He frowned. "I still had my undergraduate degree and could've gotten a job."

Her eyebrows raised at the tension in his voice. "Your parents encouraged you to marry Callie."

"I shouldn't have been influenced by them." He moved the stool away from the counter. Standing, he started pacing back and forth by the granite counter. "They kept telling me how Callie and I were close ever since we were children. I listened to their arguments, and at the time, they made sense. I had known you for such a short time. My parents said I fell for you because it was a romantic beach setting."

Lindsay turned around to stare at Harris. She pointed her index finger at him. "I guess we were never meant to be together. God had other plans."

"I wish things had been different, but I'm glad to know the truth now."

"I hope Katie will feel the same way. I'm afraid she won't be happy, but I want to see Amy and Jenna. I hope she understands how important it is since I have cancer. And it's only right you can meet them too." She walked to the sink and rinsed her cup.

Harris moved his stool to stand. His brown eyes filled with tears. "I've missed so much by not knowing you were pregnant. I wish I could've been there for you and our daughters. I'm sorry for everything, but you did so well as a single mother."

Lindsay hadn't wanted to have physical contact with Harris, but seeing his pain prompted her to draw him into a loose embrace. "It seems we both reached out to each other, but roadblocks got in the way. We can't change the past, but together we can try to find Amy and Jenna."

He hugged her back. She swayed, feeling overwhelmed by his closeness. Bolts of energy crisscrossed up her arm and through her body. "Sorry, I'm weak from the chemo."

"You need to sit." He eased her down to sit on the sofa. "I should've gone with you to your chemo."

His touch spread a warm feeling throughout her body. *Maybe the temperature in the room has gone up,* Lindsay thought. *I don't want the warmth to come from Harris. I can't fall for him and go through that heartbreak again. I can't allow him to get too close to me.* "Phoebe took me to chemo. I'm not sure about getting lunch after the appointment. I don't seem to have much energy these days."

"We can order something and have it delivered."

$\sim$

At 11:00 a.m. sharp, Lindsay and Harris were seated in chairs across from Zach Porter. He looked like he was in his midthirties. He had dark blond hair and wore a wedding band. On his mammoth desk were a couple of framed pictures. She hadn't pictured a private eye to have such an incredible office, but it wasn't a one-man business either. Porter had an attractive receptionist, an assistant, and a savvy computer person to help with searches.

"Mrs. Prescott, I started researching the Amish people. I learned they might move when a family in another location needs their help. Do you remember Katie and Roman Yoder talking about relatives living in another place? Or did Katie mention in her letters that their district had made changes they disagreed with?"

Lindsay shook her head, glancing down at the packet of letters she held in her hand. After Phoebe read the letters from Katie, she'd given them back to her. "Katie never said anything about not agreeing with their bishop or members. When they lived in Shipshewana, Katie's parents and siblings lived nearby, but Roman's family did not. When I made phone calls to businesses in Shipshewana, I heard they might have moved to Ohio. I'm not sure they did, though. I know the Amish like to go visiting and will hire drivers or go by bus. Katie wrote once that they visited her sister and husband in Lancaster, Pennsylvania. She said how Amy and Jenna enjoyed traveling there. That was when they were thirteen years old."

Mr. Porter rubbed his chin. "Lancaster, Pennsylvania, doesn't have cheap farmland. It's a popular tourist spot too. Did Katie mention her sister's married name?"

Lindsay sighed. "No, I'm afraid not. Katie probably still has some family in Shipshewana. She came from a big Amish family. Katie's maiden name is Gingerich. Phoebe and I talked about going to Indiana to see what we could learn."

"You've been a big help," Mr. Porter said quickly.

She tapped her finger against the packet of letters. "Thank you. I'm glad." A sense of relief and a positive feeling gave Lindsay hope she'd see her daughters soon. She was glad Harris hired Mr. Porter to aid them in their search.

"I've heard Kentucky is becoming a popular spot for the Amish to move to. You said Roman was a farmer, so I wonder if he moved where the land is cheaper. Land is too expensive in many areas. Or maybe he isn't farming now. He could be running a business. Did he have other interests or hobbies when you lived with the Yoder family?"

"Not really. I can't think of anything. I just remember Roman spending a lot of time reading mysteries and their Amish and Mennonite weekly newspaper, *The Budget*." Lindsay leaned forward in her chair, smiling. She anticipated finding news about the Yoder's new location from the paper. "I can't believe I didn't think of this before. We need to buy a paper because it has stories from all over the United States. They include where they live. Maybe Amy or Jenna even wrote about the happenings in their district. *The Budget* comes out on Wednesday."

Harris smiled at Lindsay. "That's a great idea."

"I'll get my assistant to buy the newspaper and read through it. That's definitely another place we can look to see if we can learn what happened to the Yoder family." After Mr. Porter wrote something on his pad, he looked at Lindsay. "Do you have any extra pictures of Phoebe? Even though Amy and Jenna will be dressed in Plain clothing, pictures of Phoebe will help."

After Lindsay removed photos from her folder, she leaned closer to the desk and handed several photos to Mr. Porter. "Here you go. By the way, Katie and Roman didn't have other children."

"Thanks." Mr. Porter looked at a photo of Phoebe. "You have a beautiful daughter. I'll keep you both updated. I don't think it's going to take long to find them. Jodi, my assistant, is already searching for them on social media. Katie could have relatives who have left their faith and are online somewhere. I know the Amish don't have phones in their houses, but I'm sure someone has to know where the Yoder family is now. If we don't get any leads soon, I'll go to Shipshewana."

"I'll look forward to hearing what you learn." *Soon I might be able to see Amy and Jenna,* Lindsay thought. *I'm happy but scared at the same time. I know Katie and Roman gave them a stable and loving home, but what if they feel I didn't love them? I kept Phoebe but gave them away.*

Harris stood, handing Mr. Porter a check. "I'm glad you're getting started on this right away."

Lindsay said, "If Amy and Jenna are found soon, I'll be on cloud nine."

Mr. Porter pushed his chair away from the desk, walked to Lindsay, and shook her hand. "I work best under pressure, especially for a lovely woman like yourself."

Lindsay felt her face get warm, knowing she was blushing at the private eye's compliment.

Harris noticed how Lindsay's flushed face at Zach's comment. *With her delicate features, blue eyes, high cheekbones, and creamy skin, she is mind-blowingly beautiful. Her honey-blonde hair brushed her shoulders. He remembered how he'd loved running his fingers through her silky hair on the beach. Even though she has cancer, Lindsay pulls it off with an inner glow. I wish I could've seen her pregnant with our daughters. I can't believe how my life had changed since I received Lindsay's letter. If she hadn't gotten cancer, would she have ever contacted me?*

The two of them left the investigator's office. "Have you ever eaten at Cap City Fine Diner and Bar?"

"Yes, I have. Phoebe and I went there. I got their meatloaf, and it was the best I have ever had. How did you know about it?"

"I was a speaker a year ago at a medical conference. I ate there with other doctors." He unlocked his black Mercedes and opened the door for Lindsay. "Is it okay if we eat lunch there? Or if you're too tired, we can get it to go."

She nodded and slid into her seat. "We can eat at the restaurant. Hearing our daughters might be located soon gave me energy. I can't believe you were in Columbus and not far from Phoebe's restaurant. I thought about mentioning eating where Phoebe works, but I don't think it'd be good to surprise her."

"I'm anxious to meet Phoebe." He shut Lindsay's car door, feeling a nervous twinge about meeting his daughter. *Would Phoebe be happy to finally meet him, or would she resent him for not marrying Lindsay?*

While Lindsay fastened her seat belt, he got in behind the steering wheel. He had to know if she'd ever missed him enough to look to see what he'd done with his life. "I wish I'd known you lived here. Did you ever check to see what had happened to me?"

"During my pregnancy, I saw you went to medical school and saw your marriage to Callie in the news. She was a stunning bride. I never did look again because it hurt to see you lied to me when I thought you had loved me. Learning you had a girlfriend back home and then realizing you married her, I knew I couldn't look again at the wonderful life you two had."

Harris left the parking lot and entered the street. "I never looked either. I figured you were still married to Paul. I didn't even know your married name."

Lindsay frowned. "That's interesting we never looked for each other, but I was busy with raising Phoebe, and you were consumed with your career. How long have you and Callie been divorced?"

"Three years, but we had already been separated for two years. Like I said before, we never should've married." He quickly turned his head away from the street to look at Lindsay. "I wish I could change the past, but I can't. I hope we can learn to know each other again and enjoy spending time with our daughters."

"Let's take it one step at a time, but I agree we need to spend time with our daughters. That's the most important priority." Lindsay grinned. "All this talking with you and the private eye has given me an appetite."

Twenty-five minutes later, they were seated at a table. Both had ordered the meatloaf.

"It looks like you love the meatloaf. I can give you some of mine when you finish yours," Lindsay said.

Harris rolled his eyes at her. "I'll slow down. Your meatloaf is safe from me. I noticed you're enjoying the mashed potatoes."

"Their buttermilk-chive potatoes are delicious. Thanks for suggesting this restaurant."

Lindsay seemed okay, but he didn't want her to do more than she should and feel poorly later on. "When we get back to your place, I want you to take a nap. I'll check in with my partners to see how it's going."

"I am exhausted, and a nap sounds wonderful." Her blue eyes widened, and a big smile stretched across her gorgeous face. "Just think, we might meet Amy and Jenna soon."

He poised his fork before his mouth, thinking what a trooper Lindsay had been and still was. In his gut, he was thrilled she was the mother of their daughters. "I hope they are found quickly. Of course, I'm sorry you have cancer, but I'm glad it made you contact me."

She sipped her water. "I wish you had said hello to me at the restaurant. I don't suppose it would've made any difference. I was married to Paul, and I wouldn't have left him."

"I couldn't forget you, and that was why I went to find you in your hometown. I decided I couldn't marry Callie until I saw you again. I wish the waitress had mentioned your pregnancy to me. Maybe I'd realized you married Paul because you were pregnant with my baby."

Lindsay shrugged. "She might not have known I was pregnant, but I suppose she did. People talked a lot in Granville, especially about my mother."

A young woman stopped by their table. "Would you like refills?"

Harris nodded. "I'd like more iced tea, please."

"I'm fine," Lindsay said. "Thank you."

"It's nice to see you, Mrs. Prescott. You probably don't remember me, but my name's Deidre Moore. You were my favorite teacher in middle school."

Lindsay smiled. "I do remember you now. I'm glad you said something."

"I'm going to Ohio State part-time."

"That's awesome. I'm not surprised. You were always a great student."

After Deidre left to get the iced tea, Harris said, "You've accomplished a lot. Being a teacher has to be rewarding, especially when a former student is happy to see you."

"I love teaching, and a couple of years ago, I became head of the math department. I wanted Phoebe to be proud of me. I had originally planned on going to college after high school. I was accepted and had a scholarship." She gave him a small smile. "Then this tall and handsome boy swept me off my feet. If I hadn't gone to work at the beach, I suppose we never would've met."

"I'd like to think we still could've met somehow." *Being part of Lindsay's life again and having plans to meet my daughters for the first time is an incredible feeling for me. We can all have a second chance to be a family. I like the mature Lindsay a lot and have strong emotions where she's concerned. I wonder if she has any feelings for me. Is it possible for us to get together after all these years apart?*

Chapter Nine

Phoebe swallowed hard, hoping that meeting her father for the first time would go okay. After she got out of her car, Phoebe stood for a moment, staring at the expensive-looking car in the driveway.

Well, here it goes, Phoebe thought as she opened the front door. Once inside, she tossed her handbag on the foyer's small table.

Her parents were seated on the sofa, so Phoebe walked to her father. She extended her hand to Harris and smiled. "It's nice to meet you. I'm sure by now you know I'm Lindsay's daughter."

"Hi, Phoebe. I'm happy to meet you too."

He seemed emotional about seeing her. His eyes were teary and wistful. It was hard to accept Harris Manning hadn't cared enough to see her mom again after their summer together. After Phoebe sat on a chair, she stared at Harris. "You could've learned about us a long time ago if you'd taken time to answer my mom's calls."

"Phoebe, your father and I both made mistakes. He didn't get my phone calls because they were deleted by Callie. He talked to her last night, and she admitted what she had done."

Phoebe still didn't think that excused her father from responsibility but kept quiet. She saw her mom's blue eyes fill with tears.

Her mom smoothed her dress over her knees. "I learned today that your father came to see me when I lived in Granville. He didn't have my home address, but Harris saw me with Paul in a restaurant. A waitress told him I was married." Glancing at Harris, her mom continued. "Harris didn't know I was pregnant and thought I had moved on with my life."

Phoebe gave Harris a dubious glance. "*Really.* You thought the love of your life had moved on at age eighteen to marry another kid who was also fresh out of high school. Didn't you stop to consider there was more to the story or wonder why your summer fling married so fast?"

"I was foolish and stupid. I wish I could change the past, but I want to get to know you and have you as part of my life." Harris gave her a searching look.

Phoebe felt relief at the sound of a knock on the door. *I won't need to reply. After all these years of it just being mom and me, it's hard to wrap my head around having another parent in my life. Mom seems too comfortable with Harris, but maybe she's drained from going through chemo and wants me to spend time with him.*

Harris walked toward the door, turning around to glance at them. "I suppose it's the pizza we ordered."

Her mom said, "I hope you're hungry. Harris ordered two large pizzas, salad, and breadsticks."

Our first family meal together, Phoebe thought, raking her fingers several times through her hair. "Let's eat outside. I'll grab paper plates and glasses. What would you like to drink, Mom?"

"Water, please." Her mom walked to the cabinet. "I'll help with the drinks. Harris wanted to order a bottle of pop, but I told him we have iced tea in the refrigerator."

Once they were seated at the patio table and everyone had food on their plates, Harris offered to say the prayer before they ate.

Her mom said, "That would be nice."

Harris bowed his head and prayed, "Our heavenly Father, thank you for bringing us together. Help Zach Porter and his assistant, Jodi, as they look for Amy and Jenna Yoder. When our daughters, and Phoebe's sisters, are found, help each of us to approach them in the best possible way. Please heal Lindsay of her lymphoma cancer. Give her the strength to continue her fight. Most of all, thank you for your son, Jesus. Amen."

"I'm guessing you're a Christian," Phoebe said. She dipped her breadstick in ranch sauce. She was glad Harris had asked for two dipping sauces.

Harris nodded. "I wasn't, but after Callie had two miscarriages, I went through a deep depression. I tried to talk with Callie about us going to therapy together or joining a group of parents who had lost babies. She didn't want to do either one. I needed to fill the void somehow. A friend told me to go to church with him. Once I accepted Christ, I felt happiness and peace."

Her mom touched Harris's arm. "I'm glad. I couldn't have made it without God's unconditional love through the years."

Harris held a slice of pizza in his hand. "Phoebe, do you have any preferences about the field of medicine you might choose?"

Why did he have to ask me that when I'm not sure I want to go to medical school now? Phoebe sipped her iced tea for a moment. "I'm undecided."

"You don't need to know yet. I wasn't planning on being a gastroenterologist, then decided it was the right choice for me. Maybe you can visit me in Cincinnati and learn more about what I do."

Phoebe shrugged. "If I can fit it in, maybe I will. I'd just hate to leave Mom right now."

"You both can visit me."

Phoebe shook her head. "I don't see it happening right now. I'm sorry, but I'm still trying to take all this in." When she saw the disappointment in Harris's eyes, she had a twinge of regret that she hadn't been agreeable to his plans. But how could she rush into visiting him so soon? He was a stranger to her.

He gave a quick nod. "You're right. Visits can wait. Lindsay needs to get through her treatments and get well. We need to focus on finding Amy and Jenna too. I'm anxious to meet them."

"I haven't had a chance to ask you how it went with the private eye. Is he going to get busy searching for Amy and Jenna soon?" Phoebe asked before taking a bite of pizza.

Harris nodded. "He's starting immediately. I hope he finds them quickly. When he does locate Amy and Jenna, I hope you can go with us."

"I want to, but I also worry about their reactions." Phoebe didn't want to hurt her mother, but she couldn't keep quiet. It still bothered her that she'd just learned about her sisters. She took a shaky deep breath and released it. "Mom, I know you and Katie decided to keep the adoption a secret, but I wish you hadn't waited until now to reveal it. It's going to be weird to meet them. What do we talk about? I wish I could've known them during our childhood."

Her mom rubbed her forehead. "There were many times I wanted to tell you, but I couldn't break my promise. When I was diagnosed with lymphoma, I knew I had to see them and have all three of you learn to be sisters together. I should've insisted Katie tell them the truth by a certain age, so you three could have spent time together before now."

"We have been close for years. You shocked me a lot when you finally told me the truth about Harris and my sisters." Phoebe paused for a moment, appreciating Harris staying quiet. "If I were in their shoes, I'd wonder why their relatives had never told them the truth. Why did all of them keep quiet? You lived with Katie and Roman, so all their close friends and relatives had to know Amy and Jenna were adopted. For being honest, Christian people, they basically lied to Amy and Jenna by keeping the truth from them."

~

After Phoebe left the patio to take a call from Haley, Harris asked Lindsay, "How are you feeling? Is there anything I can get you? You didn't eat much."

When Lindsay saw the deep concern in Harris's brown eyes, a memory came to her. In the process of being in a hurry to see Harris after her day job at the beach, she'd fallen down the steps going to see him. He'd cleaned her arm and examined it before putting antibiotic cream on it. His touch had ignited a strong flame of passion in her. Unfortunately, she still felt too much for this man. "I don't have much of an appetite these days."

He grinned. "We'll see what we can do about that. I remember how much you loved the Butterfinger Blizzard at Dairy Queen. We'll get that for you tomorrow."

"You have a good memory. Phoebe loves blizzards and ice cream too. I wonder what Amy and Jenna love to eat for dessert." Lindsay laughed. "I imagine they love whoopie pies. Katie made them a lot when I lived with her. I loved the bread she baked. It was especially delicious when it was right out of the oven."

"It's good to hear you laugh. I know today has been trying." Harris gathered the plates and placed them on top of the pizza boxes. "I'll take this in."

"I'm going in too. Harris, thank you for coming today."

"I'm just twenty-two years late."

She'd managed to live years successfully without Harris, but how much did she want him to be included in *her* life?

He wanted to be a father, so that meant he'd be visiting them a lot.

Harris held the patio door open for her. "You were too young to deal with it yourself."

Lindsay stepped into the house. "I did deal with it. Before I gave Amy and Jenna to Katie and Roman, I lived in fear they'd be kidnapped. I had to protect them. I lived in a sleazy, cheap apartment surrounded by undesirable people. I never told Phoebe about the couple who kept trying to talk me into putting them up for adoption. They said I'd get a lot of money for them because there were many couples who wanted babies. I overheard them talking one night in the hallway. They were contemplating grabbing the girls if they couldn't convince me to put them up for adoption. I heard them say they would split them up, so they could make more money. I left the next morning to go to Shipshewana."

Harris tossed the pizza box on top of the counter. "That's terrible. I'm glad you left and took the girls away. I wish you'd tried again to contact me after Paul died."

"I felt rejected by my mother, then by you, and then by Paul's parents. I couldn't take anymore rejection, so I handled it myself. It was good I did. Our daughters seemed to have had happy childhoods from the letters Katie sent me. I know Phoebe did too."

"We're going to make up for lost time. Whatever you need, you tell me. I hope Phoebe will accept me sometime. You did the best you could under the circumstances. I'm proud of everything you've accomplished."

She looked at him. "What do you think of Phoebe?"

He grinned. "She has attitude, which will be good for her in medicine. And she's gorgeous like her mother." He gave her arm an affectionate squeeze. "You need to rest. We'll talk tomorrow morning."

After Harris left for his room at the Holiday Inn, Lindsay realized two things: First, the father of her triplets was flirting with her. Second, she was not ready to become involved with Harris Manning again.

She wished he didn't have the silky-smooth voice she remembered because it made shivers dance up and down her spine. Fortunately, she could handle a few emotions where Harris was concerned. She wouldn't be swayed by him.

My focus is only on finding Amy and Jenna.

Chapter Ten

"You just had to get the stage four non-Hodgkin's lymphoma cancer, didn't you? It couldn't be an earlier stage." Harris grinned at Lindsay as they entered her house on Saturday. "I guess you get out of more housework this way. Phoebe has to cover for you."

"Hey, I'm the sick one here." Lindsay rolled her eyes at Harris. "Be nice."

Phoebe stared at her parents. "I never thought you'd come back cracking jokes after seeing Mom's oncologist."

"I can't believe Dr. Richardson made time to see us on a Saturday morning." Lindsay had agreed to him meeting with her oncologist. She decided it couldn't hurt. As a doctor, Harris might ask better questions. Even though his medical background wasn't in blood disorders, it should still be beneficial. She tapped Harris on his arm. "What did you say to get an appointment?"

"I explained to him I was visiting this weekend and that I wasn't sure when I'd be back in town." Harris sat on the sofa. "I'm glad we went to see him."

Phoebe frowned. "It seems like you could've talked to Dr. Richardson by phone instead of making him go to the office."

"I thought of that, but he mentioned going to the office." Harris noted the coldness in Phoebe's voice and wondered if they should've asked her to go with them to see Dr. Richardson.

"I know it's only been a day, but I'm hoping we'll hear something soon from Mr. Porter. I had trouble falling asleep last night." Lindsay wrapped a lock of her hair around her finger. "I wish I could remember Katie's married sisters' names, but I can't. I'm sure that would've helped."

Phoebe took a seat on the kitchen stool, bouncing her leg up and down. "Katie's parents should still be in Shipshewana. I didn't sleep much either."

"I've been praying they'll be found. I'm sure God will answer our prayers." Harris leaned forward. "If Porter hasn't called by this afternoon, I'll give him a call. I'll ask if he went to Shipshewana or if he's learned anything."

When the landline rang, they all stared at each other. "I gave him my number too," Lindsay said.

Harris heard Vickie's name called out from the caller ID and saw the frustration on Phoebe's and Lindsay's faces.

Phoebe frowned. "Did you tell Vickie and Michelle you gave two daughters away? And Roberta? I don't suppose you told Drew though."

Shaking her head, Lindsay said, "I never did. Haley might've told her mother since you chatted with her. You were the first one I told." As she walked to the phone, Lindsay said over her shoulder, "Once we find Amy and Jenna, I'll tell our friends."

"I'm glad you told me first . . ." Then Phoebe mumbled, "But I wish you'd told me years ago."

While Lindsay spoke to Vickie, Harris said, "I'm sorry we didn't know about each other until now. Lindsay mentioned her teacher friends to me and Haley's mom. Who's Drew?"

"He's our neighbor. Mom's gone out with him a few times." Phoebe crossed her arms over her chest. "Drew's in Germany, so that's why he hasn't been around."

Harris knew Phoebe wanted him to know about Drew. Was she worried he and Lindsay might become a couple? Right now, they needed to find Amy and Jenna, but he was interested in what Lindsay thought of Drew. "That's nice."

Phoebe pointed to a vase of flowers. "Drew sent her those."

He bit his lip, staring at the bouquet. Were the flowers sent because Drew missed Lindsay? Or maybe he wanted to cheer her up after the infusion treatment? He should've gotten flowers for Lindsay, but it never occurred to him. His mind had been filled with the news of having adult daughters and the secret adoption.

"I wonder how my sisters will react when they learn the truth." Phoebe blew a breath out. "I might go for a run instead of sitting around here. This is boring."

He wanted to tell Phoebe how he enjoyed running, but it didn't seem like the time to mention it. She'd made it clear it was boring being with him. He had all the time in the world to try to bond with Phoebe.

After only a few minutes, Lindsay's conversation with Vickie ended. Walking to the refrigerator, she asked, "Would either of you like something to drink? I'm supposed to drink a lot of water." She put a glass under the water dispenser. "Vickie wanted to know how I was feeling after chemo."

"I feel like baking cookies," Phoebe said. "I don't have to go to work today so I definitely have time. I might go running later with Haley, so I'll burn off the calories."

Lindsay smiled at her daughter. "I don't think you have to worry about calories, but cookies sound great."

An hour later, Harris pulled his cell phone out of his jean pocket at the sound of its ringtone. Glancing at the screen, he said, "Zach Porter's calling. I'll put it on speaker phone, so you both can hear everything."

Phoebe stopped eating her cookie at the counter. She hopped off the stool and moved to sit by Harris on the sofa.

While her mom finished filling the cookie jar, she said, "I hope it's good news."

Harris answered, and Mr. Porter said, "Jodi located the Yoder family. She went to Shipshewana yesterday. She learned the Yoder family moved about a year ago to Millersburg, Ohio. Roman Yoder bought his aunt's store there. A lot of the relatives were surprised they left Shipshewana. The Yoders sold their farm and house to someone outside of the family."

In spite of tears rolling down her cheeks, Phoebe saw her mom's eyes were filled with happiness.

"Jodi learned something else that will surprise you."

"What's that?" her mom asked as she sat on a chair by the sofa.

"I have you on speaker phone. Phoebe's here too," Harris said.

"Katie got pregnant when Amy and Jenna were nine months old," Mr. Porter said. "She and Roman had a baby boy. His name is Seth."

"Katie never told me. Why would she keep it from me? I wish she had shared with me the girls had a brother. Katie couldn't get pregnant for years, so it's nice she finally did."

A thoughtful expression crossed Harris's face. "I'm sorry she never told you."

"It's weird she didn't mention Seth in her letters to you. I wonder what he's like." Phoebe supposed he was close to his sisters. Did Katie and Roman feel closer to their biological son than to their adopted daughters?

"Jodi is still in Millersburg. She has gone to the store and met both girls and Seth. Katie and Roman are out of town and have gone to Niagara Falls. Jodi didn't mention anything about you looking for them," Mr. Porter said.

"When are they returning?" Harris asked.

"Wednesday sometime."

"Are Jenna and Amy single?" her mom asked.

"Jodi said they aren't married." Mr. Porter cleared his throat. "I have to tell you that Jodi was surprised to learn both young women are going to start taking emergency technician classes. They both want to become EMTs. We didn't think Amish women would be allowed to do something like that."

Her mom grinned at Phoebe and Harris. "It seems our daughters are taking an interest in medicine because of their father's background. And their grandparents' background too. I'm amazed neither of them is married. Amish marry young and get busy on starting a family."

"Thank you. I'm glad we know where they moved to. Give us the address, please," Harris said.

Harris ended the call. He looked at Lindsay and asked, "What do you think? We can go to Millersburg today. We won't tell them we're their birth parents. We can just visit the store."

"I'm thankful we know where they are, but I don't know if we should go yet. I hate to wait until next week to see them, though." Her mom took in a deep breath. "I wish Katie had received my letter. Then she could've reached out to me."

"It's totally up to you, Mom." Phoebe leaned forward. "If you decide to go, you can keep the secret until Katie and Roman have returned home. You don't need to tell them who you are."

Frustration crossed Lindsay's face. "I want you to meet them at the same time, but that's not possible until Katie and Roman have a chance to tell them about their birth and about you."

Phoebe was quiet for a long moment. "I'm anxious to see them. Sometimes it's hard to imagine I have identical sisters." She gave a nervous laugh. "Maybe Harris's suggestion would be okay. We could go this weekend. I'd have to change my appearance so Amy and Jenna won't question why I look like them. I could wear the blonde wig that was part of my costume in the high school play. I'll wear fake eyeglasses too."

"We'd have to go today. The Amish don't work on Sunday, and their businesses aren't open. They do the work that is necessary, like feeding the livestock, but otherwise, the women prepare food on Saturday to serve on Sunday. They don't want Sunday to be busy with kitchen tasks."

Phoebe stood. "I'll get ready. It's going to be weird to see my identical sisters. It's awesome they're going to do EMT training."

"See, you already have something in common with them. You both want to help people and pursue careers in the medical field." Her mom walked to Phoebe and hugged her. "I'm glad you're going with us."

"I'll check my emails and phone calls at work while you two get ready to leave." Harris grinned. "Phoebe, I can't wait to see your disguise."

"I'll freshen up a bit." Her mom glanced over her shoulder at Harris as she was walking away. "I can't wait to see them, but at the same time, I hope we're doing the right thing. Katie might never forgive me for going when she's away."

Phoebe frowned at her mother. "You have a right to go now. We aren't going to storm in and tell your secret. When they learn the truth later, they'll understand how we were anxious to see them in person."

Millersburg, Ohio

"Hello," an Amish man said to Phoebe as she looked at a lovely small quilt. "If you have any questions about our store or town, don't hesitate to ask me anything."

In the Yoder's store, Phoebe grinned at the tall, good-looking man with his broad shoulders and muscular build. She wondered if most Amish men were built like him. Surely, he didn't have a gym membership, so it must be from what he did for a career. He wore black pants and a blue shirt with suspenders. She noticed his charming accent when he spoke to her using English language. She read the Amish spoke in Pennsylvania Dutch, but when they started school, they learned to speak English. It was important because they needed to be able to use the language of their customers and work with English businesses.

He must be Seth, she thought. *I think it'll be fun to mess with him.* "Hi. So do you answer all types of questions? What if I ask you something you don't know the answer to?"

He blinked his green eyes quickly. "I don't know the type of question you might want to ask that you think I can't answer. In general, I can answer questions about our store. If you're not from around here and are interested in learning more about the Amish businesses in town, I can share what I know about them."

"I'm from out of town so that would be helpful." Phoebe loved his pronounced Pennsylvania Dutch accent.

"Don't give this nice young man a rough time," Lindsay said, standing beside her daughter. "You have a lovely store. I see several things I'd like to purchase to take back home."

Phoebe nodded, glancing around and noticing the place was illuminated by natural light and LED lighting. She'd expected to see food items only, but she also saw bird feeders, clocks, candles, and a children's section with toys, books, and games. She picked up a bird feeder and examined it. "The craftsmanship is excellent. Who made this?"

He gave a pleased look at Phoebe. "I did. A lot of the items in here are made by Amish individuals. The quilts hanging on the wall are all made by Amish women in our district."

A pretty girl wearing a lavender dress with a black apron entered the store. "Seth, I brought blueberry muffins. I'll put them in the display case."

Phoebe saw her mom's expression as soon as she saw her Amish daughter. It was obvious her mom was overwhelmed. Her blue eyes were misty. It was easy to see why because she shared her mother's emotions. Seeing her sister stunned her so much she was speechless.

"Hey, Jenna," Seth said, "it's about time you got here. Amy's working in the back. I've been handling the whole store myself. What did you do? Go pick the blueberries first?"

"Very funny. You know I was baking them at home, and I told you I had to run errands." Jenna smiled at Phoebe and Lindsay. "I see you met my *bruder*, Seth. We allow him in the store occasionally. I hope he hasn't been a nuisance."

Phoebe smiled at Jenna. "He's offered to answer any questions I might have."

Harris moved to stand by Lindsay. Looking at Seth and Jenna, he asked, "Where would you suggest a good place to eat for lunch?"

Lindsay grinned, staring at his load of bread and other items. "It looks like you already have enough food for lunch."

Harris shook his head, glancing down at his basket of food. "Hey, I couldn't resist, and I'm buying all this to take home. It's not every day I can buy homemade Amish food."

As Seth left to ring up a customer, Jenna said, "There's a restaurant I think you'll like."

Phoebe gave Lindsay's hand a quick squeeze when Amy appeared from the back of the store. Phoebe's heart flip-flopped at the smile that graced Jenna's face as Amy joined them. It was obvious her sisters had a close bond. Would they be able to accept her and be glad to finally know the truth about a long-held secret? Seeing how identical they were to each other was a shock. She knew they were identical triplets, but seeing them in person took her breath away.

At the sight of her daughters together, Lindsay started to fall. Harris immediately put his arm around her waist. "You need to sit down."

Amy pointed to a nearby rocking chair. "You can sit there. I'll get you a drink of water."

With an embarrassed glance, Lindsay said, "I'm sorry. I have lymphoma cancer, so I get weak sometimes."

Phoebe realized that seeing Amy and Jenna was hard on her mom. Lindsay's eyes glistened with tears. She pulled a tissue out of her crossover purse and handed it to her mom.

Harris helped Lindsay to the chair. "After you rest, we better get you something to eat."

"Okay, but I want to come back here after lunch because I saw a few things I want to buy. One thing I want is a wall clock, but I can't decide which one to buy for the living room."

Phoebe decided to follow her sisters to get the glass of water but stopped before the open doorway. She heard Jenna talking. "What's going on? Yesterday, an Englisher, Jodi, bought a lot of toys for her nieces and nephews—or so she said. I'm not sure she was in the store to buy stuff. She asked a lot of questions and seemed too nosy."

"Well, some tourists are more fascinated about our Plain life, but it does seem strange we have three more Englishers interested in us, especially the two women. They watched us closely."

Amy cleared her throat. "I better get water to the woman. She doesn't look well. That's sad she has cancer."

Alarm washed over her in a wave. *It wouldn't do for them to see her eavesdropping,* Phoebe thought, so she quickly moved away from the doorway and went back to her mother's side.

Phoebe and Lindsay were seated on one side of the booth with Harris across from them. They decided to drive to Berlin to eat at the Boyd and Wurthmann Restaurant. The town was only a few miles from Millersburg. Phoebe sipped her lemonade from a straw and sighed. "Seth was a lot of fun to tease but—"

"I know you've always enjoyed teasing Haley's brothers, but I didn't want you to make Seth uncomfortable."

Phoebe shrugged. "I'll stop kidding around then. When I saw my sisters, I was stunned. I couldn't get a smart comment out of my mouth."

Lindsay nodded. "I wanted so much to hug Amy and Jenna. It was difficult seeing them without being able to tell them I love them. I wish we could tell them who we are, but I'll wait until Katie and Roman return to tell them the truth."

"We'll go back before they close for the evening, so we can see them again before we leave." Harris sighed. "Although it's great to see the girls, I don't like pretending we're just tourists."

Lindsay's stomach tightened as she stared at her cup of soup. "This soup looks good, but I'm not hungry. Seeing our daughters was amazing, and all I can think about is them."

"Do you want me to spoon-feed you?" Harris grinned and picked up her spoon.

"Stop. I'll try to eat." After she grabbed the spoon away from him, Lindsay dipped it into her soup. She raised her eyebrows at Phoebe and Harris. "I can see you two aren't having any problem eating."

Phoebe smiled. "Harris and I need to keep our strength up in case you get faint again."

"That's right. We do. I'm surprised you haven't eaten much of your BLT sandwich. I remember that was your favorite sandwich when we dated. I'm glad we came here to eat. My steak sandwich is good."

Phoebe pushed the glossy blonde hair out of her face. "I don't know how women stand wearing wigs. It'd be worth telling Amy and Jenna I'm their sister, so I can stop wearing it."

Lindsay nodded. "I'm very thankful I haven't lost my hair. I hope the doctors are right about me not having to go through that."

"Oh, I forgot to tell you something," Phoebe said as she looked at her mother. "When I went to get the water for you, I overheard Amy and Jenna talking about how we seemed too interested in them. They mentioned Jodi had asked a lot of questions yesterday. They seem a little suspicious, or maybe I'm reading too much into it. I left before they realized I overheard them."

"Lindsay, maybe you should tell them you know their parents," Harris said.

"That will make them more suspicious. They will ask how I know them." Lindsay shook her head. "I'll write a note to Katie telling her we know where they relocated to and visited their store while they were away. I'll include it with the letter and send it again."

Chapter Eleven

The English driver dropped Katie and Roman off at their grocery store on Wednesday. Roman stood outside the front door with a bag in his hand. Staring at their business, he said, "The store is still here."

Katie laughed. "Why wouldn't it be? We left three responsible adult *kinner* in charge."

"Are you ready to work again? Or should we sneak off before they see us? We should've had the driver drop us off at home instead."

"It was *wunderbaar-gut* to get away, but I'm happy to be here again," Katie said.

Roman opened the door for Katie, then followed her inside.

"The travelers have returned." Seth took their bags from them. "You timed it just right. We'll be closing soon."

"How was business?" Roman asked.

Amy stepped from around the counter. "It was *gut*. We had four Englishers come in and buy a lot of items. We'll need to restock our shelves."

"Where's Jenna?" Katie asked.

"She went home a little early to start supper." Amy moved closer to them. "While you were gone, a letter came for you. Prescott is the name on the return address label."

Seth set the bags on the floor. "A woman and her daughter with that last name were two of the Englishers who were here."

Katie's heart skipped a beat. Could Lindsay and Phoebe have been in the store? But wouldn't her *kinner* have noticed Phoebe resembled them?

"The Prescott woman used a credit card to pay for her items. She was here in the store on Saturday, and she stared at us a lot." Amy's eyebrows shot up. "After she fainted, the woman said she had cancer."

Katie's pulse quickened, afraid it could be Lindsay. "What is her first name?"

"Lindsay. Her daughter, Phoebe, was with her." Seth grinned. "I think Phoebe liked me because she kept giving me a rough time. She's very pretty."

Amy rolled her brown eyes. "You were an easy target. She enjoyed teasing you."

Roman's jaw dropped. "What did Phoebe look like?"

"She's blonde and wore glasses." Seth rubbed his chin. "Something about her seemed familiar though."

Katie stared at Roman, knowing that what she'd been afraid of happening with the girls might occur now. Lindsay wanted Amy and Jenna to know she was their biological mother. *Is Lindsay breaking her promise after all these years because she has cancer and she wants to connect with Amy and Jenna before she dies?*

"*Mamm*, it seems you know Lindsey Prescott." Amy gave her a challenging glance and asked, "Were you friends once?"

"*Ya*, we met Lindsay when she was young, but we haven't seen her for years." Katie cleared her throat. "Let's go home."

Seth wiped off the counter. "A man named Harris Manning was with Phoebe and Lindsay. Did you ever know him?"

Roman shook his head. "*Nee*, we don't know him."

Katie realized that wasn't true. They did know Harris was their daughters' biological father, but they didn't know him personally. Katie decided to get off the topic of Lindsay. "*Danki* for taking care of everything here for us. We had a great time. I'm glad we saw the Niagara Falls."

～

After they ate supper, Katie and Roman went to their bedroom to read the letter from Lindsay. Katie's gaze landed on the wonderful cedar hope chest Roman had made for her. He gave it to her when he'd proposed. It now held quilts she'd made for Amy and Jenna to give them when they married. *Would they marry in their faith, or would they want to learn more about the English world they'd been born into?* Katie realized they had to tell the truth, but she wasn't happy about any of it.

Katie sat on the edge of their queen-sized bed covered with her mother's beautiful blue-and-purple quilt she'd made for them. As she stared at the sealed envelope, Roman sat beside her and picked up her free hand. She felt the warmth of his touch and looked into his vibrant green eyes. "What would I ever do without you?"

"I love you, and we'll get through this."

Katie gently pulled her hand out of his grasp to open the envelope. "There's another envelope inside. *Ach*, she sent the letter to our old address, and it was returned to her." She quickly read the note that had been tucked inside and opened the second envelope.

He looked over her shoulder at the note. "At least Lindsay and Harris didn't tell them our secret while we were away."

Katie waved the letter. "Sure, but she didn't need to go to our store when we weren't there."

Roman sighed. "Perhaps, she didn't know we were away, but that doesn't seem likely. I checked our answering machine, and there wasn't any message to call her."

"The one time we go on a trip, this happens." She exhaled a sharp breath. "She was sneaky and somehow found out we weren't home." Roman's jaw tightened. Katie knew what he was thinking. After being married for years, it was nice to have a sense of your husband's thoughts, but maybe not so much this time. "Okay, if I'd been in Lindsay's shoes, I'd be anxious to see my daughters, too, and wouldn't want to wait any longer. I wish the first letter had been forwarded to us."

"But it wasn't. We have to deal with it now."

Katie unfolded the letter and read it aloud to Roman.

Dear Katie and Roman,

I hope this letter finds you and your family well.

I have been diagnosed with lymphoma cancer. Having this has made me realize that if I don't survive, Phoebe will be alone, so I want her to meet Amy and Jenna. She needs to know about her sisters, and they need to know about her. I also want to meet them. I feel I have missed out on so much by keeping their birth a secret from them. I know I promised not to tell the truth to Phoebe, but things have changed. I pray you'll understand and forgive me for breaking the promise I made so many years ago.

Phoebe plans on attending medical college and is doing well. I'm thankful each day that I kept her to raise. She's been the greatest joy in my life. We are close, so I worry about how she will take the news that she has two sisters. I'm afraid she'll be hurt I never told her years ago. If I had it to do over again, I would've said we needed to tell them the truth a long time ago.

I wonder if Amy and Jenna are married and have children.

Hopefully, we can work out the details together soon about how to tell them. I have chemo each month, so that is something we need to work around.

Gratefully and your friend always,
Lindsay Prescott

"Well, Phoebe knows the truth now. You were right we should've told them before. I should've listened when you felt a nudge from God." Katie rubbed her forehead. "I was too stubborn and thought it best to never tell them."

Roman rubbed her arm. "It's okay. We'll tell them soon."

"We're being forced to, and I don't like it. Lindsay agreed to keep our secret." Katie threw the letter on the bed.

Roman tucked a strand of her hair under her *kapp*.

Leaning her head on his shoulder, she said, "I doubt Phoebe is blonde. She must have disguised herself so as to not shock Amy and Jenna. I suppose she could need glasses even though our daughters have perfect vision."

He cleared his throat. "We'll start at the beginning about how we met Lindsay."

Katie gave an enthusiastic nod. "That's *gut*. We can tell part of the story this evening and wait to tell them the rest."

"*Nee.* We might as well tell them the whole story. Let's pray before we go talk to them."

"Okay."

With bowed heads, Roman prayed, "Dear Father, we have to face our *kinner* and tell them the truth about Lindsay being their biological mother. Give us the right words to say to ease the pain of Amy, Jenna, and Seth realizing we kept the truth from them for years. Guide them as they grasp the news and for them to feel free to ask questions. Amen."

After they left their bedroom, Roman and Katie saw their *kinner* seated in the living room. As he ate carrot cake, Seth looked comfortable in their recliner chair.

Amy rolled her eyes at Seth. "If you want any cake, you better get it now before someone eats all of it."

"I'm a growing boy. I can't help it I'm always hungry." Seth waved his fork at Amy.

Katie and Roman sat on the sofa across from their *kinner*. Katie realized she might as well see their reactions when they told them what they had kept secret for years.

"We poured you iced tea." Jenna pointed to the glasses on the coffee table.

"*Danki.*" Katie smoothed her apron over her lap. "I'll explain first how we met Lindsay."

"Actually, it's interesting how we met," Roman added. "I'm sure God in his wisdom meant for us to meet her."

Katie continued. "Years ago, she was on her way to visit her girlfriend, but she stopped in Shipshewana to use the restroom. When Lindsay went back out to her car, it wouldn't start."

Roman nodded. "We noticed her condition and how upset she was."

Jenna's brown eyes narrowed. "What was wrong with her?"

"She was single and pregnant and looked like a child herself." Katie gave a small smile. "I thought, at first, she was almost ready to deliver because she was huge. It turned out she was only five months pregnant."

"We got her car towed to the auto shop and took her home with us." Roman continued. "After her car was repaired, Lindsay went to Fort Wayne to visit her friend."

"So what happened then? Did she return to visit you?" Seth asked.

"Lindsay was pregnant with triplets. She'd married Paul Prescott. He'd been her high school sweetheart, but Paul wasn't the father of her babies."

Roman put his arm around Katie's shoulders. "Paul died in an automobile accident a month after they were married.

His parents knew the babies were not their son's. They wouldn't give any help to Lindsay."

Amy frowned. "You haven't mentioned Lindsay's parents. Why couldn't they help her?"

"Her father had died, and her mother was an alcoholic." Katie sighed. "We became her family. She had a job at McDonald's and tried to make it on her own. It was hard because she had to be on bed rest for a couple of months of her pregnancy."

"If Paul wasn't their father, then I'm guessing Harris Manning could be Phoebe's father." Seth's fingers held his glass of iced tea.

"*Ya*, Harris is the father, but he never knew about Lindsay's pregnancy. She met Harris when she'd worked at a hotel on the beach. They were in love. Or Lindsay thought Harris loved her. He left to go back to college before she could tell him about her pregnancy."

"I wonder why only Phoebe came with Lindsay and Harris to see you." Amy leaned forward and gave them a puzzled look. "What happened to the other two babies? Were they girls or boys?"

Katie cleared her throat. "Lindsay gave birth to identical triplets."

"Three beautiful daughters." Roman grinned. "She came to live with us for several weeks. It was *wunderbaar* to have three babies in our house."

"We were blessed to help Lindsay. Your *daed* and I had been married for ten years, so having *kinner* in our house was such a joy."

Jenna smiled at them. "How nice you helped her out with her triplets."

Roman glanced at Katie. At her quick nod, he said, "Lindsay knew she couldn't raise three babies on her own, so during the second month with us, she asked if we would consider adopting you two."

Katie remembered the agony of not getting what she wanted. "I wanted to adopt Phoebe too, but Lindsay couldn't bear to give all three of you away."

Seeing the shock on their *kinner's* faces hurt Katie.

"I can't believe this. Jenna and I are adopted." Amy stood and paced back and forth in front of them. "And our birth parents were in our store."

Seth put his glass on the end table. "Am I adopted too?"

"Of course, you aren't." Jenna raised her eyebrows at Seth. "You look like *Daed*. You have his green eyes and *Mamm's* light brown hair."

"That's right," Roman said. "We were blessed with our daughters and then again with you."

Seth snapped his suspenders. "So I'm not Amy's and Jenna's biological brother."

"We're all family here. You're our daughters as much as Seth is our son. I'm sure you have questions about why we didn't tell you." Katie decided it was better to be honest with them. "I thought it best we didn't. I was never comfortable with sharing the knowledge you had an Englisher for a mother. It seemed it'd be confusing."

Amy stopped in front of Katie, giving her mother an indignant look. "It seems you never planned on telling us. Lindsay visiting here forced you to tell us the truth."

Jenna did a skeptical headshake. "I can't believe no one in Shipshewana told us."

"It was a closed adoption. Our friends and relatives knew this, so that's why they never mentioned it." Katie stared at her lap for a moment before giving direct glances at Amy and Jenna. "But your *Aenti* Lizzie and *mammi* wanted me to tell you when you were eighteen. I'm sorry I didn't."

Jenna swallowed hard. "It's sad Lindsay has cancer, but I don't see how a mother could wait for years to learn more about her children. At some point, it seems she would've wanted to see us."

Her voice husky with restrained emotion, Amy said, "I guess she had Phoebe, so she didn't need to know anything about us."

"Hey, wait a minute," Roman said. "Lindsay wanted to keep in touch. She asked your *Mamm* to write her a letter each year on your birthday to let her know how you were doing."

Katie nodded. "I did."

"Then why didn't Lindsay have our new address?" Amy asked. "We saw her letter went to our old address."

Oh great, I didn't want to mention that I stopped writing after they graduated from eighth grade, Katie thought. "Well, I stopped the letters after you graduated from school."

"Was that what Lindsay wanted?" Jenna's brown eyes widened.

Roman gave Katie a quick glance, turning his head back to look at their *kinner*. "I think we need to decide when you want to meet with Lindsay, Harris, and Phoebe. That is, if you want to meet with them. And remember, Phoebe just found out she has sisters. I'm sure learning she has two sisters is a big shock to her too."

Katie gave her husband a grateful look in appreciation of him stepping in so she didn't have to explain it was her idea to stop the corresponding with Lindsay.

"I don't like that she kept Phoebe. You should've insisted we were kept together. How could Lindsay afford to raise one baby when she had no support? And why did she choose Phoebe?" Amy frowned. "Never mind. It doesn't matter. I can ask her myself."

Katie drew a deep breath. "I can tell you what she told us. She breastfed all three of you, but she wanted to make sure you were all okay taking bottles before she left. Phoebe refused to take a bottle."

"There's something else you should know. When she came here with you three, Lindsay looked frightened. She lived in a cheap apartment, and a couple who lived in a unit next to Lindsay wanted her to give you all up for private adoption. They told her she could make money by giving each of you to a different family. She refused." Roman paused for a moment, then continued. "From the sound of it, Lindsay suspected they meant to kidnap you. She piled everything she could into her car and never went back to that apartment."

Katie nodded. "Lindsay drove straight to our house where she knew it would be safe."

"That had to be scary. I can see why she left that place in a rush, and I'm thankful she did. But I'm curious why she chose an Amish family when she isn't Amish." Jenna gave Katie and Roman a small smile. "You two must've impressed her a lot."

Roman said, "She wanted a stable home life for her babies. Lindsay felt certain we would give you that."

"She liked our simple life and often mentioned how perfect it was." Katie chuckled. "Lindsay loved my homemade bread, and I teased her over how fast she could put it away." She paused, remembering how Lindsay had also enjoyed being with her family. "She liked spending time with my *mamm* and *daed*. They filled a void for her since she didn't have parents."

"After the death of Lindsay's father, her mother fell apart. Her childhood hadn't been good at all." Roman took a big drink of tea. "I'm glad you know the truth now, but it doesn't change anything. We're still your parents, and we love you. Whenever you want to spend time with Phoebe and your biological parents, we'll understand."

"Where do they live?" Jenna asked.

"Lindsay and Phoebe live in Columbus." Roman ran his fingers through his hair. "Lindsay's a high school math teacher. Harris is a doctor in Cincinnati. I guess he's still living there."

At this information, Amy gasped. "Are you kidding me?"

Jenna's jaw dropped. "Unbelievable that we might have gotten our medical interest from Harris."

"Apparently, your *grandparents* are also doctors." As much as Katie hated to share this information, she tried to keep her voice normal. She hoped they wouldn't mention how they could've had different lives with established medical careers if they'd been raised by Lindsay. Relief went through her when she reflected on how she'd given permission for the EMT training before Lindsay appeared in their lives.

"I love you both, but this is a shock to learn that the two people I have trusted most in this world kept a huge secret from me and Amy." Jenna briefly closed her eyes, then took a deep breath. "Now I belong to a new family. Not even Amish, but English."

Amy placed her arms behind her back, gripping one wrist with the other hand. "It is definitely strange to learn that we're adopted."

"You know God blessed you with two mothers," Seth said. "One who gave you life and our mother who always loved you and raised you with a strong faith. You'll need this faith to get you through spending time with your biological parents."

Roman picked up Lindsay's letter from the sofa and placed it on the table in front of him. "You should read Lindsay's letter."

Katie wasn't thrilled that Roman gave Lindsay's letter to Jenna and Amy. But she knew the girls might as well read how she regretted that their birth had been kept a secret. She glanced at their simple living room with bare walls, adorned only with a clock on one wall. Their furniture wasn't spectacular, but it was comfortable. It was nice Roman's aunt and uncle had taken excellent care of the hardwood floors.

If Amy and Jenna went to visit Phoebe at her house, would they enjoy watching TV? Would they spend time on the Internet and learn a lot of English things? She felt sick and hoped they wouldn't be influenced by their English parents. It was a shame they hadn't taken the baptism instructions and joined their Amish church. Waiting for this event to happen had been eating away at her. She'd watched women younger than her daughters joyfully join their faith, but still, hers showed no interest. Fear gripped her heart. Would they be swayed from joining because they'd learned the truth about their birth parents?

Chapter Twelve

Columbus, Ohio

When Lindsay saw the Yoders' phone number on the caller ID, she bit her lower lip, wondering if Roman and Katie had told Amy and Jenna about their adoption. Since it was only Friday, and Roman and Katie had been expected home on Wednesday, would the call be good news that she could meet with them soon? Or maybe Roman and Katie wanted more time to tell the truth to Amy and Jenna?

At the third ring, she grabbed the receiver and answered. "Hello."

"Hi, it's Roman. Is this Lindsay?"

"It's Lindsay. It's good to hear your voice, Roman. I'm guessing you're calling about my letter."

"*Ya.* After we read your letter, we told our *kinner* the truth about the adoption."

She rubbed the back of her neck. "How did they take the news?"

"They were hurt, surprised, and asked questions."

"What questions did they ask?"

"Well, they were resentful to have just learned about the adoption and wondered why you waited so long to reach out to them. Katie explained it was a closed adoption. I told them how you asked for letters about them to be sent to you each year." He sighed. "It was a secret that needed to be told. I'm glad they know the truth. By the way, they realized you, Harris, and Phoebe were in the store."

Roman's voice still sounded pleasant and calm. He'd always had a laid-back personality. "I'm sorry we went to the store, but I wanted to see them so much."

"I get it. We're sorry your letter had been returned to you. Katie gave the post office the new address. She also gave it to the new owners."

"It's okay. You're actually living closer to me and Phoebe now. Just under two hours." She fondly remembered the long four-hour drive from Columbus to Shipshewana with the triplets in their car seats. They were such great babies to travel with. Except when one started getting fussy, the other two did too. "Your store is incredible."

Roman chuckled. "I heard you bought a lot at the store, so *danki* for the business."

"You're welcome. I enjoyed meeting Seth. I was happy to learn you and Katie have a son."

"We've been blessed with our three children. Lindsay, you gave us a wonderful gift when you allowed us to adopt Amy and Jenna."

"I'm glad they were raised in a loving home and you had a baby for them to grow up with." She worried about Katie's reaction since Roman was the one on the phone. "How's Katie?"

"She's okay and said to tell you hello. We're sorry you have cancer," he said in a soothing tone. "You're in our prayers."

"Thank you." She exhaled a deep breath. "Would Amy and Jenna like to meet with us? Or do they need more time?" She hoped that wasn't the case. Her patience wasn't that great these days. Seeing her daughters while they knew she was their birth mother could be the start of a wonderful mother-daughter relationship. And Phoebe would get to spend time with her sisters.

"It's hard to get away during the week, but they can visit next Sunday. Our English driver has a sister to visit in Columbus, so she'll drop them off late on Sunday morning. We don't have church in our district next Sunday. How does that sound to you?"

"It sounds wonderful. I'll be counting the days."

～

"I'm nervous. The week went by too slowly, and suddenly, it's Sunday. I can't believe we'll all be together. I never thought Amy and Jenna would come here, but I'm glad they are." Lindsay tried to hold her cup of coffee without spilling it. Her hands were shaking earlier, and she tried to hide it from Harris. It was touching how he was trying to become involved in her and Phoebe's life, but she was capable of taking charge of her own life. She wasn't the young girl he had met that memorable summer. Lindsay couldn't forget the pain of his rejection even though she'd forgiven him for leaving her before she could tell him about her pregnancy.

"It might be better that Amy and Jenna didn't know about us until now." Phoebe tucked a lock of black hair behind her ear. "They might have felt rejected, but now they're adults. I hope they realize you didn't have a choice in giving them up for adoption."

"I asked Roman how they took the news. He said they were hurt and surprised they hadn't been told earlier. I can't change the past, but we can move on and get to know each other now." Lindsay stood by the sink as she finished washing the vegetables. She put a bowl of spinach dip in the center of the veggie tray. "Roman explained to them how I requested Katie to write letters to keep me updated."

Phoebe got a mixing bowl out of the cabinet. "Since we're skipping church today, I'll bake chocolate chip cookies. Or do you think I should make something else for dessert?"

Lindsay turned her head around to look at Phoebe. "I love your cookies."

Her daughter gave her a worried look and stuck her hands in her jean pockets. "Do I look okay wearing this? Or should I put a dress on since you're wearing one?"

"Your jeans are fine, and your red blouse is perfect. I'm more comfortable wearing a dress." Her conservative, mid-length dress had short sleeves. Lindsay thought Harris looked especially handsome in his khaki pants and a polo shirt.

"I'm glad we decided to eat lunch here." Harris held a box of aluminum foil in his hand. "I'm glad you two are okay with me fixing the meat. I can fix the corn on the grill too. I wish your grill was a little bigger though. I won't have room for anything else."

Phoebe laughed. "You're already fixing steak, hamburgers, and hot dogs. What else would you want to fix on the grill?"

Harris smiled. "That's a good question. I'd wrap potatoes if I had room."

"Phoebe made macaroni salad so we'll have plenty to eat." Lindsay put the tray in the refrigerator and waited to close the door. "I should make iced tea and lemonade."

"I can do that." Phoebe motioned to the sofa. "You should sit and rest."

"I think I will." As she walked to the living room area, Lindsay murmured, "I want to tell Vickie and Michelle about your sisters, but it can wait."

"Hey, I called my parents yesterday. They're thrilled to be grandparents and want to meet you and your sisters soon." He set the foil on the counter and sat down beside Lindsay.

Phoebe removed eggs and butter out of the refrigerator. "Did you tell them Amy and Jenna were raised Amish?"

A reluctant smile appeared on Harris's face. "That was a hard one to explain to them."

"I wonder if Amy and Jenna will question why I chose an Amish life for them." Lindsay's mind went back to the first time she was on the Yoders' farm in Shipshewana. "When I was pregnant and staying at their house, I fell in love with their strong focus on family. Katie's siblings and parents were so sweet. They supported and helped each other in every way imaginable." Lindsay put a throw pillow behind her back. "I'm sure Amy and Jenna must realize how blessed they are to be able to work alongside their parents, and they seemed happy working at the store together with Seth."

Phoebe cracked the eggs into a bowl. "I hope he's doing okay with the adoption news."

Lindsay sighed. "I hope so. It seems impossible that so much time has passed." She darted glances at Phoebe and Harris. "I'm sorry for everything. When I first got sick, I should've contacted you, Harris, and told both of you everything then. At least we'd have met them two years earlier. You both missed so much by not knowing the truth."

Harris's brows shot up, and he ran his fingers through his hair. "You have nothing to apologize for. It's my fault for being a jerk. I know I can't make up for missing years of our daughters' lives, but we both can look forward to spending as much time with Amy and Jenna as they want. I suppose it'll be easier to be a part of Phoebe's life." He smiled at his daughter. "At least I hope we can spend time together."

After Phoebe measured the sugar, she grinned at Harris. "I'm warming up to you."

Lindsay noticed Harris looked like he wanted to tell her something. His expression reminded her of years ago when he was quiet and had a serious expression, and it was right before he told her that they were over as a couple. Sometimes she wished her recall of sad events wasn't so vivid. *I certainly have a lot of heartbreaking memories, and now I'm ill with lymphoma cancer. But God is good. He is my strength, and I leave nothing to chance and everything to God.* A meaningful verse from Proverbs came to her mind. *"Commit to the LORD whatever you do, and He will establish your plans."*

Harris went to the coffeepot and refilled his cup. "Would you like another cup?"

Lindsay shook her head. "No, thank you."

As he walked to the sofa, Harris said, "There's something I have wondered." His eyebrows drew together. "I hope you don't mind me asking you how you chose your oncologist."

"My family doctor recommended him. Why are you asking?" She wasn't sure why Harris wanted to know this information.

"I'm only mentioning this for you to consider, but if you don't like my suggestion, it's fine," Harris said. "I think you should get a second opinion about your treatment from another oncologist."

Phoebe stopped stirring her cookie dough and tilted her head upward to stare at Harris. "That's a good suggestion."

"I've already started treatment. I had the PET scan, too, before the chemo started. Why would you want me to get a second opinion?" She hated that irritation laced her voice, but she wasn't going to switch doctors at this point in her treatment. Harris wanting her to get another opinion wasn't going to sway her to do it. "That's something you do before you start chemo."

"Well, you can always switch. Since you ended up in the hospital from problems with the first chemo treatment, I thought I'd suggest it."

When he stiffened, she noticed the wrinkle lines on his forehead were more visible, but she remained quiet as he continued. "I wouldn't be offended if a patient of mine decided to get a second opinion. Something else bothers me. Dr. Richardson should've realized you were in the beginning stages of lymphoma cancer when you had the enlarged spleen two years ago."

"I asked Dr. Richardson about that, but he said the blood tests didn't show I had cancer when I first went to him. The only thing I had was low platelets. I like him and his staff. Dr. Richardson told me if I had to get cancer that lymphoma cancer was one of the better ones to have. It responds well to chemo. Hopefully, I can tolerate the next chemo treatment so that some of my cancer cells will be killed."

Phoebe opened a drawer and removed two cookie sheets. "I thought that before you started treatments you should've gotten another opinion, but Dr. Richardson seems fine to me."

"Other than my primary doctor, a teacher friend recommended Dr. Richardson. I don't need a second opinion," Lindsay retorted with a critical tone in her voice. She didn't want to hurt Harris's feelings but she wasn't about to change doctors. "Now we need to do the finishing touches to get ready for Amy and Jenna."

~

At ten o'clock, Lindsay saw a white minivan pull into their driveway. "They're here." She felt a warm glow flow through her while she waited for them to get out of the vehicle. Having her daughters actually at her house seemed remarkable. God was good to have Amy and Jenna come see her, especially after her dishonesty. Now the secret was out, and hopefully they all could move forward.

Harris pulled her away from the front window and spoke in a rushed, excitable voice. "Let's open the door."

Lindsay turned her head, wanting her daughter with them to greet Amy and Jenna. "Where's Phoebe?"

"I'm coming, Mom," Phoebe yelled. "I decided to change into another top."

At the appearance of Phoebe in a blue blouse with white polka dots, Harris opened the front door.

Once they were out of the van and walking on the sidewalk, Harris murmured, "I know they're identical, but seeing them look exactly like Phoebe takes my breath away."

Lindsay saw one had on a lavender dress while the other wore a bright blue dress. Such beautiful daughters . . . Bouncing on her toes, she waved enthusiastically. "I probably look like a crazy person, but I can't help it. I'm so excited."

Touching her arm, Harris said, "You're allowed."

Lindsay smiled tentatively at the girls as they drew closer. Once within reach, she extended her hand to each daughter. "We're glad you could come."

Briefly, Lindsay saw Harris's eyes were misty and thought he might cry, but then he returned their daughters' smiles and greeted them.

"Hello, I'm Jenna. It's nice to be here." She gave them a timid smile, touching her blue dress.

"And we meet again," Amy said in a guarded voice.

Harris said, "Please come on in," and led them into the room by the gray sofa.

"Something smells good," Phoebe said, smiling at Amy as she held a container by its handle.

"It's Amish cinnamon bread." Amy grinned at Phoebe. "Hey, you look better without your blonde hair."

"I loved eating Katie's delicious bread. I couldn't get enough of it." Lindsay wondered if Katie had mentioned anything about her likes and dislikes to Amy and Jenna. What had Katie told them about her and Harris?

"*Mamm* baked it for you. Would you like some now?" Amy asked Lindsay and remained standing.

"How thoughtful of Katie. I'd love some, but I'll wait until a little later. I feel like we need to talk. I want to learn so much about your lives." Lindsay had eaten little at breakfast but was too nervous to attempt eating.

"*Ya*, we do need to talk." Amy exhaled a deep breath and glanced at Jenna. "We didn't sleep well last night. Jenna and I have a lot of questions."

Harris bit his lower lip. "I know this must be difficult for you both to learn you were adopted."

Once Amy and Jenna were seated, Phoebe stood near and asked, "Would you like something to drink? We have lemonade and iced tea."

"*Nee, danki*." Jenna clasped her hands in front of her, sitting on the sofa next to Amy.

Phoebe sat on the other side of Amy while Harris and Lindsay took seats together on the smaller sofa across from their daughters. Lindsay appreciated Harris by her side. She loved seeing the triplets seated together. *They are so beautiful.*

Amy lifted her chin, meeting Lindsay's gaze straight on. "Why did you and our *mamm* decide to keep it a closed adoption? Jenna, Phoebe, and I shouldn't have been kept in the dark. We had a right to know years ago."

Lindsay noticed the defiance in Amy's brown eyes but also couldn't miss seeing the hurt in Jenna's. "Katie suggested it, and it seemed like the right thing to do at the time. I'm sorry you're only now learning the truth."

"In spite of the closed adoption, I wished you'd insisted on seeing us earlier rather than now." Jenna frowned. "*Mamm* might not have agreed, but *Daed* would have."

Lindsay noticed that Amy and Jenna looked at each other. She could see the silent conversation being held between her two daughters. *What is it they want to ask me?*

"Did you ever wish you could come see us in Shipshewana? It's hard to believe you went for years without having any contact with us. We know *Mamm* wrote you a yearly letter until we finished eighth grade, but that isn't really getting to know us. To be honest, it's hurtful," Amy said, hardening her voice.

Lindsay's heart plummeted at hearing the anger in Amy's voice. Of course, it was hurtful that she'd waited years to let them know she was their birth mother. *Why hadn't she reached out to Amy and Jenna earlier? Why hadn't she broken her promise to Katie and Roman a long time ago? Had she been afraid of her daughters' reactions?* "I did want to be a part of your lives. I wanted to tell Phoebe that she had two sisters, but I felt I had to honor the promise I made to Katie and Roman. I was thankful your parents agreed to adopt you. But it was always difficult for me to keep quiet through the years. I had many moments of sadness on each holiday. I wished with my whole heart I could've spent those days with you."

Harris grasped her hand, then looked away from Lindsay to stare at his daughters. "We can't change the past, but I'm glad to know I have three beautiful daughters now."

Lindsay exhaled a deep breath and leaned against Harris to soak in his strength. Should she tell them how she saw them once in Shipshewana? It might make them feel a tiny bit better that she'd made an effort to see them once. "When Phoebe was in fourth grade, I had a day off at my school. Phoebe was spending the day and night at a friend's house. I decided to visit you both. You were at your school, and I saw you outside during recess. You both were playing kickball."

Jenna gave Lindsay a startled glance as she moved forward slightly. "I remember. I kicked the ball too hard, and it went to you. I thought you were pretty. And you said, 'You have a strong kick.' Then you kicked it back."

"We didn't think much about you watching us because other Englishers were interested in our school." Amy's brown eyes shifted from Jenna to Lindsay. "Wait a minute. I remember now being surprised you left the playground to go into our school. Did you ask our teacher about us?"

"No, I didn't. That might have raised suspicions if I had asked about you two. I did ask if I could visit the classroom a day during my spring break. I said I was interested in the Amish teaching methods. I thought I could see you again. Your teacher said that wouldn't be possible."

"We never had English visitors in our classroom. I'm sorry you couldn't visit our school. That would've been something if you could've been in the room with us." A pained expression crossed Jenna's face.

A tightness seized her chest as she realized more needed to be said to Amy and Jenna. As Harris put his arm around her shoulders, she said, "I had trouble leaving because I wanted to take you both home with me. I loved you so much and knew I couldn't go to see you again. It wasn't fair to your parents. On my way home, I cried, but I was glad I saw how happy and healthy you both looked. I knew I did the right thing giving you to Katie and Roman to raise." Tears pooled in her eyes from the pain of reliving years of missing her daughters.

Amy's expression softened. "We have had a happy life. Our parents have been *wunderbaar-gut.*"

"You picked wisely." Jenna's eyes glistened. "We love our parents and our brother. Family's so important in our faith and one of the many things I love about being raised in an Amish home."

Amy nudged Jenna and chuckled. "You haven't loved everything, sis." Turning her head away from Jenna, she glanced at Phoebe, then at Lindsay and Harris. "Jenna used to hate cleaning out the horse stalls, but she got out of it because she forgot to close the barn door once. We had to look for two horses for hours."

Jenna frowned at Amy. "You're exaggerating. It wasn't for hours."

Phoebe cleared her throat. "I think it's interesting we all live at home. I stayed at home while attending college instead of living in a dorm." With quick glances at her sisters, Phoebe continued. "It's great you live with your parents and work in their store."

"It's pretty normal for Amish girls to remain at home until they marry." Jenna smiled. "Well, they might stay at home after marriage too. Newlyweds sometimes live with the bride's family until enough money is saved to have their own house."

"You have a lovely house," Amy said, looking around the room. "I like the openness with the kitchen and living room."

Nodding, Jenna said, "It's cozy. Your shelves of books in here remind me of our *daed*. He loves to read."

Lindsay was sure they noticed her large-screen TV, but she was glad neither had mentioned it. Amish would never have a TV in their houses, so reading, playing board games, and doing puzzles were common pastimes. "I remember Roman and I discussed what books we had both read. We both had the same interest in reading mysteries, especially Agatha Christie."

"When *Mamm* sent you letters, was this where she sent them?" Amy squinted her eyes at her. "Have you always lived here?"

Lindsay shook her head, wondering if Amy thought it looked like there would've been plenty of room to raise three children in her house. "No, Phoebe and I lived in apartments for six years. The first apartment was only a studio, but it was all I could afford. I had a wall bed I slept on at night. After I taught school for four years, I was fortunate to get this house for a good price. It needed renovation. Teachers from the vocational school helped me with updating the electricity and plumbing. I started doing the painting myself until I realized I was getting more paint on me than the walls." She laughed. "I hired a painter then."

With an embarrassed look, Amy said, "Of course, I should've realized you wouldn't have had this house when Phoebe was a baby."

"Now that we know the truth, it makes sense *Mamm* never wanted to talk much about our births." Jenna rubbed her chin. "She must've been afraid to reveal too much because she could've given away the secret."

"After you learned the truth of your birth, did Katie show you any pictures? I gave her a few of all three of you together." Lindsay wondered if Katie had even thrown the photos away, so they wouldn't be found accidentally.

Amy shook her head. "We never saw any photos."

"I'll get them." Phoebe left the sofa and walked to the end table. After she opened the drawer, she lifted out a photo album and handed it to her sisters. She grinned. "I have to say that we look pretty adorable."

As they peered at each page, Lindsay said, "I had you at thirty-three weeks, so you were around five or six weeks early. You probably ran out of room in my womb. Amy, you were born first. You weighed three pounds and eleven ounces."

"*Mamm* said I weighed three pounds and nine ounces. Is that right?" Jenna asked.

Lindsay nodded. "Yes, you did. Phoebe was born last and was the smallest at three pounds and two ounces. I had a C-section. I'm glad I breastfed all three of you, but that created a deeper bond. I cried for months after I left you both with Katie and Roman. Your birthdays were especially hard. I wished all the time I could've raised you three together."

As they continued looking at the baby pictures, Harris said, "I wish I could've been there when you were babies and all through your lives."

Jenna raised her chin to stare at Harris. "You could've been part of our lives if you hadn't broken up with Lindsay. I won't claim to understand your past treatment of her, but it happens occasionally in our Amish community. When a single woman becomes pregnant, a small wedding usually follows instead of a large celebration. You can't make up for lost time, but it's *gut* you're making an effort to be part of our lives now."

Lindsay said in a gentle voice, "Harris didn't know I was pregnant." She saw his brown eyes full of tenderness as he glanced at her.

Turning away from her, Harris faced his daughters. "It's true I didn't honor your mother, but I promise I will from now on."

～

A couple of hours later, they were outside on the patio filling their paper plates with food. Amy scooped a big spoonful of macaroni salad onto her plate. "Everything looks delicious. You went to a lot of trouble. I love corn on the cob. We haven't had any yet from our garden."

Lindsay slid a slice of the cinnamon bread next to her steak. "I know Katie's bread will be yummy. Please tell her thank you for me."

"I should warn you I made the macaroni salad," Phoebe said.

Jenna laughed as she followed Phoebe with her full plate of food. "Now you say it after I took a lot of it."

"Don't pay her any mind. It's always good." Lindsay had to tease Harris about the food he'd prepared for their lunch. "It's a shame you didn't have a bigger grill for more food to fix. I don't want our daughters to starve."

"Hey, don't speak that way to the chef." Harris slid patties on a plate. "These hamburgers have my special hot sauce. They are not for the fainthearted."

Phoebe returned to the side table of food and picked up a bun. "I'll take one. I like hot stuff."

"Be sure to have plenty of water to drink with it." After Harris got his plate filled, he sat at one end of the table. "Let's say grace. Lindsay, do you want to say it?"

Nodding, she bowed her head. "Dear God, thank you for Amy and Jenna being here today. It is such a blessing to have our three daughters together with us and for this special time to learn more about each other. We give thanks, too, for the food and our beautiful weather. In Your Son's Name, we pray. Amen." Lindsay raised her head. "I remember how nice it was your parents prayed silently before a meal."

"*Ya*, we still do." Jenna concentrated for a moment on cutting her steak into pieces. "It's always been that way in our home, but I liked hearing your prayer said out loud too."

Amy sipped her lemonade and looked at Lindsay. "You have a lovely yard."

"It is beautiful with all the flowers. It's such a nice day to be surrounded by nature and the sounds of birds chirping above us." A sad look flashed across Jenna's face. "I wonder what it would've been like to grow up here. It's hard for me and Amy to think about all these years, not knowing we were adopted."

Lindsay swallowed a bite of food, then carefully put her fork beside her plate. She reached across the table and grabbed each Amish daughter's hand in hers. "I felt God meant for me to give you to Katie and Roman. Life is never perfect, but my choice was based on God's guidance. Even with the heartache, He always knows what is best for our lives."

Amy squeezed her hand. "I can see why you couldn't keep all three of us, but I wonder why you chose to keep Phoebe." She grinned at Phoebe. "It couldn't be because you were cuter."

"Phoebe was the smallest, and she lost weight when she wouldn't take a bottle. I wanted to make sure you all would switch to the bottle after I had breastfed you. Phoebe refused to take a bottle from me or from Katie." Lindsay wiped her mouth with a napkin. "Actually, Naomi tried the bottle with Phoebe too. I decided I needed to keep one baby, and it seemed Phoebe had to be the one I took home with me."

Amy nodded. "Mom mentioned the bottle refusal, so it makes sense. I have to admit that if you'd kept me instead of Phoebe, I would've gone to college, I'm sure. My education wouldn't have stopped at eighth grade. My life would have been very different."

Lindsay heard jealousy in Amy's voice. *It might be a good thing for Amy to express her feelings about not being raised in my English home instead of keeping them bottled up.*

Jenna said, "Keeping Phoebe must have been hard in its own way. You knew Phoebe would've loved knowing she had two identical sisters, but you kept your secret. I can't imagine going through this. You're a strong woman, Lindsay."

Her daughter's words touched her greatly. "Thank you. My faith gave me strength."

After he swallowed a bite of hamburger, Harris gulped down a long drink of iced tea. "Whew, I might have gotten carried away with the sauce. Be careful, Phoebe." He stared at her from his end of the table.

"Mine's fine." Phoebe grinned. "But I've been taking tiny bites."

"Something occurred to me that I haven't asked you yet. I hope you don't mind me asking, but I was surprised you haven't taken your baptism classes. Why have you waited? And Seth too?" Lindsay was anxious to hear their answers because most took their vows by age twenty-two.

Harris sat up straighter. "Is it because you want to do your EMT training before you join your church?"

"I plan on taking my baptism classes next year." Jenna shrugged her shoulders. "Our bishop gave us permission to become emergency medical technicians, so that isn't a problem. I just haven't gotten around to it."

Amy sighed. "It's complicated because I want more education. I'm interested in becoming a nurse after I spend time as an EMT."

"Does Seth want to take his church vows soon?" Phoebe asked.

"*Ya*, he wants to join our faith but wants to wait too." Amy's face stretched into a broad smile. "He's probably afraid it will make him more available for marriage. We have to be a church member before we can marry."

Phoebe stood and went to the side table to grab the desserts. Over her shoulder, she said, "It's cool you both are going to become EMTs and I'm going to be a medical student."

"I wonder if other triplets who aren't raised together have the same career interests. Before we found you, I wondered if you had married and if I had also missed out on grandchildren," Lindsay said, watching Phoebe put a plate of her chocolate chip cookies and slices of Katie's bread on their table.

"*Mamm* wishes we were married by now. I'm not in a hurry to get married, and Amy isn't either." Jenna took a bite of cookie. "Did you make the cookies, Phoebe? They're delicious."

Phoebe nodded. "Thank you."

"Everything was good," Amy said. "Thanks for preparing a *wunderbaar* lunch for us."

Harris grinned. "It looks like none of us are vegetarians."

Phoebe laughed. "I'm surprised there was any meat left for us. I saw you eating some while you were grilling it."

"Shush, don't tell on me," Harris said, waving his fork at Phoebe.

Lindsay sighed. "The afternoon is going too fast. I wish you could spend the night."

Amy smiled. "It's been nice getting to know you."

"We're glad you looked for us. I wish *Mamm* or *Daed* had told you we moved to Millersburg." Jenna bit her lower lip. "None of our Amish relatives ever mentioned we were adopted. We even asked why we had black hair when no one else did."

"I guess everyone thought it best to keep your adoption a secret," Phoebe said. "Could I visit you sometime?"

"Of course. We'd love for you to come to our house." Amy grinned. "You've already seen our store in your disguise, but I'm sure we can find other things for you to see and do."

Phoebe said in a hopeful voice, "Would next Friday be too soon? That is if it's okay with you and your parents. I could leave after work and spend the night."

"I'm sure it'll be fine, but I'll check and call you tonight," Amy replied. "It'll be *wunderbaar* to have you at our house."

"I don't want to offend you, but could I take a photo of you three before you go home?" Harris cleared his throat. "I understand it's against your faith to have pictures taken, but I thought since you aren't baptized, maybe it'd be okay."

"Sure, you can." Jenna patted Harris's arm. "We can't pose for a photo, but you can snap one of us with Phoebe."

"That's great." Harris ran his fingers through his hair. "If you ever have any questions to ask me about the medical field, I'll try to answer them. I'm sorry I wasn't around for you when you were younger, but I'm here now."

Chapter Thirteen

As soon as Amy and Jenna were picked up by their English driver, Harris walked Lindsay to her bedroom. He noticed how pale her face looked. "Lindsay, you need to rest. You've had a stressful day in many ways. Is there anything I can get you?"

"I am exhausted, but it's a good kind of exhaustion. It was a day well spent." Lindsay gave him a big smile. "Amy and Jenna hugged me before they got in the car with their driver. I wanted to hug them but didn't know they'd feel about it, so it was nice they made the first move. And they said they'll pray for me daily."

"It went well, I think. They definitely connected with you."

Lindsay nodded. "I'm glad you think so. I could tell they're interested in you too. It was a wonderful day."

"I got the impression they're disappointed in Katie and Roman for keeping the secret from them." Harris wasn't going to mention it, but he thought Amy sounded a bit jealous when she heard about Phoebe's childhood. Was she disappointed Lindsay had kept Phoebe instead of her? To him, it would make sense because Amy wanted more out of life than an eighth-grade education. He was glad it came out how

Katie made Lindsay promise never to tell the truth about their birth. But still, it had to hurt that Katie and Roman never told them the truth until they were forced to, and Lindsay hadn't broken her promise before now.

Once in her bedroom, Lindsay kicked off her shoes and sat on the bed. "Amy and Jenna are going to call me when they get home. I'll take a nap while they're making the trip home."

He fluffed her pillow. "I'll be in the living room if you need anything."

"Phoebe left quickly, but that's nice she wanted to see Haley. I'm sure she'll be sharing about her Amish sisters. I hope Phoebe can have a strong sister relationship with Amy and Jenna, but it'll take time."

"It's all going to work out for them. They are sensitive and kind daughters. And I'm sure they want their mother to rest. I'll go check my emails."

Lindsay touched his arm. "I'm glad you're here."

After he left Lindsay's bedroom, Harris wished Phoebe hadn't left. It would've been nice to chat with her while Lindsay took a nap. What would it have been like to have memories of our daughters as children? He'd seen all the photo albums of Phoebe and some of the schoolwork Lindsay had kept through the years. He'd read the letters from Katie too.

His guilt had been weighing on him ever since he'd received Lindsay's letter. Or maybe it had happened years ago when he'd rejected a beautiful young woman. He'd taken a lot away from her. She'd tried to reach out to him, but he'd been selfish. Why didn't he do what his heart told him and return quickly to tell Lindsay that he wouldn't marry Callie? Ironically, he was twenty-two years old—the same age his daughters were now. Amy and Jenna showed courage and made an effort to learn more about their past. It had to be a major shock to Amy, Jenna, and Phoebe to learn the truth about their births as triplets. What they had believed their whole lives had turned out to be a big lie. Jenna and Amy immediately made the trip to Columbus to learn more about their past.

Sure, he was a successful physician, but what did it matter? He hadn't anyone to share his life with for years.

Recalling how Lindsay had said they needed to look forward reminded him of what he'd read once about what Jesus expected when it came to past mistakes. In his heart, Harris knew Jesus never wanted him to look back at his decisions that had turned into mistakes. Jesus wanted him to stop wasting time dwelling on the past because wishing what he could change was pointless. He couldn't change what he'd done years ago.

Instead, Jesus wants me to release my mistakes to Him. He can bring joy and beauty out of my mistakes. But only if I trust Him and allow Jesus to bring beauty out of my failures.

Lindsay and I are older and wiser now, and life smoothed over our youthful mistakes and gave me the courage to accept God's purpose for my life. Is Lindsay in God's plan for me? He brought us together again after so many years apart. That has to mean something.

Harris grabbed his cell phone from the coffee table and opened it to look at the picture he'd taken of his three daughters.

They might have my black hair and brown eyes, but their beautiful features remind me of Lindsay.

Harris put his phone down on the table. He wanted to peek in to see if Lindsay was asleep. If she was awake, maybe he'd tell her something that was of utmost importance to him.

The burning question in his heart was to ask Lindsay if she could love him again. He sighed, knowing the question would have to wait. It was too soon to ask, but hopefully, he wouldn't have to wait too long.

Millersburg, Ohio

"They should be here soon," Katie said to her parents, Naomi and Clarence Gingerich. They were seated at the kitchen table, enjoying her mother's delicious cake with cups of *kaffi*. "I'm glad you both came. Amy and Jenna will be *froh* to see you." Katie wanted her parents there to ease the situation between them and their daughters. Katie heard the hurt in her daughters' voices before they left to visit Lindsay. If only Lindsay hadn't gotten cancer, the truth could've been buried forever.

That's selfish of me to wish things could return to the way it was, but I'm afraid we will lose the girls to the English world. Maybe becoming EMTs will be enough for them to be content here. I hope and pray they'll still join our church. Tucking the loose tendrils of her light brown hair under her *kapp*, Katie glanced at her son.

"*Danki* for bringing the chocolate cake." Seth jabbed his fork into his dessert. "You make the best cakes, *Mammi.*"

Naomi smiled at her grandson. "*Daadi* and I have missed you. You should visit us sometime."

"Work is busy with a lot of building going on, but I'll visit on a weekend when I can get a Saturday off." Seth took a big drink of milk.

Stroking his white beard, Clarence said, "It's too bad about Lindsay's cancer. I remember how much she loved her triplets."

"I can't believe how Phoebe is their sister," Seth said. "I never noticed she looked like Amy and Jenna when she was in the store."

Roman chuckled. "I heard you were busy chatting with the blonde Phoebe."

"Well, I didn't realize who she really was. Of course, Phoebe isn't related to me, so there was no harm in having a little conversation with her." Seth took another bite of cake.

Katie tapped a spot by Seth. "I hope you go to a singing again and meet a young woman to court. It shouldn't be hard for you to meet someone in our faith. I heard several young ladies are interested in you, especially Veronica."

"I'll attend another singing." Seth grinned. "I'm not sure about several ladies being interested in me, though."

"Sorry to change the topic, but I've been remembering Phoebe and her sisters when they were babies." Naomi fingered the rim of her coffee cup. "Lindsay had put a tiny, pink bracelet on Phoebe's wrist. Jenna's bracelet was yellow while Amy's was lavender. Even though we don't believe in wearing jewelry, I thought their bracelets were a great way to identify the baby girls." Naomi glanced at Katie. "I'm glad Lindsay gave you Amy and Jenna to raise, but it's good the secret is out now."

Katie frowned. "I hope it works out. Amy and Jenna feel betrayed that we never told them until we had to." She hadn't slept last night with the knowledge they were going to visit their birth parents and Phoebe. *How will they feel about me and Roman when they return home? Will they want to spend more time with Harris, Lindsay, and Phoebe? I hope not.*

"It'll work out. You and Roman raised them as your daughters. Things will settle down." Clarence took a long sip of his coffee.

"I hope so. I keep wondering if they'll take their kneeling vows or wait even longer." Katie's anxiety soared whenever she considered how none of their *kinner* had joined their Amish faith.

Roman ran his fingers through his hair. "I hope they take their baptism vows, but maybe that won't happen. They were born to English parents. And sure, they came to us as babies, but Amy and Jenna definitely haven't shown an interest in becoming Amish. It's like something has been holding them back. While we have been *gut* examples to them—well, I shouldn't say it like that because I sound prideful, but I wonder at times."

"I'm going to join, but I want to wait a couple of years. I'll pray about it, but I'm planning on waiting until I'm twenty-three." Seth stood and walked to the sink. "I just don't feel ready to make a lifetime commitment."

As Katie watched her son rinse his plate, relief flooded her soul. At least Seth would commit to their faith. Maybe he'd even decide to not wait a couple of years. He could meet someone at one of their youth events and decide to settle down with a wife.

Naomi grinned. "I'll have to make you another cake. You're such a *wunderbaar-gut* grandson." She paused for a moment, then stared at Katie and Roman. "When I become troubled, I remember the verse in Peter, and I feel better when I give all my worries to God. Being dependent on our Father is what is necessary in this life. I think it says to cast all my cares, worries, and anxieties on God because he cares for me."

Katie nodded, thinking her mother had added a few words to the verse from Peter, but it was a good one to remember.

Seth opened the kitchen door. "I'm going to go to the phone shanty to check the answering machine to see if we have any messages." He paused at the door and said, "Hey, Amy and Jenna are back."

Seth held the door open for his sisters. Amy entered the kitchen first. "I guess you were watching for us. You must've missed us."

Seth laughed. "I did, and I saved you some chocolate cake."

Jenna followed Amy into the kitchen. "It's *gut* to be home. It was a bit much traveling four hours in one day."

"Next time, we'll spend the night. Lindsay invited us to stay overnight, but we hadn't planned on doing it this time." Amy hugged Naomi. "This is a nice surprise to see you."

"Where's my hug?" Clarence asked.

After the girls hugged their grandparents, Jenna removed plates from the cupboard. "I can't wait to eat a piece of your cake, *Mammi*."

While Naomi slid the cake on their plates, she asked, "How's Lindsay? I heard she has cancer."

"She looked exhausted and pale," Jenna said, sitting in a chair by her grandmother.

"Harris was attentive to Lindsay. I think he loves her. You should have seen the way he looked at her." Amy cleared her throat. "He offered to answer any medical questions we might have. I'm still going to the EMT training, but I've always wanted to pursue a medical career. When I was younger, I thought I'd like to become a doctor. Not now, though. It'd take too long. Maybe I'll think about becoming a nurse or a physician's assistant. Phoebe's lucky she will start medical school soon."

Katie studied her daughter for a moment. "That might be difficult if you want to join our church. Have you decided not to take your kneeling vows?"

"Is that why you didn't tell us the truth about our birth?" Amy took a seat by Roman. "You were worried we wouldn't join the church?"

"*Nee*, I thought it best you didn't know. See what it has caused now? It's overwhelming and confusing to you girls." Katie hoped her parents or Roman would step in and give her support, but they remained quiet.

"I can receive my education and still join our church later. Just think how I can help our church members if I have a nursing degree." Amy swallowed a mouthful of cake. "This is delicious."

"*Danki*." Naomi pushed a lock of her white hair away from her face. "It sounds like you've thought about what you might do, but be sure to pray and ask God what He wants for you."

"Amy, I never knew you wanted to become a nurse." Katie glanced at Roman and asked, "Had you ever heard this before?"

"Amy mentioned it to me recently," Roman said. "I think becoming an EMT might be the best thing, and fortunately, it has the bishop's approval."

Jenna walked to the refrigerator. "Amy, do you want a glass of milk?" At her sister's nod, she poured a glass of milk for each of them. "I didn't want to like Harris since he broke up with Lindsay. But he's a nice man. It's a shame he never knew about us until now. He had tears in his eyes several times."

As Amy took the glass from Jenna, she said, "Phoebe's nice and easy to talk to. I'm glad we got to spend time with her. She wants to visit us next Friday. I hope that's okay."

"That's great you had a nice visit, and I'm sure it meant a lot to them. Friday should be fine for Phoebe to come." Roman looked away from Amy to look at Jenna as she returned to her seat. "Seth wants to join the church. What are your feelings about taking your baptism vows?"

"I'm going to join our faith," Jenna replied. "I don't want to this year but probably will next year."

Although Katie was happy to hear two children wanted to become Amish, she was concerned about Amy. What if she attended college? Then she wouldn't want to join their faith. If that happened, it would break her heart.

Clarence grinned. "Okay, enough talk about serious stuff. What did you eat at Lindsay's house?"

Chapter Fourteen

Phoebe was in a hurry to get home after work on Friday to check on her mom and get cleaned up before leaving on her road trip. Following her sisters' visit on Sunday, they had arranged for Phoebe to visit them today and spend the night. She felt yucky because a toddler had accidentally dumped a glass of Hi-C punch on her. When she noticed her mom was on the phone, Phoebe went to her bathroom and quickly took a shower. Then she packed an overnight bag. Well, she packed and unpacked it. She wanted to make a good impression on Katie Yoder. She sounded like a tough person to please. Finally, she packed a conservative blouse and a long skirt to wear on Saturday. To travel to Millersburg, Phoebe decided to wear a deep rose dress with cap sleeves.

She waited until her father arrived from Cincinnati even though she didn't want to arrive late to the Yoders' house. Fortunately, Harris had left his practice in the afternoon. After visiting with him briefly, she carried a bouquet of flowers and a pan of brownies to her car. Harris carried her bag while her mother looked worried.

Before getting in her car, Phoebe said, "Mom, don't worry. I'll be careful driving. I'll call you when I get there."

"They'll love your brownies." As Lindsay's blue eyes took in her appearance, she said, "You look pretty in your dress. You made a good choice."

Harris nodded. "You look lovely. Have a good visit with your sisters."

Lindsay grinned. "And Seth."

Phoebe shrugged. "He's fun to tease is all. Besides, he's younger than I am."

"He's not that much younger than you." Lindsay hugged her. "You better get started. It's a long drive. Tell the girls I said hello."

After driving for several minutes, nervous thoughts popped into Phoebe's mind. She would be meeting Roman and Katie for the first time. Even though they had also wanted to adopt her, it might be awkward to meet them now. Maybe she should've waited to visit. Would it be unsettling to the Yoders to see her spend time with Amy and Jenna? She was with them last Sunday at her house. Since her sisters haven't joined their Amish church, it has to be a concern to Katie and Roman that they might decide to include English activities in their lives.

After two hours of driving, Phoebe pulled into the driveway of her sisters' house. After she turned the key off in her ignition, she called her mom. "I'm here."

"You made good time. I'm glad you made it there safely," her mom said.

"Say a prayer that it goes well. I hope I can fit in okay."

"I'll say a prayer, but I'm sure it'll go fine."

"I better get in there, or they might think I changed my mind about visiting. I love you. Bye, Mom."

As soon as she shut her car door, Jenna was by her side, hugging her. "It's *gut* to see you again. Thanks for coming."

"I'm happy to be here." Phoebe grinned. "You can help me by carrying the brownies."

"Brownies sound delicious."

"The flowers are for your mother. I hope she'll like them."

As they walked toward the house, Jenna said, "I'm sure she will. I like your dress."

"Thanks. I thought I better avoid wearing pants."

"*Ach*, that's thoughtful of you, but you can wear pants or jeans around us. We see English tourists wearing all kinds of clothing in our store." Jenna giggled. "I'm glad you aren't wearing your fake glasses and wig, though. I wonder how Seth will respond now that you look like our sister."

"I'm sure he'll tease me."

"Everyone's in the kitchen. *Mamm* thought you might like a snack." Jenna took her to the back porch and opened the kitchen door for her.

Amy smiled at Phoebe as soon as she entered the room. "Hi, sis. We had a disagreement about where you'd sleep. Jenna wants you in her room this time, but on your next visit, you'll be in my bedroom."

Phoebe loved hearing how her sisters were happy to have her at their home. She glanced at an older woman standing by the kitchen counter, holding a dishcloth. She must be Katie Yoder. Phoebe assumed Roman Yoder was the man standing next to her. "Hello, Mr. and Mrs. Yoder."

Roman smiled at Phoebe as he put a coffeepot down on the stove. "Please call us by our first names. It's *wunderbaar-gut* to have you here."

"*Ya*. Welcome, Phoebe, to our home." Katie began wiping down the countertop with the dishcloth.

Roman stood and grabbed her overnight bag. "I'll take your bag upstairs for you."

"Thank you." Phoebe noticed how Seth resembled his father. They both had the same brilliant green eyes, strong jaw, and chiseled cheekbones.

Amy opened a cabinet door and removed a vase. "I'd better get your flowers in water."

"Phoebe, you look different without your disguise." Seth grinned. "I liked you as a blonde."

"I used to want to be blonde like my mom when I was little. I loved her hair and blue eyes." Phoebe turned to smile at her sisters. "Now I love looking like my sisters."

Seth shook his head. "But you don't seem like Amy and Jenna at all. I don't mean because they're dressed in our Plain clothing and you're not, but your personality and other things are different."

Amy nodded. "And Phoebe's hair is shorter than ours since we have never had our hair cut. Another difference is you don't have our Pennsylvania Dutch accent."

"It'll be fun to see if we have some things in common. I've heard of twins being separated and raised in different environments, but they have many of the same food preferences and interests." Phoebe wanted Amy and Jenna to feel a connection to her, and her sister pointing out their differences wasn't helping.

"You must be hungry and thirsty after your long drive." Katie walked quickly to the kitchen counter. "We have apple pie, and I can put a scoop of ice cream on it. Or there's carrot cake."

"Both sound yummy, but I'll take the pie with ice cream."

Leaning against the counter, Jenna said, "*Mamm,* we should go to the living room instead of staying here. There's more of a breeze in there."

Katie frowned. "I don't think it's warm in here, but you're right, it'll be more comfortable in there."

Within a few minutes, they were all in the living room with their desserts and drinks.

Roman said, "Let's bow our heads and pray."

"We pray silently," Jenna whispered to Phoebe.

Once they lifted their heads, Phoebe took a bite of her pie. She couldn't believe she was seated in an Amish living room with her sisters and their family. How her life had changed in a matter of weeks. There were two sofas covered in a blue fabric. Seth and Jenna joined her on one sofa while Katie and Amy sat across from them. Roman sat in a tan recliner. There was a ceiling lamp that looked like it was a battery-operated light. There were smaller battery-operated lamps on the end tables. "You have a lovely home."

"Fortunately, we got away from gas-powered lights when we moved here." Jenna rolled her brown eyes. "They made our house too hot in the summer. When we moved here, there were already battery-powered ceiling lights in the rooms. The table lamps also use batteries. I was surprised *Daed's* relatives didn't take the table lamps with them when they moved."

As Katie gazed at Phoebe, she said, "I'm sure this is different for you being in an Amish home without electricity. When Lindsay asked us to adopt Amy and Jenna, she explained how she wanted a stable home for her daughters because she never had one. It touched our hearts how she wanted a simple life filled with love."

Phoebe held her glass of iced tea tightly in her hand. "Harris and I both were amazed when we learned about the adoption to an Amish couple, but it makes sense to me now. It obviously was a difficult time for my mom. I'm glad God directed her to you and Roman." She hoped what she said sounded good to Katie and the rest of the family. She didn't want to offend anyone.

Out of the corner of her eye, Phoebe glanced at Seth. After he swallowed a mouthful of her chocolate brownie, Seth said, "This is so *appeditlich*."

Phoebe giggled. "I guess that means my brownie tastes good."

"*Ya*, it means delicious." Seth grinned. "I'll have to teach you some Deutsch words, or otherwise, my sisters might gang up against you and tease you by talking in our language."

Amy gave Seth a frustrated glance. "*Ach*, you know we'd never do that to Phoebe."

Phoebe took another bite of pie. She couldn't believe how the apples were sweet, tart, and just the right texture for eating. She smiled at Katie. "Your pie is *appeditlich*. I love the cinnamon crumb topping too."

"Hey, stop showing off," Seth said. "I see you are learning our language quickly."

Katie stared at Phoebe for a moment, then she straightened her back. "I'm glad you like my pie. How's Lindsay feeling?"

"She has a lot of fatigue from the cancer and chemo." Phoebe tucked a lock of her black hair behind her ear.

"That has to be rough. Does she have to have chemo much longer?" Concern clouded Roman's eyes.

"She's supposed to have it for six months. She couldn't tolerate the first chemo treatment and ended up in the hospital. It was scary. I was with her for the first treatment. They rushed her to the ER when she had chest pains. She had low hemoglobin, low blood pressure, and other things that had gone wrong. After Mom was admitted to the hospital, the ER doctor ordered a blood transfusion. Fortunately, the following week, she tolerated the chemo without any problem."

Seth stopped eating his brownie, giving Phoebe a compassionate glance. "I'm sorry about your mom. I enjoyed meeting her when she came to our store."

Jenna sat straighter in her chair. "I remember how Lindsay felt faint that day. Was it also because she saw us for the first time since we were little? That had to be overwhelming."

"It was a defining moment for her. For all of us. I couldn't believe I had two sisters, and I also learned I had a father who had never died." Phoebe tried to keep her voice normal, but she didn't like being the focus of the Yoder family's attention.

It was a relief to Phoebe when they went upstairs to get ready for bed. When she'd made plans to visit, her sisters said it was church Sunday this weekend. Otherwise, Phoebe might have stayed a second night. She wasn't crazy about attending an Amish service, but maybe she would in the future. She found it interesting they only had church every other week at someone's house or barn. They didn't have a church building for their services.

Jenna wore a coral capri pajama set, which was interesting to Phoebe. She expected to see a long nightgown. When Amy entered the room, she also wore capri bottoms with a short-sleeved pajama top. "Your pj's are cute. Where do you shop?"

"Walmart, usually, but we've gone to other stores." Amy smiled as she plopped down on Jenna's bed. "Okay, confess now. Do you wish you'd grown up with us in an Amish family?"

Looking at their waist-length hair, Phoebe grinned. "I'm not sure I could've handled never getting my hair cut, but I wish we could have been together as children. It would have been fun and wonderful to have sisters. But at least we know the truth now and can spend time together."

"In some ways, it must've been nice to be so close to Lindsay, but I'm sure there were times you would've loved having a father and a brother or sister in your family." Jenna propped a pillow and rested her head against it. "I wish we'd known about you and Lindsay years ago. I don't think our parents should've kept it a secret."

Amy nodded. "We only learned everything because of Lindsay's letter."

"It was a shock when I accidentally found the fourteen letters Katie wrote to Mom. I saw they were sent each year on my birthday. She was in the hospital, so I waited until she came home to explain why she had them."

"You never read them?" Jenna asked.

Phoebe shook her head. "I read the letters after I knew about you." She sat in the corner where there was a chair. As she glanced at Jenna's lavender-and-white quilt on her bed, she asked, "Did Katie make your quilt? It's beautiful."

"*Nee*, I did." Jenna touched the quilt. "I can make you a quilt for your bed. That'll be something for you to have from me."

Phoebe was touched Jenna wanted to make her a quilt because that would be a labor of love. It would take Jenna hours of work to make one. "I'd love to have a quilt."

"We should make a quilt for Lindsay too." Amy sighed. "It's sad she had to give us up. I admit I sometimes wish she'd kept me instead of you, because then I could've attended high school and even college. Yet, I can't imagine growing up without Jenna, Seth, and our parents."

"I can understand that." Phoebe was glad Amy was being open about her feelings. "There were times when I wished I could've had a dad and siblings. Mom seldom dated while I was growing up. I think she never got over Harris. She did go out a few times with our next-door neighbor, Drew, but then she got sick. He's also still hurting from the death of his wife, and he travels for his job a lot."

"I saw how Harris looked at her," Jenna said with a sigh. "It's sad how everything went wrong for them."

Phoebe shrugged. "Maybe they wouldn't have made it when they were so young. Harris had years of medical college ahead of him. Even if his parents had helped them financially, it would've been stressful to raise three babies while attending classes."

"Speaking of college, I'm definitely interested in becoming a nurse. I'd never mentioned it before to my *mamm*. It's a miracle she said Jenna and I could become EMTs. If I'd been the one Lindsay had raised, I'd probably be a nurse by now or even studying to become a doctor."

"You can still become a nurse," Jenna said, "but you might have to confess going to college."

"Why would you have to confess going to college when you haven't been baptized into your church?" Phoebe thought this whole concept sounded absolutely wrong.

"It'd be considered wrong to go to college with non-Amish adults. Pride becomes relevant because I'd think I required more schooling than an eighth-grade education. It would seem I thought myself better than everyone."

"I hope it works out for you if you decide to become a nurse." Phoebe twisted the ring on her finger. "Harris said he or our grandparents would pay for us to attend college."

"Are you going to have him pay your tuition?" Jenna asked.

Phoebe shrugged. "I don't know. I want to become a doctor, so that will cost a lot of money."

"I don't even have my high school diploma." Amy smiled at Jenna. "Maybe being an EMT with you will be enough for me."

Phoebe nodded. "I think it's awesome you two are going to start training to become EMTs."

"Enough talk about education," Jenna said. "What would you like to do tomorrow? I know Seth's taking you for a buggy ride in the afternoon, but is there anything special you'd like to do in Millersburg?"

"Just spend time with my sisters." Phoebe's eyes filled with tears.

Amy leaned closer to Phoebe and grasped her hand. "That sounds perfect to me."

"We'll start making memories," Jenna said in a choked voice. "I'm glad I have another sister."

Chapter Fifteen

A warm breeze brushed against Phoebe's face. Riding in Seth's new buggy was fun, but maybe it was because he was the driver. As she sat close to him, Phoebe suddenly laughed at an image of Seth's mom. Poor Roman was probably getting an earful from Katie. When she'd left with Seth for their ride, Katie had looked displeased. She'd said to Seth, "How can you take Phoebe for a ride? I thought you were supposed to work."

"You better not be laughing at the driver here."

"I'm not. I'm afraid I was thinking about how unhappy your mother looked that we were going for a buggy ride."

Turning his face toward her, Seth scrunched his face. "Why is that funny?"

She shrugged as her brown eyes met his green ones. "It seemed humorous because I know Katie would prefer you to take an Amish girl on a ride instead of me. But she doesn't have to worry about *us* going for a ride."

"*Mamm's* okay with me giving buggy rides to Englishers. I do it sometimes when the construction business is slower. It gives us extra money, and it's great talking with the tourists as I show them the sights in town."

"I saw some of the stores in town when we first came to Millersburg. It's a charming town with cheese shops, antique stores, and fine-art galleries. Well, some of it was in neighboring towns. I'm glad you're taking me on a scenic route." She glanced at the rolling hills. "I love how this road is mainly used for Amish buggies. It's nice it's paved and well-maintained."

"The road will take us back to Millersburg." Seth waved to a woman riding her bike as his buggy passed her. "That's Veronica. She's the daughter of friends of my parents. Many Amish ride their bikes into to town."

"She didn't look happy to see you." Phoebe noticed how pretty Veronica was in her purple Amish dress, and she looked to be around their age.

"Maybe she thinks I should be at home building the birdhouse she wants to give as a gift."

Phoebe cleared her throat and decided to be blunt. "Maybe she didn't like seeing you with me."

He grinned. "Could be. I'm a charming guy."

She laughed. "Also, a conceited guy."

"Were you surprised I asked you?" Seth asked after a moment of silence. He sneaked a glance at Phoebe.

"A little bit surprised, but I'm glad you did." She saw the serious expression on his good-looking face. He wanted her to enjoy what he'd done for her. It was sweet he'd gone to the trouble of showing her a new experience. "Riding in a buggy is nice and relaxing."

"Do you regret not growing up with Amy and Jenna? And me, of course." Seth gave her a broad smile.

Phoebe pressed her lips together. *Oh no, another Yoder asking me the same question. Do I seem like I had an unhappy childhood? I guess because we are identical triplets it's normal for them to wonder if I wish Mom had given me up for adoption too.* "I wish I could've known I had sisters years ago. It'd been nice to do what we're doing now and visit each other's homes. But I had a great childhood with my mom. Don't take this the wrong way, but I can't imagine growing up in an Amish home without electricity and the many things I now realize I have taken for granted. It's probably the same thing for my sisters. I'm sure they're glad they grew up with you and your parents."

Seth frowned. "I don't think Amy is. She isn't upset with Lindsay but is with our *mamm*. She told me and Jenna that when she was a teenager, she could've lived with Lindsay and attended high school with you."

"Do you think Amy would want to live with us and go to Ohio State with me?" She couldn't keep the excitement out of her voice. "She could get her GED and apply to college. I can help her do both. It'd be wonderful to have Amy live with us."

He shook his head. "I don't think *Mamm* will allow her to live with you and Lindsay."

"But she's an adult." Phoebe wondered if it was because of finances. "Is it because your parents need Amy to work in the store?"

"*Nee*. We've been raised to stay separate from the world."

"But Amy and Jenna are going to train to be EMTs. And you have a store where tourists shop. That's not keeping separate from Englishers."

"That's true, but we live at home," Seth said in a light tone. "We keep separate by not having electricity in our homes, and without having quick transportation, we spend more time together as a family." He gave her a direct look. "Did you miss watching TV?"

She took in a cleansing breath. "I have to admit how I loved hearing the sounds from the farm animals in the barn. No dings from cell phones and the silence of the rooms without a TV on was relaxing."

"I'm glad." After a moment of silence, he asked, "Could I visit you sometime in Columbus? I like spending time with you."

Phoebe wasn't expecting Seth to be interested enough in her to drive to Columbus. Well, not drive exactly. He'd have to hire a driver because he wouldn't be able to take his buggy for a long trip. It'd be fun to spend time with him on her home turf. "I'd like you to visit sometime."

His eyes flashed with humor. "Wow, don't sound so thrilled for me to see you again. I want to get to know you better."

"You just mentioned staying separate from the world, yet you want to visit me in Columbus. Of course, you surprised me. And it's not weird to you that I look exactly like your sisters?"

His eyebrows rose as he drew in a breath. "You don't look like Amy or Jenna to me. It's not just because your hair and clothing are different. It's more than that."

Relief went through her. She didn't want to remind him of his sisters. Or *her* sisters. She gave a nervous laugh. "It's confusing but fascinating."

He took his eyes off the road to look at her. "I've taken girls home from singings, but I never had a steady girlfriend. I know we can't be serious about each other right now, but to be completely honest, I want to see what happens if we learn more about each other."

"I don't know if that's a good idea right now. Your parents aren't going to like you visiting me. It'd be different if I wasn't English. I've only been around you and your family for a short time, but I can see how Katie doesn't want you to become close to me. And I get it. I'm not Amish. I'm not sure your mother wants Amy and Jenna around me and my mom very much."

Seth frowned. "I'm in my *rumspringa* and have been since I was sixteen. I started attending youth get-togethers then. I don't have to join my faith until I feel ready or I decide to get married. I'm free to do things that I can't do if I join the church. I can even get my driver's license, and I'm happy to have a cell phone. Amish parents are wise to give their children the opportunity to experience non-Amish things, so we can make the right decision for our lives. Some men might even wait until they are twenty-four or twenty-five to join the church."

"I get that, but I don't want to upset your mom."

Pulling the buggy off the road onto a side country lane, Seth turned to her. "I'm an adult. *Mamm* needs to understand that I can choose what to do with my free time. Do you have a boyfriend back in Columbus?"

She shook her head. "I had a boyfriend, but we aren't together any longer." There wasn't any point in telling Seth that Jared had originally broken up with her because she hadn't wanted to take their platonic relationship to a sexual one.

"Then we are free to date each other. I hope you'll change your mind about seeing me again."

Phoebe hadn't expected Seth to mention dating her. *How should I handle this new development? Do I want to become involved with Seth? I'm going to medical school, and he's Amish.* She cleared her throat. "I don't think we should date, but we can be friends. We come from different worlds. I can't imagine you leaving your Amish lifestyle, and I don't want to leave mine. I enjoy talking with you. That day we first met in your parents' store, you made me feel carefree again. I hadn't felt that way since before my mom was diagnosed with cancer. It's been hard seeing her ill and suffering from the chemo treatments. The chemo might kill the cancer cells, but it also kills the healthy cells."

"I'm sorry Lindsay has cancer. I've been praying for her."

"Thank you." Phoebe liked that Seth had been praying for her mother and felt it was sweet he was interested in dating her. What could it hurt to spend time talking with Seth on the phone? *Even though Jared hurt me, it's not likely Seth will. We'll be friends and nothing more.* "Maybe we can talk a couple of times a week on the phone."

She could tell by the way he looked at her that he wanted to kiss her, which was crazy because they hardly knew each other. A warm rush of emotion moved from her chest through her whole body. His closeness caused a nervous awareness within her. It might not be possible to remain just friends with Seth. When he didn't kiss her, a wave of disappointment hit her. Should she kiss him? No, that might shock him too much. What was she thinking anyhow? She shouldn't kiss her sisters' brother. And kissing definitely wouldn't keep them at a friendship level. Could they keep their relationship as friends and nothing more? "I like you too."

"I suppose we better head to the restaurant. I hate that our ride is ending, though." Seth grinned. "You're an interesting girl, Phoebe Prescott."

"It's been fun having my first buggy ride. My mom said how much she loved riding in a buggy when she stayed with your parents."

"*Gut* to hear you like it."

Before she couldn't understand how her parents had fallen in love during one short summer, but now she could see how it had happened. She felt something for Seth that she shouldn't. Especially since he was Amish. She would never consider becoming Amish,

and it didn't seem likely that Seth would abandon his faith.

～

"I don't like it at all," Katie said as soon as the two customers left their store. Now that it was just the two of them, she could freely speak. She was sure her blood pressure was rising with the knowledge that Seth was on a buggy ride with Phoebe. "Why is he spending time with her? Seth should be taking a nice Amish girl on a buggy ride. Amy said Seth talked to Veronica at the singing they all went to recently. If Phoebe hadn't come to visit us this weekend, maybe Seth would be taking Veronica for a buggy ride instead. We hear the bishop and other ministers speak constantly in their sermons to remain separate from unbelievers."

Roman straightened several cans on a shelf. "Phoebe's leaving today to go home. She's not planning to return anytime soon. She usually works on Saturday but asked to get off today."

"How do you know she won't be back again on the weekends? She might even quit her job to spend more time with our family." Katie continued. "And Amy and Jenna went quickly to spend time with her, Lindsay, and Harris. Then Phoebe immediately came here this weekend. I don't think the only reason she came was to bond with her sisters, though. I think she likes Seth, which is crazy. They seem to glance at each other a lot. Our daughters said how Phoebe teased Seth when she first met him in our store."

Roman turned away from the shelf and fingered his beard. "It's just a buggy ride during the daytime. You're making a big deal out of it. Phoebe never had a younger sibling to have fun with, and she likes teasing Seth. Amy and Jenna are always ribbing their *bruder*."

"I don't see why Seth couldn't take a bigger buggy, so Amy and Jenna could go too."

"He wanted to drive his new buggy. Amy and Jenna said they had a couple of errands to run while they went on the ride. It's not like they're going to be by themselves for long." Roman put several bags of Amish noodles back on a wide shelf. "I thought the customer would buy the noodles. She said how they reminded her of the ones her grandmother used to make."

Katie drummed her fingers on the store's counter. "Don't you see what's happening? Our *kinner* enjoy being with Phoebe. I can see why. She is a likable and kind person, but it worries me that she's very different because of her English upbringing. We've taught them their whole lives to keep separate from the world. Now Amy and Jenna have an Englisher for a sister and exciting new birth parents." Katie's panic rose when she thought about how the English world might be too appealing to her daughters and Seth. She couldn't lose any of her *kinner* to the secular world.

"I don't think we need to worry. Phoebe's a nice young woman, and she has a life. When she starts medical college, she isn't going to have time to drive here."

"If Amy and Jenna want to visit Lindsay and Phoebe again, we should go too. We could find an Amish bed and breakfast nearby to stay at. I'd like to see Lindsay again."

"Or we could go with them but come back the same day. I hate to leave the store overnight. It's only a two-hour drive from here by car." Roman raised his eyebrows, giving her a doubtful glance. "That's great you want to see Lindsay. I'm sure Phoebe would also enjoy us visiting them."

"I also want to see Lindsay's home and see what is there to tempt our daughters to leave our community. We can have Seth watch the store. Of course, we'll need someone else to help him." As she looked around at their store, Katie sometimes wished it wasn't such a huge place to manage. It was hard to get away during the busiest tourist season.

"Harris might be at Lindsay's home. Phoebe said he's involved in Lindsay's cancer treatment since he's a doctor, but I'm sure he wants to be there for Lindsay during her illness too. I suppose it'd be *gut* to meet him."

Katie rubbed her forehead. "*Ach.* You don't think they'll start living together, do you? That would be a terrible example for our children. And for Phoebe too."

He expelled a breath. "Geez, Katie, I don't see that happening. For one thing, they live in different cities. And Phoebe lives with Lindsay. Jenna said Harris is a Christian, and we know Lindsay accepted Christ years ago."

"I hope you're right." She moved a stack of pot holders closer to the register, trying to collect her thoughts. Her brain was racing with images of Lindsay committing adultery again. She had to get a grip on herself and stop thinking about Lindsay doing something wrong. She had raised

Phoebe and done a great job with her. "For years, I wanted to avoid all this drama with the birth parents, but now we have to make the best of this situation that we can."

Roman walked closer to Katie and pulled her into his arms.

"What if someone comes into the store?" She lifted her head slightly from his chest to look into his green eyes.

"Then they'll see me hugging you. Before we went to Niagara Falls, I felt like God wanted me to tell you that we needed to call Lindsay and make plans to tell the girls the truth. I was going to ask you for Lindsay's phone number. I planned on doing it when we returned, but it was too late."

Guilt entered Katie's soul. In her heart, she knew why Roman had waited. He knew revealing the truth would upset her. "I'm sorry I put a burden on you. If only Amy and Jenna had joined the church and married Amish men, then I wouldn't have to worry about them. And giving us grandchildren would've been even better."

"God has a plan for them. Right now, it seems His plan is for them to become EMTs."

"I love you. I shouldn't worry. God gave me the best husband. And you're right. They're taking their training right here in Millersburg. They will be occupied in learning how to do their new jobs." The kids had mentioned getting pizza before Phoebe left for home. If they went to the restaurant, Katie could see if Seth and Phoebe had gotten closer during their time spent together. "Maybe we should go to the pizza place, so we can join our *kinner* for supper."

"I am hungry. That's a great idea. I'll put the Closed sign on the front door. We should leave now. It's great being the owners. We can do what we want. I feel free."

Katie laughed. "When we go under with no profits, you might not feel so free."

~

"It smells *gut* in here. I'm glad they ordered for us. I'm hungry," Katie said as her and Roman entered Joe's Pizza.

Roman smiled at her. "You always want the same toppings on your pizza. You never want to try something new."

She grinned, knowing he referred to her love of bacon, pepperoni, and mushrooms on her pizza. "I'm a creature of habit. We better go sit. Jenna is busy waving at us." Before she walked toward the round table, Katie glanced down at her dark purple dress and was relieved it looked presentable because a young man was next to Jenna. "I'm glad we came straight from the store. We saved time."

Roman put his hand on her elbow. "I see two empty seats for us. Let's grab them."

"We ordered chicken wings and pizza," Amy said when they were close to the table.

"*Mamm* and *Daed,* I'd like you to meet Eli Zimmerman," Jenna said, turning to a handsome Amish man with dark blond hair.

"It's nice to meet you," Katie said as she took a seat by Amy.

Before Roman sat down, Eli stood to shake his hand. "I'm happy to meet you both."

"He's been telling us about the recent medical emergency calls and transporting the patients to the hospital." Amy gave a bewildered glance at Eli. "It's amazing how many calls come from our Plain people."

"*Ya,*" Jenna said, "that might be another reason our bishop said we could do the training. I wish we could start classes now instead of waiting until September."

Eli sipped his Coke from a straw. "It'll go fast. You'll take around 120 to 150 hours of classroom training, and they in-clude hands-on learning."

As a male server came to their table, he asked Katie and Roman, "What can I get you to drink?"

"I'd like an iced tea," Katie said.

"The same for me," Roman added.

Phoebe pushed a plate toward Katie and Roman. "You must try these garlic knots. They're so good."

Seth nodded. "You better grab some before Phoebe eats all of them. The buggy ride gave her an appetite."

Amy rolled her eyes at Seth. "Phoebe, ignore him. He has eaten most of them."

"How was the ride? Did you enjoy it?" Katie asked before turning her head to take a peek at the server. As he set glasses of iced tea in front of her and Roman, she said, "Thank you."

"I loved it." Phoebe's face lit up, and her eyes filled with happiness. "Thank you for having me. It's been great being here."

"What did you like best?" Seth ran his finger under his suspender.

"I can't pick one thing." Phoebe tucked a lock of her black hair behind her ear. "Every minute's been awesome. Spending time with my sisters, great food—" She glanced at Seth. "—the buggy ride, and meeting your wonderful parents." She smiled mischievously at everyone. "Oh, this is important. I learned my mom was right about the straight pins. I couldn't imagine using them to hold dresses together. I thought she had to be kidding."

Both of her daughters chuckled, and Jenna said, "It was hilarious when I did a fake scream and said I stuck myself with a pin. You should've seen your face."

Katie's heart became lighter, realizing what a charming young woman Phoebe was. Maybe she should enjoy her visit instead of worrying about Seth's attraction to her.

Anyhow, nothing would happen with Phoebe leaving soon for Columbus.

Chapter Sixteen

Columbus, Ohio

On Wednesday morning, Harris was glad to drive away from the treatment center. He hated seeing Lindsay having to endure her chemo. He glanced at her after stopping at a red traffic light. His chest tightened at the thought of her dying from cancer. He loved her but was afraid to tell her his feelings.

"Harris, I'm glad you went with me when I had my treatment." Lindsay giggled. "Oh, you did more than go with me. You drove me. I can drive, you know."

Hearing Lindsay laugh reminded him of their carefree time on the beach that amazing summer. Meeting her had been a breath of fresh air. Before that, his life hadn't had any meaning. He'd been going through the motions of making his parents happy. As an only child, he'd felt pressure to meet their high, rigid standards. Sure, he'd wanted to become a physician, but his life had been basically dictated to him.

"I enjoy doing things for you. I hate that you have cancer, but I like that you only have chemo for two days every twenty-some days." Even though Lindsay hadn't gotten a second opinion from another oncologist, Harris decided that as long as everything went well, there wasn't a need to see another doctor. The trip to the hospital had worried him, but since the blood transfusion, Lindsay's color was better. And she didn't have any more serious issues, like a heart or kidney problem, that would mean she'd have to get her chemo in the hospital. This was her third chemo treatment, counting the first incomplete one.

Lindsay hesitated, then said, "A twenty-three-year-old man at church had the same type of non-Hodgkin's lymphoma cancer a year ago that I have. He now has cancer again, but it can't be treated with chemo this time. His chances of surviving are only twenty percent. I hope that doesn't happen to me."

"That seems unlikely that will happen." He squeezed her hand right before the traffic light turned green. As he drove through the intersection, Harris said, "You're going to be fine. Remember, Dr. Richardson said lymphoma cancer is very responsive to chemo. He seems confident you're going to do great."

She gave him a skeptical look. "I want to believe that, but I'm afraid it'll always be in the back of my mind that I'll get cancer again. The follicular type of non-Hodgkin's I have can return later."

"We'll pray and think positive." She looked thinner than usual in her gray capris and blue blouse. "Have you lost more weight?"

She shook her head. "Not recently."

"How about we eat at Phoebe's restaurant? Then we can go to an afternoon movie or watch a movie at your house."

Lindsay glanced at her watch. "I never ate breakfast. I felt too nervous. The menu at her restaurant has the best pancakes. And we can tell Phoebe what the doctor said."

"I didn't realize you never ate breakfast. You should eat a high-protein meal before treatment. I'm glad I got you a granola bar and a bottle of juice at the treatment center."

They had a refrigerator stocked with bottles of water, juice, and shelves with various food items available for the patients and caregivers.

"I don't know about the movie. You need to get back to your patients."

"I forgot to tell you. I rearranged my schedule. I'm going to stay overnight." He laughed. "I know a lot of the staff at Holiday Inn by first name now." He thought about how special it was to be with Lindsay. Because he wanted to spend more time with her and Phoebe, he'd made plans to stay overnight at the hotel and return early in the morning to Cincinnati. He'd go straight to the office in the morning.

～

After eating, they found a bench to sit on while walking on a short trail in a nearby park. For a moment, Harris was distracted by Lindsay's sweet fragrance and her closeness. He took a deep breath and exhaled it. Taking Lindsay's hand in his, he said, "I'm glad you suggested going for a walk instead of watching a movie."

"It's too nice of a day to be inside. There's a nice breeze to keep the temperature from feeling too warm."

Harris nodded. "It's pleasant being here in Columbus. I hope you and Phoebe visit me sometime in Cincinnati. I want to show you where I live and work. You'd love Ault Park in the city. I go there frequently."

"I'd like to visit you sometime."

"My ranch has four bedrooms. At the time, I thought it was too big for me, but now I'm glad I have it. I'll have room for any visits from you and our daughters."

She turned her head, giving him a mischievous smile. "Maybe we should visit the beach when I'm well. I'm sure you remember all the walks we took by the ocean. You complained I liked to walk too much."

He laughed. "Only because we ran each day too."

"Before cancer and the chemo treatments, I ran with Phoebe," she said with a sigh. "I hate having this fatigue. I'm hoping I'll feel better by the time school starts in August. I need to talk to the principal soon about my job. I did finish the school year, but I took a few sick days when I had my first chemo treatment and had to go to the hospital. It was hard to teach some days since I wasn't sleeping with all the night sweats, and my skin was so itchy."

"I can't see you going back to teach now, but I'm hoping you'll feel better soon. You should be able to take off from school for your two days for chemo plus extra days to recover from it. You'll be done with chemo anyhow in October."

"A few years ago, I switched from middle school to high school. I love teaching upper-level math classes. I don't want to lose my position as a teacher and as head of the math department."

"I'm impressed. You're already a big shot at your school, and you're young."

Lindsay laughed. "I wouldn't say I'm young but thank you."

"You've accomplished a lot with getting your degree, raising Phoebe on your own, and remodeling your house." *Since Lindsay has done well in her life, she might not want to marry me and move to Cincinnati.*

"Not well enough to pay for Phoebe's future medical school expenses. Fortunately, in the past, she received several scholarships. We also saved money with her living at home for all four years."

"I was serious when I mentioned paying for medical school."

"That's going to be expensive and too generous. Maybe you can just pay a portion and I'll pay some too."

He stared into Lindsay's blue eyes. "Okay, we can do it that way, but I feel it's my turn to cover her expenses."

"I'm glad I finally got the courage to write to you." She shrugged. "At times, I can't believe you're back in my life. I keep waiting for you to disappear again."

He put his arm around her. "I'm never going to leave you again. I was a foolish young guy, but now I know better. When I'm around you, everything takes on a clean brightness. I don't like having to go back to Cincinnati because I hate leaving you. I want to always be a part of your life. And hopefully, I can be a father to our daughters."

"I like it when you're here," she said. "I know it's a lot of driving back and forth, but I hope you still plan on coming back this weekend."

He nodded. "I'll leave Friday after I see my last patient." Phoebe said she'd take Lindsay to Thursday's chemo treatment, so he could be at work. Her second day of treatment would be shorter.

"I'll miss you until I can see you again."

His heart flipped over in his chest when he saw her tongue run over her lips and a flash of desire in her eyes. He drew her face to his in an embrace. When his lips met hers, there was a dreamy intimacy. He wanted to savor the kiss. For the first time in years, everything seemed right.

When they broke apart, Lindsay tilted her head. "You kiss better now than you did when you were in your twenties."

He grinned. "Is that right? I guess I've improved with age."

"I tried dating a few times. Recently, I've dated Drew. He's a nice man, but he's not over losing his wife in a car accident. Phoebe likes him and his son. Matthew is like a little brother to her." She raised her eyebrows. "Are you sure you have strong feelings for me? It's not because I have cancer, is it?"

"I wish you didn't have cancer, but it's not the reason I've been spending time with you. I love you, Lindsay."

She smiled. "I love you too, but we are older and wiser now. We aren't the same people we were on the beach. We have both grown and have separate lives. We need to focus on our daughters."

Lindsay was correct in what she said, but he didn't like hearing it. He knew what he wanted more than anything. He wanted to marry Lindsay and spend the rest of his life loving her. They had already wasted too many years by being apart, but how could they marry when they lived in different cities? Phoebe wanted to continue going to Ohio State, and more importantly, Lindsay's chemo treatments were here in Columbus. That wasn't a huge problem, because if everything went well, the treatments would finish by the end of the year. Even if Phoebe decided to live on campus, there was also Lindsay's job. He doubted she'd want to move and apply for a teaching job in Cincinnati. If he moved to Columbus, he'd be only two hours from Amy and Jenna, so that was another reason to relocate. He'd love to be more available to his three daughters.

But could he leave his established practice and his partners?

Chapter Seventeen

Although Phoebe worried about Harris hurting her mother again, she'd enjoyed running with him at the park. She'd planned to have a serious conversation with him during their run, but it hadn't happened. The timing hadn't seemed right. Instead, they had a fun banter between them. They were now in his car, so she needed to have the courage to question him before they arrived back home.

"Thanks for running with me this evening," Harris said.

"I'm glad I went with you." Phoebe took a deep breath, then exhaled it. "Something is bothering me. I noticed Mom is falling for you again. I don't want to see her hurt. I know you're both mature adults now, but I worry you two are rushing into a relationship that might not work for you two later. And she was seeing Drew before you arrived in our lives." She had to mention their neighbor. She liked him and his son, Matthew, but in her heart, she knew her mother wasn't the same person with Drew as she was around Harris.

Harris gave her a quick glance. "I hate that I broke up with her. I wish I could go back and make it right and marry her. I regret so much that I was never around for Lindsay or for you and your sisters. I love your mom, and I promise I won't desert her again."

Phoebe studied her father's face as Harris drove quickly through a yellow light. Was he trying to hurry back to the house to avoid further questions? "I don't understand how Callie managed to delete Mom's calls and messages from your phone. I'm sure you didn't share a cell phone."

"Unfortunately, Callie said she lost her phone, so she gave my number on her résumé for when she was applying for jobs. I had one of the early Blackberry cell phones my parents bought for me. She used my phone for a few weeks. Back then, I never used it much anyhow. Cell phones were not as popular as they are now. I had a landline phone in my apartment and should've given that number to Lindsay before I left. But I wasn't expecting her to call me since I broke up with her. Before I left, she told me I was the biggest jerk ever and a liar. Lindsay didn't have a cell phone and never gave me her mother's phone number. I was an idiot."

Phoebe replied, "I wish when you saw my mom in the restaurant with Paul, you would've said hello to her. You were still single, and even though she'd married Paul, she would have at least known you cared enough to look her up. After he died, I'm sure she would've called you."

Harris stopped at a traffic light and turned to look at her. "She'd told me Paul had been her boyfriend and they'd gone to the Prom junior and senior years, so I guess that was why I accepted her marriage to him."

"I wish Mom had tried to call you again when we were born."

"I wish she had too."

Phoebe said, "I'm sorry I brought up painful memories. I'm happy you're in our lives now, and it's great you went with Mom to her chemo treatment."

After Harris pulled into the driveway, he patted her arm. "I'm committed to your mom. I'm not going away this time. I hope we can eventually build a life together, and I want you to be part of it. I wish Amy and Jenna could be part of our life too, but with them being Amish, it might be not as close as I'd like. But whatever time they have for me in their lives will make me happy."

"That's true. I see the closeness Amy and Jenna share, and I wish I could have that deep relationship with them. I doubt I ever will, though. They grew up in the same family and have many wonderful memories. I have to admit it was a shock Mom gave them to Katie and Roman, but I also get her reasoning behind it. I love many things about the Amish life."

"As an only child, I never experienced the type of intimacy you have always had with Lindsay. I'm glad you voiced your feelings to me and hope you'll continue to do so in the future. I'm glad you're my daughter. I understand what you feel about your sisters because I'm jealous of the father-daughter relationship Roman has with Amy and Jenna. All we can do is try to forge ahead and develop new memories with each other."

Phoebe nodded and was quiet for a moment. After she took her seatbelt off, she said, "You came here as soon as you learned Mom's secret, and you've been awesome to us for the past month. I'm glad I was able to hear your side of the story."

"It's good you drilled me." He was proud of Phoebe for not letting him get off easy.

"I always wanted a father in my life." She cleared her throat. "Now I have one."

"Hey, that deserves a hug for my daughter."

As they hugged, she whispered, "Is it okay I call you Dad instead of Harris?"

"There's nothing that would make me happier."

She pulled away from their embrace and gave him a broad smile. "Thanks, Dad."

"You don't have to change your last name. But maybe you could think about doing it in the future. I'd be proud to share my last name with you."

Lindsay tapped on the driver's seat window. "What's going on? Are you two plotting something? By the way, I have lasagna in the oven, so I hope you both are hungry."

Harris unbuckled his seat belt and opened his door while Phoebe hopped out of the car quickly. "I love your lasagna. I'll jump in the shower first," Phoebe shouted over her shoulder as she ran toward the house. "Dad, you need to take a shower too. You're drenched in sweat."

Lindsay's jaw dropped. "Did I hear her correctly? She just called you dad."

He nodded, grinning. "I hadn't expected to hear Phoebe call me dad yet. She also said it in the car. I love being called dad. Phoebe must approve of me now. She questioned me about my intentions. She doesn't want me to hurt you."

"I'm glad you convinced her she can trust you." Lindsay took his hand. Staring at his wet T-shirt, she said, "I'll give you a hug after you have dry clothes on. It's good I didn't go with you two, then. It gave you time to bond and gave me time to fix dinner."

As they walked toward the house, he said, "Next time, you should go with us."

~

When the three of them finished eating Lindsay's homemade lasagna, Harris said, "I only want to eat your lasagna from now on. It's the best I've ever had. You did too much."

She shook her head. "I didn't. We have carrot cake for dessert. Phoebe made it from Katie's recipe. The last month I stayed in Shipshewana with our triplets, I copied her recipe. Whenever I baked the cake for us, I realized Amy and Jenna could be eating the same cake."

Harris looked at Phoebe as she entered the dining room. His daughter wore a skirt with a pink blouse. "You look pretty."

"Thanks, Dad."

Lindsay smiled. "She cleans up well. It's nice you're double-dating with Haley and Scott."

Harris vaguely heard the women chatting about Phoebe's evening, but he was lost in his own world of happiness. *Wow, I can't believe I have a family now after wanting one for years. Thank you, Lord, for Phoebe and Lindsay. And thanks for bringing Amy and Jenna into our lives,* Harris prayed silently.

He gathered the dirty plates and carried them to the sink. As he rinsed them, Harris realized it'd be great to have a family holiday together. As an only child, his holidays were not memorable. In fact, he remembered how boring and quiet the Manning traditions were for both Thanksgiving and Christmas. However, he'd enjoyed a couple of the Fourth of July celebrations. His parents had invited over the neighbors, the few relatives they had, and the medical staff from both their practices.

The Fourth of July would be in a couple of weeks. He wondered about planning something for it and having the triplets, Seth, and both sets of parents spend time together as a family. He couldn't see Katie and Roman visiting him or Lindsay's house, though. They'd invited them twice, but they'd been busy with the store. Tourists swarmed the area during the spring and summer months. Whenever Seth wasn't working at his full-time job, he gave buggy rides to the Englishers. He'd heard Phoebe was disappointed her sis-ters hadn't been back to see them. It was up to him to get them all together.

"Hey, before you leave. I was wondering what you both think of us going to Millersburg to celebrate July Fourth. I'd like to meet Katie and Roman and spend time with Amy and Jenna."

"I'd love that," Phoebe said, putting the leftover lasagna in the refrigerator, "but do you think the store will be open? The holiday is on Thursday. I'll have to see if I can get it off too."

"One of my partners told me about a new hotel recently opening a few miles from Millersburg. It has a pool. We could ask them to go swimming, but if they don't want to do that, we can enjoy biking or hiking. There are trails for both near the hotel. It's a scenic area." Harris noticed Phoebe's face lit up at his suggestion to get together. "We can leave here on Wednesday night. I'll come after work. I'll reserve three rooms in case Amy and Jenna want to spend the night with you, Phoebe."

"I'll call them while I'm waiting for Haley and Scott and my date." Phoebe pulled her phone out of a little purse. "Or I can call Seth. He has a cell phone."

"Wait, Lindsay hasn't said anything." He looked across the kitchen counter to where she had moved to the sofa.

Clutching a pillow against her chest, she frowned.

"If you don't think it's a good idea, it's okay. We can do something else for the fourth," he suggested.

"I like it, but I'm not sure we can get Katie and Roman to close their store," Lindsay said. "We should make it on Sunday instead of the fourth. And here's another thing. I don't know if they'll want to go swimming, especially in front of non-Amish guests. Some Amish will wear conservative swimsuits, but others won't go swimming. I did see an Amish young woman wearing a two-piece suit once in the pool, but I'm guessing she was in her *rumspringa*. I saw her later at the motel, and she was dressed in her long dress, apron, and wore a *kapp*."

A thoughtful expression was on Phoebe's face. "I remember that was when we went to the beach. You kept glancing at her. I guess she made you think of Amy and Jenna."

"She did, and I wondered if Amy and Jenna ever got to go swimming in a pool."

Phoebe shrugged. "They might have church on that Sunday. They won't want to miss it. I'll leave a message on their answering machine about the fourth, but I'll tell them we can plan on a Sunday if they want to keep the store open."

"If everything works out, do you think they'll feel comfortable enough for me to take them out to eat at a restaurant? There's a hotel restaurant." Harris ran his fingers through his hair, wondering if Katie and Roman would even want to meet him.

Lindsay laughed. "You certainly have surprised me with your eagerness to make arrangements. I'd love to see Katie and Roman again. I wonder if I should call instead."

At the sound of a knock on the door, Phoebe said, "Well, it looks like I don't have time to call. You should go ahead and call, Mom. Mention both days to them."

"I'd like to meet the young man before you run off."

"Mom already knows him pretty well." Phoebe walked to the door and opened it. "Hi, Drew. It's great seeing you. We didn't know you were back from Germany."

"We got back last night. Is it okay if I come in? I'm bearing gifts."

Phoebe said in a cheerful voice, "You must come in then."

Drew chuckled. "You'll have to check with your mom to see if she'll share with you."

Upon entering the house, Harris noticed Drew was an extremely good-looking guy—something Phoebe and Lindsay hadn't mentioned to him. He stared at his well-proportioned body and wavy, dark hair.

Instantly, Lindsay walked to Drew, smiling. "The neighborhood hasn't been the same without you. I'm glad you're home."

Harris's eyebrows shot up when Drew kissed Lindsay's cheek.

Drew put a basket on the coffee table. "This is heavy, so I'll set it down for you. It has all kinds of goodies for you."

Lindsay followed Drew to the table, bending over to peek at the basket covered with cellophane wrap. "Thank you so much. I feel special. I can't wait to dig into it." She glanced at Drew. "Where's Matthew?"

"He went swimming with his friends. Matthew liked meeting his relatives, but he's happy to be home again."

"A lot has happened since you were away. I now have a father and two sisters." Phoebe grinned and walked to Harris, touching his shoulder. "Drew, I'd like you to meet my dad, Harris Manning. And Dad, this is Drew Morrow."

Surprise filled Drew's gaze as he stared at him. "I'm confused. I thought your father wasn't alive."

Lindsay rubbed her forehead, looking flustered. "It's rather complicated. Why don't you sit? Would you like something to drink?"

"No, thank you, but I'll sit."

"Mom's husband wasn't my dad. I'll get my phone so you can see a picture of my identical sisters," Phoebe said.

"I want to see your pictures." Drew took a quick breath. "I can't believe you have identical sisters, but I know how you like to kid." He seemed caught off guard by Phoebe's announcement.

"She's not kidding," Lindsay said. "I gave birth to identical triplets."

While Phoebe shoved her phone at Drew and tapped on the picture to make it larger, Lindsay briefly told the story of why she had to give two babies away.

A second knock sounded at the door, Phoebe said, "I'm sure this must be my date."

"Hi," a young man said as he stepped inside the house.

"This is Jared Walker." Phoebe pointed to Harris. "This is my father, Harris Manning."

Jared raised his eyebrows but in a polite voice said, "It's nice to meet you."

"You remember our neighbor, Drew Morrow." Phoebe waved her hand at Drew.

Jared nodded. "Hi."

"Hello, Jared," Lindsay said in a firm voice. "I'm surprised to see you."

Harris noticed Lindsay spoke in what he imagined had been her teacher's voice, and she hadn't smiled at Jared. Apparently, Jared and Phoebe had dated before. He wondered if he'd missed something when he was daydreaming during the women's earlier conversation. "It's nice meeting you, Jared. Did you and Phoebe meet at Ohio State?"

Jared nodded. "We were in a class together."

"We better go. I don't want to miss the movie previews." Phoebe pulled on Jared's hand.

After quick goodbyes, they left, and Drew said, "I better go get Matthew. You have beautiful daughters, and your Phoebe is a handful."

Lindsay laughed as she walked with Drew to the door. Harris could tell Drew was disappointed to learn he was in Lindsay's life, but what concerned him at the moment was Phoebe's date.

When she returned, Lindsay plopped down on the sofa. "I wasn't expecting to see Drew, and Phoebe didn't hesitate to introduce you."

"It was nice she did. Okay, what's up with Jared?" If it was something bad, he wouldn't think Phoebe would've gone out with him. "I could tell you weren't crazy about him. I'm guessing you know him."

"He broke up with Phoebe when she wouldn't sleep with him. I never expected her to go out with him again, but she said earlier they're just friends now."

"That's good she had the strength to say no," Harris said. "It's great Phoebe shares stuff with you. You have such a close mother-daughter relationship. You did a good job raising Phoebe."

"Yes, we are close. It's only been the two of us, and Phoebe knew she could depend on me." Lindsay frowned. "But she hadn't mentioned to me earlier that it was Jared taking her to the movie." She gave a little laugh. "Even with my chemo brain, I doubt I would've missed that part of the conversation."

"I guess chemo brain is a real thing. I hope you haven't forgotten what I said to you at the park."

"Oh no, what did you say there?" Lindsay gave him a deadpan look. "Was it something important?"

After a moment, he laughed. "I can tell you're teasing me. You just want me to say it again. I love you."

"I can't fool you. I love you too." She stood. "I'll get our carrot cake, then I'll call the Yoders."

"How about we wait on the cake and the phone call? I want to hold you in my arms. We can cuddle on the sofa and kiss all we want. Our daughter is out of the house for a few hours." Harris took Lindsay's hands in his and pulled her down beside him. "Besides, I want to show my appreciation for the awesome meal you fixed."

"I like how you think, Dr. Manning." She drew his face to hers in an embrace.

His arms encircled her, one hand in the small of her back. He kissed her, and she returned his kiss with a sweet tenderness.

When they stopped kissing, Harris stared at Lindsay's lovely face and ran his finger along her cheekbone. Her radiant smile warmed a part of his soul. His heart was full of happiness and love. He wished he'd thought of giving her a gift like Drew's. But his regret didn't stop him from feeling he could give his love freely to Lindsay. He would give them the necessary time to continue to grow as a couple and fill as many precious moments as possible with their daughters. Nothing would stop him from loving this remarkable woman.

Chapter Eighteen

Millersburg, Ohio

On a hot summer evening, Katie was enjoying sitting by Roman on their porch swing. He pushed the wooden swing gently back and forth with his foot. It'd be perfect if they didn't need to talk about what Harris wanted to do on the Fourth of July. Why did he and Lindsay want them to spend time in Millersburg for the holiday? She understood they missed twenty-two years of having Amy and Jenna in their lives. Harris had to be a little bitter because while Lindsay raised Phoebe, he had a lonely life without children. Oh boy, spending a day with the birth parents was not her idea, es-pecially on a day their store was closed.

She released a deep breath. "I do want to meet Harris and see Lindsay, but I'm not crazy about their invitation to go to their hotel on the Fourth. Going swimming sounds nice, but what was Lindsay thinking inviting our *kinner* to swim in their hotel pool? She should realize that's wrong for them to be in their suits and swim with non-Amish guests."

Roman rolled his eyes. "She invited us too. Besides, Amy and Jenna have conservative swimsuits. It'll be *wunderbaar* for them to have fun with Phoebe. "

Seth opened the screen door and stepped onto the porch. "Hey, *Mamm,* I want to go swimming. I can't wait until I can push my sisters into the pool." Seth grinned. "I'm just kidding. I'm excited to eat at the hotel's restaurant. The guys at work have already taken their wives there, and they said the food was good at Getaway Resort."

Katie shrugged. "I know Harris wants us to eat lunch and dinner there, but I think that is a little much. He's showing off that he has money to spend."

"We could have them come back here for dessert and coffee in the evening," Roman suggested.

She nodded. "We should do that. Hopefully, I'll still want to after spending a day with them."

"*Mamm,* you'll have fun with Harris and Lindsay. You obviously already know Phoebe and Lindsay. I think it's nice Harris has booked three rooms. One is for the girls and one for Lindsay. If Amy and Jenna don't spend the night, I'll take a room." Seth leaned against the porch post. "I wish I'd already met Harris because then I might have been able to stay in his room. I've never spent a night in a hotel."

"I don't think that's wise." Katie touched her prayer covering and pushed the ribbons past her shoulders. "I wonder if Phoebe is staying in the room with Lindsay or with Amy and Jenna."

"I think Phoebe will want to spend more time with her sisters, so she'll share a room with them," Roman said. "Their room has two double beds. Personally, I'm glad Harris is making an effort to meet us."

"I'm going to head out to the barn." Seth's green eyes had a sheen of purpose. "I need to get a birdhouse done for Veronica. She wants to give it to her brother for a wedding gift."

As Seth started down the steps, Katie said, "Don't stay up too late. We have church tomorrow morning."

On the last step, Seth turned around to look at them. "I won't." With a grin, he said, "I might stay up until Amy and

Jenna return from their double date. I can't wait to tease them about it."

Once their son was out of sight, Katie said, "Veronica's definitely interested in Seth. Now if he can just spend time with her. He'll see what a *gut fraa* she'll make."

"You could be right. She'll get to see Seth again when he's finished with the birdhouse. That could be what she's hoping for."

"Thank goodness Amy and Jenna went out tonight. Even though they said it was just to go over what they've learned so far in their EMT classes, I think they might be using that as an excuse. Maybe moving here is where they will find their life partners. I never would've thought they'd both would meet two Amish men by going to their EMT classes."

"You could be right about Jenna. She's talked a lot about Eli, but Amy seems more interested in what knowledge Ira has. I'm proud they want to serve our community."

"It's nice Eli and Ira are friends. I'll see if Amy and Jenna might want to start their instruction classes to join our church. The bishop has already started the classes, but they could catch up." Katie grabbed Roman's hand. "Wouldn't that be something? Then I won't have to worry anymore about them being influenced by Lindsay and Harris. I couldn't bear them to become English."

"Sure, they need to be baptized before they can marry, but I don't see it happening yet. All we can do is pray about it. Whatever happens is God's will."

"I can't imagine it is His will that they leave our faith. I hope they don't desert their Amish upbringing." Katie moaned. "We did everything for them and made sure they always put God first in their lives. If they leave our faith, I won't forgive Lindsay and Harris for butting into our lives. It's one thing for them to meet their daughters, but Harris seems too eager to pay for anything they need. We don't need his money."

"I think he's trying to find a way to bridge the gap between them. Harris wants to do the right thing by them since he missed their childhood," Roman said.

"If that isn't bad enough, his parents are too interested in them. Amy and Jenna have grandparents and don't need Harris's snotty parents trying to interfere now. They thought Lindsay wasn't good enough for their son. I'm sure they won't want Amy and Jenna to remain Amish. The elderly Mannings will try to bribe them into their world."

"I don't think they will. They're pleased to have grandchildren."

Katie put her foot down on the floor to stop the moving swing. "The breeze feels *gut* here, but how about we go to the kitchen to eat dessert? We never had any."

He nodded. "The kitchen should be cooler now. I'll come in soon. I want to see how Seth's doing on the birdhouse."

~

After he talked to Seth for a few moments, Roman trudged back to the house. *How can Katie be so clueless about my mood? She goes on and on without caring about my feelings.*

Slowly, he opened the screen door and stepped inside. He saw Katie had a piece of lemon pie ready for him with a glass of water on the table. He sighed as he pulled a chair out to sit.

Roman sipped his water and stared at the pie. He wasn't sure he could eat any of it. He hadn't liked Katie complaining about Lindsay, Harris, and his parents. Frustration mounted whenever Katie showed jealousy where the birth parents were concerned.

"I suppose we can go swimming if it's private enough. I can make sure nothing happens with our *kinner*. Or maybe I'll sit on a chair under an umbrella by the pool and keep my dress and apron on." Katie carried her piece of pie to the table, then crossed her arms over her chest. "We can eat at the restaurant and be a happy group with our English visitors."

He ignored the sarcasm in her voice about being happy to spend time with Harris and Lindsay. At least his opinionated wife seemed on board about the holiday. Unless she changed her mind later. "It'll be something different for us to do on the Fourth."

"My sister, Lizzie, invited us for the holiday too." Katie frowned as she sat on a chair across from him. "Or did you forget that?"

Roman rested his elbows against the tabletop and let his fork dangle over his pie. "We couldn't go there anyhow. It's a long trip to go to Shipshewana, and who would want to keep our store open for us while we were away for a few days? This way we're only closed on the Fourth."

Katie shrugged. "I hope Harris is right that the pool won't be crowded. I don't like that there will be men and women both in the pool. I know our children aren't baptized so they can go swimming, but I don't like it. Seth needs to wear a shirt with his trunks. The girls could wear cover-ups over their suits in the water."

"It's a new hotel, and Harris said there are a lot of rooms still available. The pool was finished only a couple of weeks ago." He grinned. "We can take our suits and towels in case we get a chance to swim by ourselves. Remember how we enjoyed swimming in the neighbors' pond?"

"*Ach*, we did that a lot. It was the two of us for a long time." Katie took a bite of pie. "I enjoyed being with you at Niagara Falls. And I have that new swimsuit I bought for the trip."

"You looked lovely in your suit at Niagara Falls. If we go swimming at the hotel, you'll get to wear it again. You have that cover-up too."

"We only went swimming once because we had to wait until no one else was in the pool. It's hard to believe how immodest Englishers are when they go swimming. The bikinis I saw were too revealing." Katie wrinkled her face. "My only regret about our trip is I wish Lindsay hadn't visited while we were away. Maybe I could've talked her into keeping the triplets' birth a secret."

How could Katie even think this way? Lindsay had a right to get to know Amy and Jenna. He expelled a deep breath. "Katie, you surely don't feel this way. It's *gut* they know the truth about their birth parents."

"I know they're unhappy I made Lindsay promise to never tell Amy and Jenna that she gave birth to them. They should blame Lindsay more than they do. She agreed to a closed adoption. I think Amy regrets being raised by us."

"Whatever Amy and Jenna decide to do with their lives is their choice, and I pray they will be guided by God's will for their lives. I don't think they regret having us as their parents. They're *froh* to be serving their community by learning to be EMTs. That alone will keep them here in Millersburg." Roman knew there was nothing more he could say on the matter. He hoped Katie would be kind to their visitors on the Fourth.

"Praying for them is important."

"Your pie is light and *appeditlich*. It'd be good to serve it when we have Lindsay and others here."

Chapter Nineteen

"I can't wait to see you," Seth said. "I'm relieved *Mamm* hasn't changed her mind and has agreed to go to the hotel to spend the Fourth with you and your parents. It's going to be amazing to go swimming and not have to work."

Phoebe stretched out on her bed as she held her phone. "I'm excited too. I'm glad it's finally July. It's been years since my mom has seen your parents, and my dad will meet them for the first time. I hope everyone gets along and has a great time."

Phoebe and Seth had been speaking every night. She'd been surprised when Seth mentioned he had a cell phone. The bishop had given him permission for his construction job. Sometimes the boss liked to be able to get a hold of him and didn't want to wait until Seth checked their answering machine in the shanty. Roman seldom used it for the store but liked having a cell phone for emergencies. Phoebe was sure Seth wasn't supposed to use his phone to call her all the time, but he liked to remind her he was in his *rumspringa*.

"My parents seem *froh* about seeing all of you. *Mamm's* started cleaning our house and wants it to look perfect when you all come for dessert in the evening. What time are you going to get here on Wednesday?"

Phoebe readjusted her pillow behind her head before answering. "Probably in the middle of the afternoon. I don't think we can check in until three at the hotel. Dad's going to leave his house in the morning. He said we'll stop for lunch on the way to Millersburg." *I have to tease Seth a little.* "I can't wait to see Amy and Jenna. I've missed my sisters a lot."

"Hey, what about me? Haven't you missed me?" Seth said in an indignant voice.

She giggled. "It's fun to kid you. I miss you. It's going to be great to see you too."

"I wish you could stay longer and go to church with us on Sunday."

"Dad and Mom want to check out on Saturday. We're going to a cookout in the evening at my friend Haley's house. Her parents are anxious to meet Harris."

Phoebe didn't want to hurt Seth's feelings, but deep down she was relieved they were leaving Saturday morning. Going to an Amish three-hour church service spoken in High German with an opening sermon in the Pennsylvania Dutch dialect didn't sound like something she wanted to experience yet. In the future, she might go with her sisters and Seth to their church. Of course, if her sisters married Amish men, she would definitely go to their weddings. It'd be sad if she couldn't be a bridesmaid, but she seriously doubted an Englisher could be an attendant in a Plain wedding.

Since learning about her sisters and meeting them, Phoebe had wished they were not Amish. It was hard to have the kind of sister bond with them that she wanted. Although their accent was cute, it was a constant reminder they had grown up in a different environment. And the Plain clothing was difficult to understand. When she'd spent a night at their house in June, Phoebe couldn't believe Amy and Jenna used straight pins instead of buttons or zippers in their dresses. Phoebe couldn't discuss movies she'd enjoyed seeing because her sisters hadn't gone to any. At least Jenna had read some of the same sweet romances she had. Amy only liked to read nonfiction that was usually on science topics. Since none of them had seen a movie, Phoebe would suggest going to one when Seth or her sisters visited next time. None of them had been baptized, so it should be fine.

"How much longer are you working before you start college?"

"July twentieth is my last day. Dad said I could quit now, but I want to get another two weeks of pay before I quit working."

Seth cleared his throat. "How do you feel about me visiting you on Sunday, then? I can get a ride to Columbus and see if I can get a couple of days off work."

"I'd love for you to come to Columbus. Do you think it'll be okay with your parents?" She knew Amy and Jenna wouldn't be surprised because they knew about her brother's nightly phone calls to her.

"*Ya*, they'll be glad to be rid of me for a couple of days. They'll save money on food while I'm gone."

She laughed. "That's true. I can't believe how much food you put away and not gain weight. But I'm sure you burn a lot of calories building houses."

"We could go to the fair. I went once to the Ohio State Fair. That was a lot of fun."

"The fair won't be open until the end of July, but we could go to the Columbus Zoo and Aquarium. I'll even fix my brownies for you." Should she mention how he'd have to ride in her car? While trying to learn more about the Amish faith, she'd read about all the buggy accidents that occurred in Ohio and other states. Her dad had mentioned to her how that was something worrying him. He didn't like that Amy and Jenna traveled to work and other places in a buggy. "It's nice I have a car and we can drive places when you visit. Does it ever worry you that you might be in a buggy accident and be injured or killed? I've heard how dangerous it is to drive a buggy. People aren't paying close enough attention and hit the buggies on the roads with their vehicles. There was a recent buggy accident I heard about on the news. A truck rear-ended a buggy, and three young children were killed. The mother is in critical condition. They were ejected from the buggy."

Seth cleared his throat. "When a buggy accident happens, we think it's God's will, but it's extremely sad when it occurs. I have headlights and taillights on my buggy. I've never been in a buggy accident. My grandparents were once hit by a truck and were thrown out of the buggy. Fortunately, they were not injured. I don't worry about it. I trust God to keep me safe."

She loved Seth's strong faith in God, but she worried that might be what would eventually tear them apart. How could they ever have a serious relationship when they were from two completely different worlds? Was there a way to bridge the gap without her becoming Amish?

"Well, I hope you don't ever get in an accident. I never want to be in a car accident either. There are too many drivers drinking while they drive. Do the Amish drink?"

"Some teenagers on their *rumspringa* like to drink beer and stronger alcohol. Some Amish might drink at weddings to celebrate. I remember a few times when my parents drank wine. Otherwise, Old Order Amish seldom drink. Does your mom drink?"

That's what I get for asking Seth about the Amish drinking habits. "She has drunk wine with her friends but not that often."

"I better not tell Amy and Jenna too much about visiting you, or they'll want to crash my time with you."

"Wait a minute. Speaking of my sisters, one is at the door now," Seth said.

She heard some mumbling from Seth before her sister came on the phone. "Hi. It's Amy. How are you?"

"I'm fine. How are your EMT classes going?" She remembered they decided to start a class before September since there was a shortage of paramedics in the area.

"*Gut*. The classes are interesting, and the instructor is great. Jenna's happy, too, that we're taking classes earlier than we expected."

"That's awesome."

"I don't need my GED to be an EMT, but I still want to get it. I've talked to our bishop. He gave his approval as long as I keep attending our church. If you have any high school books I can borrow, or if you can get any for me, that'd be great."

"I'll try to get you some books," Phoebe said. She didn't have any high school books because they were returned to the school at the end of the year, but she could borrow some.

"I just thought of something," Amy said. "Lindsay teaches at the high school. She might be able to get me the books I need to study."

"We might not be able to get the books until after the holiday, but I'll check with the school to see when they will be open."

"Thanks so much. How is Lindsay?"

"She gets tired but is doing okay."

"I can't wait to see her again. Tell her I said hello. Seth's eager to talk with you, so I'll get off here. We're looking forward to seeing all of you soon. Bye, Phoebe."

She barely got out a goodbye to Amy before Seth was back on the phone. "I'm back."

"You should come on a weekend instead so you don't miss work. I won't be working the following weekend, and you could come Friday evening on the twenty-sixth."

"Then I'd have to wait another week to see you, but that is more sensible."

It was sweet Seth wanted to see her a week earlier, but she hated for him to miss work. It was a busy time of the year for the construction company he worked for, and Seth's boss might not like him to take off work again. He'd missed a few days already to help in the family store.

Glancing at the clock in her bedroom, she saw it was ten o'clock. "You better get to bed. I know you start work early. We'll see each other in two days."

"*Ya*, I better get some sleep or I might hammer my fingers instead of the nails."

"Geez, I hope not. Goodnight and pleasant—."

"I wish we lived in the same town," Seth said wistfully. "It's good I have pictures of you on my phone. I'm starting to forget what you look like."

She chuckled. "I'm sure that isn't true. You have two mirror images of me living with you."

"To me, my sisters don't resemble you."

"I've heard you say this frequently, so I'm starting to believe you." She sighed. "I miss you too. I'm glad you have a phone so we can chat. I can't wait to see you."

"*Gut nacht*, my sweet and beautiful Phoebe."

Leaving her bed, she placed her phone on top of the dresser. Disturbing thoughts invaded her mind as she went to the adjoining bathroom to brush her teeth. It was obvious she and Seth were falling in love. She had years of medical school ahead of her, so how could it ever work out between them?

Chapter Twenty

Lindsay sat on a bench next to Katie, hating the tension between them. During lunch, Katie had been quiet and a tad moody, while Roman seemed like the same man she remembered. Easygoing with a sense of humor and a deep faith in God was Roman's personality. Katie's silence continued. Lindsay wondered, *How can anyone be unhappy with all this beauty surrounding them?* A garden of bushes and a large variety of different sizes and colors of flowers were spaced with enough room for the hummingbirds to fly between. There were several red bird feeders. Lindsay remembered keeping sugar water in them since that was what the tiny birds liked. Because of the vibrant purple-and-red petunias, bright pink impatiens, and red charm peonies, hummingbirds flitted around the garden to get nectar out of the flowers.

Lindsay noticed Katie's blue dress made her eyes look even bluer. She saw there were a few gray hairs in her light brown hair. She smiled at Katie. "I remember watching the hummingbirds at your house in Shipshewana. It was soothing to watch them and hear their sweet noises as they flapped their wings so quickly."

Katie nodded. "You breastfed the babies sometimes while gazing at the birds. You said the tiny birds needed to eat a lot like the triplets."

Relief went through Lindsay when Katie finally spoke to her. "You have a good memory. It seemed like I ate a lot too. I couldn't get enough of your freshly baked bread. Everything you made tasted great. My mother used to cook tasty meals while my father was alive. After he died, everything changed in our lives. My mother became a shell of a person without him."

Finally, Katie grinned. "Don't say I was like a mother to you. I was more like an older sister when you met me. I was thirty-two years old. We don't have hummingbirds at our house here. And I miss my kitchen. It was much bigger than the one here. I thought it would be *wunderbaar* to stay in the house where we raised our *kinner,* but God had other plans for us." She sighed. "I miss a lot of things about living in Shipshewana, especially not seeing my parents, siblings, and the rest of our families often. But I do enjoy working with Roman in our store."

"You have an awesome store." Lindsay remembered Roman had mentioned during lunch that their crops hadn't done well for three years. Lousy weather during the planting and growing seasons had caused them to have little corn and soybeans to sell. He'd also wanted to do something different and not farm any longer. When his aunt and uncle wanted to retire a year ago, Roman was elated to buy their store and house.

"Our *kinner* help a lot, but once Amy and Jenna complete their EMT training, I suppose we'll have to hire some help. Amy does the books and orders what we need to sell. Jenna loves waiting on the customers, so she's busy answering their questions and ringing up their purchases. Seth only works in the store when he isn't working at his construction job."

"Amy said the EMT training will last five months."

"That's what I understand. It's hard to believe our bishop approved for them to become paramedics when they're women. It's good they want to serve our community, and I had to say yes when Jenna felt called by God to become an EMT. Then I learned Amy has always been interested in working in the medical field." Katie smoothed her apron over her dress and exhaled a deep breath. "I'll admit I'm disappointed they haven't joined the church and gotten married."

Lindsay felt differently because she was happy they were not married. Without husbands taking their time, she was given the chance to get to know Amy and Jenna better. "They are still young. I'm sure Amy and Jenna will get married sometime."

"I'm sorry you have cancer. I wish you hadn't gotten it. I pray daily for your healing."

"Thank you for your prayers." Lindsay tucked strands of her blonde hair behind her ears.

"You still have beautiful hair. That's *wunderbaar* you haven't lost any. One of my friends lost her hair soon after she started chemo for breast cancer."

"My doctor told me I shouldn't lose my hair, so that's a blessing."

Katie's stared at her. "There's something I have wondered."

"What is it?"

"If you hadn't gotten cancer, would you have written a letter to meet our daughters?"

Her heart skipped a beat. "I don't know. Getting cancer was definitely a turning point for me, and I knew I had to see Amy and Jenna . . . in case cancer took my life. I felt God wanted them to know the truth about their births. I couldn't keep my promise to you any longer. I knew you and Roman raised them in a Christian home, and I'm thankful for you taking them when I needed help, but it's been heart-wrenching not having been able to raise my triplets together."

"I wish you hadn't gone to our store while we were away. Roman and I were put on the spot immediately after returning from our trip." Katie's lips tightened.

"I was in the hospital when Phoebe gave the returned letter to me. I tried to find you but was unsuccessful, so Har-ris hired an investigator to save time. Then we learned you had Seth. He's a wonderful young man. Why didn't you tell me about him? All those nice letters you sent me had no mention of God blessing you with Seth."

Katie frowned. "It wasn't any of your business." Frustration filled her at Katie's comment. How could she say it wasn't any of her concern? "I thought we shared a bond with you raising my daughters. It would've been great news for me to hear you were finally able to have a child. I'm glad Amy and Jenna have a brother."

Katie shrugged. "When we adopted your babies, we were childless. I didn't want to take a chance you'd decide to ask for them back because we were blessed by having Seth."

Pain laced through her at Katie's words, hurt she hadn't trusted her enough. "I'm sorry you thought so little of me that you couldn't share your happy news. I wouldn't have done what you feared. For one reason, I struggled to raise Phoebe. Second, I'd given you my word that you would raise Amy and Jenna. You having Seth wouldn't have changed anything."

Katie said, "We live by the verse in 2 Corinthians, *Be not unequally yoked with unbelievers.*' As Amish, we try to stay sep-arate from the world. I don't know what your relationship is with Harris, but it seems pretty cozy. I wouldn't think you'd fall for him again and sin. If any of my *kinner* leave our faith for your secular world, it'll break my heart. It'll be your fault."

Exhaustion and anger swept over Lindsay. *How could this person—the person she'd entrusted her babies to—spout such mean things?* "Harris and I aren't sleeping together. He has been an immense help to me with my illness and with finding daughters. And that is all. Harris, Phoebe, and I are Christians. We believe in the same Jesus Christ who died on the cross for our sins as you do. Obviously, it won't be my fault if your adult children decide to leave your Amish faith. There must be some doubt in their minds already if they haven't joined yet. I'm sorry you dislike me for spending time with my daughters. You had them for twenty-two years, and I've kept my promise all that time, but I don't regret breaking it now." Lindsay stood and put a hand on the bench corner to steady herself. "The truth needed to come out, but it seems you can't accept Amy and Jenna knowing I'm their birth mother and Phoebe is their sister. I feel sorry for you."

As Lindsay walked away from Katie, tears flooded her eyes, and she bit her lip. She should've remained quiet, but it wasn't right what Katie had said to her.

⁓

Everyone was in the pool except Katie. She sat in a lounge chair by the shallow end, sipping a lemonade. Glancing at Katie, Phoebe asked Seth, "Doesn't your mother like to swim?"

"She used to enjoy swimming in a pond when we lived in Shipshewana, but we have never gone swimming in a pool." Seth yelled, "*Mamm*, join us! The water's perfect!"

"I'm fine here." Katie put her lemonade on a small white stand and picked up a book. "I'll read a little before I get in the pool."

Phoebe whispered to Lindsay, "I don't think Katie approves of my swimsuit."

Lindsay didn't have the heart to tell her it didn't matter what kind of suit she had on. Katie had made it clear she didn't want Phoebe and Seth spending time together. "Your swimsuit's fine. It's not a bikini, and it isn't revealing."

"It's a two-piece, though, and Amy and Jenna are wearing one-piece suits with a longer part at the bottom to cover more skin."

Lindsay noticed they had their hair in buns on top of their heads with no prayer coverings. They must've decided it looked better that way since they were wearing suits and not dresses.

Phoebe widened her eyes. "Or I should've gotten what you're wearing. I love your navy-blue wraparound bottoms, and your swimsuit top is so cute on you."

"I had to get something new to wear. Remember when I tried on my old suits last week? They were too big on me."

Phoebe nodded. "I know."

"Hey, Phoebe, get over here. Amy is trying to dunk me."

Phoebe laughed at Seth. "I'm sure you deserve it."

"Go to the other end of the pool." Lindsay gave her daughter a little shove. "I'm going to swim a few more minutes, then I think I'll get out of the pool."

"Okay, Mom. I'm glad Harris planned this trip. Isn't it great being with the Yoders?"

"It is." She didn't want to complain about Katie. If she did, someone might overhear her. Katie had kept her distance since their conversation, so she was glad for that.

Harris appeared in the deep end next to Lindsay. "Glad you're having fun."

After Phoebe left to join her siblings and Seth, Harris put his arm on the edge of the pool. "Do you feel okay? You don't look happy."

"I'm going to get out. I'm tired. I think I'll rest before we go to dinner."

"There's a spot with your name on it by an umbrella."

Why does Harris have to look so handsome in his trunks? The first moment she had laid eyes on Harris on the beach, he'd taken her breath away. Years later, he still had the same effect on her. She should tell him it wasn't a good idea for him to keep traveling to Columbus. She still loved him, but did God want them to be together? Harris needed to spend time with Phoebe, but she could visit him in Cincinnati.

Sure, I forgive him for breaking up with me, but I haven't forgotten how much it had hurt to give our daughters up for adoption. I appreciate his interest in my cancer treatment plan and the support Harris gives me as I fight my illness, but where is our relationship going? He told me he loves me and I told him the same, but are we trying to recapture what we lost and make up for the years we were apart? I love my teaching job, and he has a wonderful practice two hours away, so one of us will have to move if we decide to marry.

First, I need to go into remission. I pray I will beat this lymphoma, but if I don't, I definitely won't be moving to Cincinnati.

Chapter Twenty-One

Harris knew they shouldn't stay too long at Katie's and Roman's house because Lindsay looked exhausted as she moved slowly to sit on the sofa next to him. She had dark circles under her eyes, and her skin was so pale he could see small blue veins on her thin face. When Roman and he had returned from their walk on the trail near the hotel, he'd sensed something unpleasant had occurred between Lindsay and Katie. He hadn't a chance to ask her about it as there hadn't been a moment for them to be alone.

While Harris swallowed a bite of his lemon meringue pie, he glanced around the living room at its bare, white walls. He'd expected to see kerosene lamps, but he noticed the ceiling light, as well as the lamps on the end tables, looked like a battery-run lamps. The Yoder children were on the sofa across from them while Katie and Roman sat in chairs. Phoebe had started to sit next to Seth, but once she saw there wasn't enough room for her, she took a spot next to Lindsay. He'd noticed his daughter seemed a little too interested in Seth. Granted, the young man was likable, but he knew Phoebe had big plans to become a doctor. Her interest was more due to him being a brother to Amy and Jenna.

"The hotel receptionist mentioned there are going to be fireworks tonight," Harris said. "She said we should be able to see them from our balconies. We'll be high enough so that the trees around the hotel won't interfere in seeing them."

Jenna nodded her head. "I'd love to see fireworks."

"I don't know. It might be too late," Katie said. "The store's open tomorrow."

"I think we can handle the morning until they come to the store. They can watch the fireworks." Roman grinned. "I didn't expect them to come in early anyhow since they're spending the night at the hotel. I'm sure they'll be busy chatting until late."

Katie traced the rim of her cup with her finger. "Phoebe and the girls can stay here tonight. I'll fix a big breakfast for them."

"*Mamm*, I don't want to miss the fireworks. It'll be easier to just stay at the hotel since we're already there," Amy said.

"If Seth goes to the fireworks, he can bring you home." Katie stared at Seth. "How's that sound?"

Seth wiped his mouth with a napkin. "I don't care if Amy and Jenna stay at the hotel. Harris said I can stay there too."

Harris saw Katie looked troubled. Is she worried about Phoebe and Seth spending too much time together?

Phoebe leaned forward in her chair and looked at Katie and Roman. "Could I work in the store tomorrow? I've rang up orders before at the restaurant where I work. Or I can do anything you need. I'd love to work with my sisters."

Looking at Phoebe's eager face, Harris hoped Katie and Roman would accept her offer. She'd be crushed if they refused. Phoebe wanted to have a closer connection with her sisters. On the drive to Millersburg, she'd mentioned how she felt left out at times because Amy and Jenna had grown up together.

Fork hovering before her mouth, Katie said, "*Danki*, Phoebe. It's fine with me if you help us in the store. We can always use extra help, especially with the holiday tourists in town."

Seth grinned at Phoebe. "I wish I didn't have to go to work. I'd like to see you wait on the customers. Some are disagreeable if they can't find what they want to buy."

"I've waited on annoying customers in the restaurant when they've complained about something that never happened." Phoebe said, "Maybe I should borrow a Plain dress and *kapp* to wear for tomorrow. Someone might wonder why I look exactly like Amy and Jenna and I'm not wearing Amish clothing. Or would that be wrong since I'm not Amish?" Phoebe asked.

Amy said, "I don't see a problem with you dressing like us. You can borrow clothing from me or Jenna, but it might feel more comfortable for you to wear your own."

"You can take our clothing to the hotel with you and try it on." Jenna laughed. "I better help you with the straight pins because I can't see you doing that yourself. I don't want blood on my dress."

"Your lemon pie is delicious," Lindsay said.

After Roman sipped his coffee, he put his cup down. "I love all Katie's desserts, but her lemon pie is one of my favorites." He stared at Harris and Lindsay. "*Danki*, Harris, for lunch and dinner today. It was a nice day, and I'm glad we met."

~

Harris brushed the wispy strands of hair from Lindsay's face. His warm fingertips sent a jolt to her toes. They were sitting in Lindsay's hotel room on a small couch.

"I think today went well. I like Roman," Harris said. "He's easy to talk to, and the kids seemed to enjoy the pool and fireworks."

"You did a great job choosing this beautiful hotel. The restaurant's service and food are wonderful." She sighed.

"I'm afraid Katie isn't happy with me. She said she'll blame me if her children leave their faith." Lindsay then told Harris about the conversation they had earlier when he'd taken a walk with Roman.

"I'm sorry for the things Katie said, and she's wrong. None of this is your fault. Roman even talked to me about the possibility of Amy and Jenna leaving their Amish faith. He said he'll be understanding. And the girls won't be shunned as long as they haven't joined their Amish church. After all, Amy and Jenna were born into our English world. Roman trusts they'll make the decisions God wants for their lives. Whatever happens, he'll accept it."

Lindsay couldn't see Katie being so understanding if that happened, so she didn't comment on it to Harris. *God will change Katie's heart if the girls leave their Plain lifestyle.*

"What do you think about Phoebe and Seth?" Phoebe had confided in her about how much she liked Seth, but she was afraid they could never become serious about each other.

Harris frowned slightly. "I know she enjoys spending time with Seth, but it's hard to imagine anything coming of it."

She nodded. "That's what I told Katie. I think it's nice Phoebe and Seth are friends. I'm glad the girls decided to share a room. At first, I hoped Amy or Jenna would want to share my room, but I'm tired, and it's nice spending some alone time with you." She grinned. "You're cuddly and sweet."

Harris arched his eyebrows. "I sound like a teddy bear. I better up my game here." He leaned even closer and gently pressed his lips to her cheek.

"Is that the best you can do? I need you to take my mind off of Katie. A kiss on the cheek was nice but—"

Harris covered her mouth with his. When his passionate kiss stopped, he smiled. "Was that better?"

"A little bit, but it could still use some improvement."

After several minutes of kissing, Harris said, "I think I improved because you seemed to enjoy it. I love you."

"I love you. I'm not happy to have cancer, but I'm glad it's what brought us together. God brought joy out of my illness." She put her head on his broad shoulder.

"My parents are excited to meet you and the girls. They're going to shorten their European trip and be back in a couple of weeks."

"I'm looking forward to meeting them."

"You better get to bed. It's been a long day for you. You need to get some sleep. Do you want me to rub lotion on your arms? I've noticed you rubbing them several times today. You should take Benadryl. That might help with the itchy skin."

"I'm going to take a shower first. That seems to calm down my skin. Then I'll put anti-itch cream on my arms, and thanks for the reminder to take Benadryl. Even my face is scratchy."

"After a few more treatments, that symptom should go away from what the nurse practitioner said." Harris gave her a quick kiss and said, "I'll see you in the morning."

Lindsay walked with Harris to the door. She hugged him and whispered, "Pleasant dreams, my love."

Lindsay took a shower and put on her pajamas. Squeezing cream onto her hand, she rubbed it onto her arms. Lindsay thought how she'd contributed her night sweats to her spleen problems. If she hadn't gotten the lumps on her collarbone, she might have waited even longer before going to the doctor. The night sweats should've been a sign something was wrong, but she assumed it was early menopause.

She prayed, "Dear Heavenly Father, thank you for today and for the precious time with our triplets. Having them together was a blessing for me and Harris. Be with Phoebe and help her to have a closer bond with Amy and Jenna. Guide her in making wise choices when it comes to Seth." Lindsay chuckled a little. "Isn't it something, Lord, that Seth is interested in Phoebe when she looks like his identical sisters? Please forgive me for snapping at Katie. I want to have the friendship I had with her years ago. If it's Your will, heal me from my cancer, so I can get my strength back and continue to enjoy my family. In Jesus' name, I pray."

⁓

Irritation filled Katie's soul because of the day she had with Harris and Lindsay. Even though she wore her favorite pink nightgown, she couldn't shake her negative feelings. As she continued to brush her long hair, Roman crawled into bed.

"What a *wunderbaar-gut* day we had. I enjoyed the trail Harris and I walked on. Everything went great."

Katie left her chair and carried her hairbrush to the nightstand. *Is Roman clueless that I didn't have a terrific time today?* "Next year, we're going to Shipshewana to visit my family on the Fourth."

He sat up in bed and positioned his pillow behind his head. "Okay, we can do that. Didn't you have fun today?"

"Not really. For one thing, I didn't like that Harris paid for our lunch and dinner."

"I offered to pay and leave a tip both times, but Harris insisted we were his guests. Sometimes it's important to be gracious when someone is determined to serve you in a kind way. We had them here this evening for your *appeditlich* pie. We can send some vegetables from our garden and whoopie pies back with them. Our organic produce will be appreciated by Lindsay and Harris."

Katie peered out their window facing the barn. "I wonder if Seth ever came home. I asked him not to spend the night at the hotel."

"He came home when you were taking a shower."

She exhaled a deep breath. "Thank goodness, he's here. I don't have to stay up until he gets home."

"That was sweet of Phoebe to offer to work in the store tomorrow. It'll be nice to have her there."

"I'm glad Seth will be at work and not around Phoebe while she's at the store. I need to invite Veronica over for supper sometime."

Roman yawned and patted a spot next to him. "Come to bed. I need some loving from my *schee fraa.*"

After she climbed into bed, he hugged her. "You seem tense. What's wrong?"

"I'm afraid I told Lindsay my feelings about a lot of things, and she didn't like what I said."

"What did you say to her?" He cocked his head. A hint of annoyance hovered in his eyes.

How much should she tell Roman? Well, they needed to be a united front against Lindsay, Harris, and Phoebe, so she should tell him everything. She had told him the same stuff before, but he never grasped the importance of protecting Amy and Jenna from their birth parents.

She cleared her throat. "I told her if Amy and Jenna should leave our Amish faith, I'll blame her. I wish I had gotten it off my chest that I don't like Seth and Phoebe spending time together. He shouldn't be talking with her constantly on his cell phone. His cell phone is for his job." She wouldn't mention how she said Lindsay might be having a sinful relationship with Harris.

Roman's eyebrows shot up, and he stared at her for a moment. "*Ach*, Katie. How could you? Don't you have any feelings for Lindsay and how she was separated from Amy and Jenna for years? She has cancer, and you were rude to her. You didn't show compassion."

"I'm sorry Lindsay has cancer but—"

Interrupting her, Roman said, "I don't need to hear anymore. *Gut nacht.*"

With his back to her, Katie remained quiet. Roman was right. She'd said plenty.

For years, she'd worried Lindsay would break her promise and reveal their secret of the triplets' births. Now they'd have to live with the consequences if Lindsay's selfish decision caused trouble for her family.

Chapter Twenty-Two

When nurse Suzanne called her name, Lindsay immediately stood from her seat in the waiting room. She was the same nurse Lindsay who had done her vitals before treatment the last time. Harris followed her and went to sit in a bigger waiting room closer to the nurse cubicles.

Lindsay felt like talking to Suzanne about something that had been bothering her. She hated to ask Dr. Richardson because he might think she was questioning his decision. After she got off the scales, she followed Suzanne to her small room.

Suzanne took her blood pressure, her pulse, and her temperature. Then she did the dreaded prick on Lindsay's finger to get a blood sample. It seemed strange a little prick could cause her finger to hurt and be tender hours later. They did it the first day of each chemo treatment to check platelets and white blood count. If both were too low, then the chemo would have to be postponed.

When Suzanne asked if there had been any change in her medications, Lindsay shook her head. "Everything's the same. I'd like to ask you something, though. I had a lot of pain in my left arm during the last chemo treatments because I have small veins. After the last treatment, my arm still hurt when I went home. Why do you suppose they didn't surgically put a port in for me instead of using an IV?"

"I'm not sure, but I know the port is usually inserted around your large veins near your neck." Suzanne stared at her neck and collarbone. "You're so thin there. That might be one reason he decided against a port. And there are disadvantages to a port."

Lindsay thought about the disadvantages to an IV being inserted the first day of chemotherapy. A port would be implanted under her skin to allow easy access to her bloodstream.

"Thanks. I'll ask them to use my right arm this time and see if that helps."

Suzanne stood. "I hope it goes better today and you don't have any pain. I'll take you to the room to see Dr. Richardson."

As soon as they were in the hallway, Suzanne stopped by the lab and gave the lab technician the blood sample. She said, "Here's Lindsay Prescott's blood sample."

Harris left the waiting room to follow them to a room where they'd meet with the doctor.

Once they were seated, Lindsay smiled at Harris. "Let's hope the CT scan shows the chemo is killing my cancer cells."

Harris said, "I hope so. I thought we'd get a late lunch afterward."

Dr. Richardson stepped into the room and greeted them. He had dark brown hair and a friendly smile. Lindsay guessed he was around her age. After Dr. Richardson sat across from them, he said, "Your white blood count is low, but you can still have your chemo treatment. When you get home, you might run a fever because of the low blood count. If you do, an antibiotic will be called in for the infection. I have good news. The cancer cells are responding to the chemo. You're making progress and heading toward remission."

"When do you think her last chemo treatment will be?" Harris asked.

"Probably October," Dr. Richardson said, looking at Lindsay. "Even though you didn't have two days for your first treatment, you received a lot of the medication that first day before you went to the ER."

She smiled. "That sounds wonderful that I'll be finished before the holidays."

Dr. Richardson smiled. "I thought that would get a smile out of you." He glanced at his paperwork. "Your spleen has shrunk from twenty-two centimeters to sixteen centimeters, so that's an improvement."

She didn't say anything. Her spleen was larger than it should be. A normal size for a spleen was around ten centimeters, but she'd just started her treatment in May. Hopefully, it would continue to shrink.

Ten minutes later, she was in the infusion room, waiting to get her IV inserted. As she glanced around the room, Lindsay saw many elderly people. They looked like they were in their seventies or eighties. *Could they be that old? What if I end up getting cancer again?* She saw several women with scarves covering their heads and some without anything covering their bald heads. Lindsay wondered if they suffered from breast cancer. Before more depression could settle into her soul, Harris returned with a bottled water and a few bags of snacks.

She smiled. "You fixed me a huge breakfast."

"You need a high protein breakfast before chemo. I want you to keep your strength up."

"You shouldn't have taken off work today. Phoebe planned on bringing me."

"It's okay. I covered for my partners several times throughout the years when they needed to take time off from our practice. Besides, it's only one day. Phoebe told me that even if I come tomorrow, she's driving you to your treatment."

"I feel popular."

She saw Karen walking toward her and said a silent prayer of thanks. She'd been her nurse for the first couple of times, and she'd never had trouble with pain from the IV. "Hi, Karen."

"Good morning." Karen handed her a plastic cup with white pills. "Here's a couple of Tylenol tablets to take. I'll be back with the anti-nausea medication. Then you'll get the Benadryl and steroids."

Lindsay knew the Benadryl would make her sleepy, but that was fine with her. Harris had brought a book to read, but knowing him, he'd be busy on his phone. "Thanks."

"Hey, you don't have a girlfriend in Cincinnati, do you?" she teased Harris. "You spend lots of time on your phone."

"You're my only one. Sometimes I play games, which is too addictive. If you need anything, let me know."

When Karen returned with her supplies to insert the IV, Lindsay said, "I'm thinking it might be better to put the IV in my right arm. I had a lot of pain and burning in my arm after the last two treatments."

Karen nodded. "It's better to switch arms. Inflammation happens when you use the same arm too much. The last vein used for the infusions has probably been irritated by the drugs. Also, some veins are more sensitive than others. You might not have any soreness and pain if we use your right arm. I'll slow the infusion. It sounds like it was too fast for your vein last time, and that might have caused the burning sensation."

After the infusion started, Karen returned with a warm blanket. Lindsay grinned and said, "Thank you. You know me too well. I'm always cold here."

Harris squeezed her left hand. "I'm proud of you. You're doing great."

"It's because of all the people praying for me. My church group, your prayer warriors, my teacher friends, and of course, Tony and Roberta."

"I enjoyed meeting Haley's parents."

"I don't think I ever told you I made a friend at Kroger. Right after I was diagnosed with cancer, I was at the store. When I was checking out, the female cashier asked me how I was, and I didn't give her the usual response that I was fine. I told her how I'd just learned I had lymphoma cancer. Deep inside, I was so scared about having cancer, and I suspect that's why I blurted it out to her. She took my hands in hers and said a prayer for me." Lindsay felt moisture in her eyes but wasn't surprised. She would never forget that moment. "I was touched a stranger cared enough to pray for me and try to lift my spirits. She even asked one of the baggers to take my groceries out for me."

"That was a blessing on a day you needed one."

"It's ironic I received more compassion from a stranger than I did from Katie. I expected so much more from her when we were in Millersburg. Here, she's the adopted mother of our daughters. I do wish I hadn't gotten upset with her. It seems I lose control of my emotions suddenly these days."

"Katie has no right to blame you for telling the truth. Every day, I'm grateful you told me. I know it was eating away at Roman." His eyebrows shot up. "He'd talked to Katie before your letter, telling her it was time for the truth to come out, but she wouldn't hear of it. Roman told me he planned on calling you when they returned from Niagara Falls. He'd felt a nudge from God."

Lindsay laughed. "That's interesting that Roman had God telling him to contact me." She was quiet for a moment.

Two friends, Michelle Turner and Vickie McCartney, stopped by her chair. With big smiles on their faces, they said hello.

Michelle said, "Phoebe sent us a text saying you were here today."

"Oh my gosh, I'm glad you both came. I want you to meet Phoebe's father." Lindsay turned to glance at Harris. "These two are my best friends from school." Lindsay turned her face back to look at them and said, "Michelle and Vickie, I'd like you to meet Harris Manning."

Harris stood, extending his hand to each woman. "It's a pleasure to meet you. I remember hearing about you both from Lindsay when you gave her the care package of goodies."

"I couldn't believe all the wonderful stuff in the tote bag. You two are so thoughtful." Vickie and Michelle had visited her last month and given her a Burt's Bees hand lotion and lip balm, gel beads eye mask, popcorn, fruit snacks, and devotional material with wonderful Bible verses.

Lindsay noticed Michelle looked great—as she usually did—with her brown hair in a stylish short cut. She wore jeans with a blue-and-white-striped top. Vickie was pregnant with twins, looking ready to pop at any moment. Her blonde hair was pulled back in a ponytail, and she had circles under her eyes. "Vickie, please sit down." Lindsay waved her left hand to an empty chair next to her. "How much longer do you have?"

Vickie exhaled a deep breath and sat in a chair by Lindsay. "I have a doctor's appointment tomorrow. I hope it'll be my last one. Since I'm thirty-six weeks pregnant, it should be fine to go into labor anytime. I don't have to worry now that they'd be born too early, and my doctor said twins born around thirty-six weeks generally do well. I'm miserable. I can't sleep at night. They're probably bumping into each other. I doubt there's much room left."

"Michelle, take my seat." Harris tapped the chair. "I'll get you ladies something to drink. Would you like water or juice?"

"Thank you, but I'm fine," Michelle said as she sat in Harris's empty chair.

"I'd like a bottle of water." Vickie smiled at Harris.

After he left them, the women gushed over how good-looking Harris was. Lindsay had told them about him and her having triplets earlier when they'd visited her at home. When they'd all started teaching the same year, Lindsay had become friends with them instantly. Michelle taught history while Vickie taught English.

Michelle said, "It's awesome you and Harris are together."

"You two make a cute couple." Vickie grinned. "Don't get married too soon. I want to be available to be a bridesmaid."

Lindsay looked to see if Harris was on his way back and felt relief that he wasn't. "I don't think that will happen. We haven't spoken about marriage. I love Columbus, and he has a practice in Cincinnati."

"He can start a practice here. That's what he should do to make up for the lost years." Michelle frowned. "I still can't believe how you were cheated out of raising your triplets."

Would Harris move to Columbus? Lindsay wondered. It seemed unlikely, but there was an established practice with gastroenterologists who were looking for another partner. *Geez, why am I even thinking about marrying Harris? Sure, he said how he loved me recently. I might have chemo brain, but I haven't forgotten how Harris told me he loved me when we were both young. I've forgiven him, but can I truly trust Harris this time? But more importantly, is it God's plan we have a life together?*

⁓

Within hours of returning home from chemo on Thursday, Lindsay's face became flushed. Itching was bad, and she tried hard not to scratch her face. After a restless night of her face feeling hot and itchy, Phoebe insisted she should call the cancer clinic and tell them about her symptoms. The nurse called her back and asked if she had a fever, but she didn't have a fever with a temperature of ninety-nine degrees. The nurse explained that white blood cells help to prevent infection and to be sure to call if she started running a temperature. With a low white blood count, there was a chance she'd get an infection.

Phoebe plopped beside her on the couch. "Well, what did the nurse say about your side effects?"

Lindsay shrugged. "Not much really. She wanted to know if I have a fever."

"I think your face should be back to its normal color in another day or so. At least your platelets must be okay this time. You've had low platelets before too."

"Now I wish Harris wouldn't come tonight. He was just here on Wednesday. All this driving back and forth has to be tiring. I don't think he sleeps as well in the hotel room either." Lindsay picked her cell phone off of the table by the couch. "I'll send him a text to tell him I'm tired and he doesn't need to come tonight."

"You know he's going to come here anyhow, even if you tell him not to. You look fine. Your face looks like a sunburn."

"You're probably right. Harris will still come. When I feel better, we need to visit him and meet his parents. They got home last week. They're anxious to meet you and your sisters."

"Amy mentioned they want to go to Cincinnati sometime soon." Phoebe drew a deep breath. "I still can't believe I now have a dad, two sisters, *and* grandparents."

"I'm glad you're happy. I am too, except I miss Amy and Jenna. Now that they are a part of our family, it's hard for me to believe I went so long without them."

Phoebe glanced at her phone. "Dad's been texting you. He's asking if it's okay to pick up Chinese food on his way here. He's already left Cincinnati."

"Oh, I haven't looked at my phone. Tell him that sounds good, but also tell him not to text while he's driving."

"I doubt he is."

A couple of hours later, Phoebe threw the empty Chinese containers away and rinsed the plates to put in the dishwasher. Harris and Lindsay remained seated on the high stools by the gray-and-white counter.

Harris asked, "Phoebe, would you like to go running with me tomorrow morning?"

"Sure. I'd like that."

She was elated that Phoebe enjoyed running with her dad. It probably was for the best that she wasn't running with her. Phoebe could have that special time with her dad. "I hear your ringtone. I wonder if it's Seth."

Phoebe walked to the edge of the counter and glanced at the screen. "It's Seth. It might be about when he can visit. He was disappointed he couldn't come this weekend and has to work tomorrow."

Lindsay knew another reason Seth decided against visiting was because of her chemo treatment. *He's such a thoughtful man. He must take after Roman.* She whispered to Harris as Phoebe put the phone next to her ear and walked away from them. "Seth let her take a picture of him, and she has it on her iPhone."

Harris looked at her with a curious expression. "I thought they don't allow Amish to pose for pictures."

"They aren't baptized, so it's okay for them to appear in pictures. Of course, each Amish district has their own *Ordnung* rules, but Jenna told me they'll have their pictures taken for their EMT training." Lindsay sipped her lemonade.

Phoebe rushed back into the kitchen. "Something's awful has happened. There was a buggy accident. Seth said a car slammed into the back of their buggy. Jenna and Amy were sent to the hospital."

Chapter Twenty-Three

Wooster Community Hospital, Ohio

As soon as they entered Amy's hospital room, Seth walked to Phoebe, giving her a hug.

Lindsay rushed to Amy's side and grasped her left hand. "We're so sorry this happened."

Amy gave Lindsay a weak grin. "I guess I'll get to see what doctors and nurses do. Maybe I'll become a hospital nurse. This is the first time I've been admitted to a hospital."

Harris said, "I'm so sorry you were injured. Be sure to tell them about your pain. I know breathing is painful with broken ribs. Did they take X-rays? And a CT scan?"

"I've had both."

"Are you in a lot of pain right now?" Lindsay asked, noticing Amy's pale face and her uncovered black hair.

"The nurse started me on medication for the pain. It's been severe." Amy tightened her jaw and paused as a frown crossed her face. "I'm glad all of you are here. *Mamm* and *Daed* left to get the instructions for Jenna. I have to stay in the hospital, but Jenna gets to go home tonight."

While it was a relief to hear her sweet daughter speak, it took Lindsay several moments to sort her feelings. "I'm sorry about your injuries, but I'm so thankful you, Jenna, and Seth are alive."

Harris grabbed a chair and pulled it close to Amy's bed. "Lindsay, you should sit down."

As he touched her shoulder, she murmured, "Thank you."

Seth plowed his fingers through his hair. "A car rear-ended our buggy. We'd just finished making home deliveries. There are a few elderly customers who can't make it to the store, so we take their orders to them. It wasn't dark and the weather was nice, but the driver was going too fast on the rural road. The woman and Dan weren't hurt."

"Who's Dan?" Harris asked.

"Our horse." Seth looked forlorn. "I hate that Amy and Jenna were hurt. I should've made the deliveries myself."

"*Nee*, Jenna and I wanted to help." Amy patted Seth's arm.

Upon entering the room, Jenna glanced at them. Her left arm was in a sling. "Hi. It's nice to see you guys, but I'm sorry it's under these conditions."

"We're glad Seth called Phoebe. I'm sorry about your wrist, Jenna." Lindsay thought again about how they all could've been killed in the buggy accident. *How could I have lost them after just finding my girls?*

Jenna looked at Amy and said, "I'll stay with you tonight."

"*Nee*, you don't need to do that. I'll be fine. I'm sure you have pain in your wrist, and you should sleep in your own bed."

Phoebe said, "I can stay with Amy."

Amy grinned at Seth. "Do you want to stay with me too?"

Seth raised his eyebrows. "Hey, I was going to offer before Phoebe said she would."

"You just had chemo this week. Did it go okay?" Jenna sat on the edge of Amy's bed. Her brown eyes filled with concern as she looked at Lindsay.

"I can't believe you remembered after all that's happened." Lindsay smiled. "I did have it. My face is flushed and itchy from the steroids, but I'm doing okay."

Amy raised her head. "What about your arm? Does it hurt like it did the other time you had treatment?"

"I had them use my right arm for the IV, and I didn't have any pain this time." A thought occurred to Lindsay on how she could help her daughter while she recovered. "Once you're released from the hospital, you could stay with us. Phoebe will be home for a few weeks before she starts college. Harris's car is wonderful, and you won't feel any road bumps while traveling to our house. My car isn't smooth riding."

Phoebe looked pleased at Amy spending time at their house. "That's a great idea. We can take care of you. You won't be able to work at the store, and you won't be alone at your house during the day. And, if you want, I can help you study for your GED."

Katie entered the hospital room. Surprise flashed in her eyes at seeing them. "I didn't know you were coming to the hospital."

Roman had followed Katie into the room, and he stepped around her. "It's great you made the trip. I'm sure Amy and Jenna are grateful you came. We have never had any buggy accidents and are thankful to God that no one was killed. Well, Katie's parents were in an accident once, and they were also thrown out of the buggy. They weren't injured though."

"It was scary when we were ejected out of the buggy. We landed in a field at the edge, so that was better than the road." Amy looked at Seth. "You were great rushing to check on me and Jenna."

Lindsay was sorry to see Katie looking at them like they didn't belong in the room. Why couldn't Katie have compassion in her heart for them? She should realize they had a right to visit their daughters. And, of course, Phoebe would want to see her sisters. Katie definitely didn't want to share Amy and Jenna with them.

"It's too bad the accident happened, but there is a blessing out of it. Amy can spend time with Phoebe and her mother." Harris stared at Katie. "Before you came into the room, Lindsay mentioned Amy staying with her and Phoebe when she's discharged."

"*Nee*, Amy shouldn't go to Columbus," Katie insisted, adamantly shaking her head. "She should come home to recover. Besides, she'll have medical appointments."

"I'd love to go to Lindsay's and Phoebe's home since I can't work with my right arm broken. It's too bad it wasn't my left arm." Amy glanced at Lindsay. "Is it okay with you?"

"Definitely, I'd love to have you." Lindsay turned away from Amy to stare at Jenna. "I hope you can come for a visit too."

"Maybe your parents can visit all of us in Columbus," Phoebe mentioned, giving an encouraging look at her dad.

"It's getting late," a nurse said as she entered the room. "I want to take Amy's vitals, so everyone needs to scoot out of here."

Lindsay kissed Amy's forehead. "I love you."

Harris squeezed her shoulder. "We'll be in touch. You're in our prayers."

Once in the hallway, Harris turned to Lindsay and whispered, "If Phoebe wants to stay, it's okay with me."

When Phoebe and the Yoder family members exited Amy's hospital room, Katie said, "Phoebe, that was sweet of you to offer to stay tonight, but I'm going to stay with Amy."

Millersburg, Ohio

On Monday, Amy was discharged from the hospital. As she sat in a chair in the corner of her bedroom, Katie looked up from packing Amy's clothes. "I don't see why you have to go to Columbus your first day home. You've been in a lot of pain from your broken ribs. I don't approve of this trip. It'll be okay if you change your mind. I'll call Lindsay and tell her you can't go to her house."

"You didn't mention Jenna. Why aren't you objecting to Jenna going? Is it because she's not going to study for her GED?"

Katie stopped folding the pajama bottoms and was quiet for a moment. The truth was she hated her daughters visiting Lindsay and Phoebe. *If I wasn't a truthful woman, I'd fake an illness so Amy and Jenna would stay home.* "I worry the trip will be tiring. You'll be in too much pain. And I don't like that Jenna is going either. I'm hoping she'll only stay a week."

"I have pain medication. I'll follow the doctor's orders to take it easy and ice my ribs regularly."

After she put the rest of the clothing in the black suitcase, Katie closed the lid and pulled the zipper around it. She sat on the edge of the bed so she'd be close to Amy. She needed to convince Amy to come back when Seth went to get Jenna. "I'm not thrilled you're studying for your GED. I hope it doesn't lead you to wanting more education with Englishers. We're to keep separate from the world."

Amy said, "My ribs hurt and need to heal. I can't do much in the store, and *Daed* seems happy to do the bookkeeping and ordering."

Jenna entered the room with her arm in a sling. "Our friend Caroline is happy to work in the store. She said it's a blessing to have a job while we're away. I have pain in my wrist, so I think this is a good time for me to visit Phoebe and Lindsay."

"Just think about staying a week instead of two. That's all I ask. I worry about you two being away from home and around temptations." Katie wished Seth wouldn't be the one to go to Columbus to get the girls, but she knew he wanted to spend time with Phoebe. At least he would only be there Saturday and leave on Sunday. Although Roman and she had talked about visiting Lindsay sometime, it hadn't happened. Katie knew she'd feel uncomfortable at Lindsay's home. Otherwise, she'd go with Seth to get Jenna. After the July visit at the hotel, Roman had told her to write a nice letter to Lindsay, but she couldn't. What she'd told Lindsay on the Fourth had been the truth. She would blame Lindsay if Amy and Jenna left their faith.

Jenna glanced at the luggage. "I just finished packing too. *Ach*, *Mamm*, I don't want to leave you shorthanded for too long at the store, so that's why we'll only be gone for two weeks. Amy and I can heal just as well at Lindsay's. And it's a good opportunity for Amy to study for her GED. If Amy decides to become a nurse, she needs to have her high school diploma before going to college."

Amy nodded. "Face it, *Mamm*. Jenna and I can't separate completely from the world when we were born to English parents. That has to mean something now in our lives. It'll be an ideal time to meet our English grandparents and spend time with our birth mother and Phoebe. And I look forward to getting to know Harris better. I might decide that being an EMT is enough for me and not become a nurse."

I'm glad Lindsay's parents aren't in the picture, but still, I'm not happy Amy and Jenna will be meeting Harris's parents. "You might be disappointed when you meet Mr. and Mrs. Manning. After all, they encouraged Harris to marry Callie and convinced him Lindsay was a summer fling. That was nasty of them to influence Harris like that."

Amy bit her lower lip. "It seems you have something in common with them when it comes to Lindsay. You aren't happy I know the truth about my birth. I heard your unkind comments about Lindsay and Harris. It's obvious you don't want Jenna and me to spend time getting to know them. While we're gone, I hope you'll realize God brought our birth parents into our lives for a reason. There might a chance they will get their happy ending and marry each other."

"I'm sure God didn't do it so you can criticize me."

Amy leaned forward. "I love you, *Mamm*, but I do wish you and *Daed* had told us years ago about Lindsay. She was young, and it's obvious it was a burden for her to keep quiet to Phoebe about us."

Katie responded with a calmness she didn't feel. "I didn't want to lose you two. Lindsay was too young to have raised you. She realized it and wanted us to adopt you both. I didn't want you influenced by the English way of life. If you don't join our church, you'll break mine and your *daed's* heart. I'll worry about your salvation if you dismiss our faith."

Jenna frowned. "I'm going to join the church. But I don't believe that if I don't join I won't be saved and not go to heaven."

Amy stood. "I'll check to see if Harris left any message on our answering machine. I don't want to say words I might regret later." Amy touched Katie's arm. "I'm sorry you feel the way you do. You raised us to be Christians, and Lindsay gave us life. Don't worry about what the future brings. It says in Matthew we shouldn't worry about tomorrow. I'll be sure to follow the path God wants for me. It might be the same one you wish for us, or it might be another path He has in mind for me."

Chapter Twenty-Four

Columbus, Ohio

Lindsay put the newspaper she'd been reading beside her on the sofa. She pushed her long blonde hair behind her ears. She loved being able to watch her triplets make whoopie pies together. Jenna had decided Phoebe needed to learn how to make them since she loved eating them so much. It was awesome they all three loved to bake. It gave Phoebe another chance to bond with her sisters.

"Mom, I think we should offer some of these pies to our grandparents when they arrive today." Phoebe frowned. "I wonder if they'll want to be called by their first names or by Grandma and Grandpa."

Jenna put a piece of parchment paper on a cookie sheet. "I'm nervous about meeting them. I hope they'll like us even though we're so different from you."

Phoebe chuckled. "It could be they'll like my Amish sisters the best. They'll be fooled by your sweet personalities, but I know the real Amy and Jenna."

"Hey, we only played one joke on you," Amy said and then glanced at Lindsay. "We couldn't fool our mom. She knew I wasn't Jenna."

Hearing Amy call her mom again warmed Lindsay's heart. Jenna and Amy had started calling her mom earlier in the week. They mentioned how they were blessed with two fantastic mothers. "Geez, I'm sure Helen and John will love all three of you. How could they not love my beautiful and amazing daughters? Be prepared, though, to be spoiled by them. Harris said they are bringing science books since all three of you are interested in the medical field." Lindsay laughed. "Poor Harris said they are going to make him look bad because he didn't think of all the stuff his mother bought. Oh, I hate to spoil their surprise, but I should warn you they bought Kindles for all three of you so you can buy e-books. Harris mentioned you might not want them, but I think you could get them charged where Seth charges his cell phone."

Jenna sighed. "I don't think I can accept a Kindle. We're Old Order Amish. My friend Caroline has an e-book reader, but her parents are more lenient."

Lindsay nodded. "Harris said they're e-book readers only, but if you can't keep them, I'm sure they'll understand."

"I'll keep mine," Amy said. "I don't see the big deal about having an e-book reader. It's not like we can make phone calls on it. I'm sure *Mamm* will have something to say about it though."

"I'll keep my reader too. It'll be nice to have it instead of using my cell phone for reading e-books." Phoebe licked the cookie dough off her big spoon. "This pan of chocolate cookies is ready for the oven."

As her daughters continued chattering to each other, Lindsay hoped Harris was correct in that his parents wouldn't be judgmental about her decision to give Amy and Jenna to Katie and Roman to raise. She knew they'd been shocked to have two granddaughters that were raised in an Amish home, but it was not uncommon for the Amish people to adopt children of various nations and races. It happened frequently, so obviously other single mothers must see the value in having their children adopted by the Amish. *Helen and John surely won't be rude and complain that I did the wrong thing in front of Amy and Jenna.*

Lindsay left the couch to walk closer to the kitchen area. "I purchased a subscription to *The Budget*. I noticed how the Amish and Mennonites love to travel. I was thinking we could go on a cruise when I get through my chemo treatments and Phoebe and I have a Christmas break from school. I know the Amish don't fly, but we can drive to the port to get on the cruise ship. I think it'd be fun for all of us to take a cruise to the Bahamas together. It'll only be for a few days."

"Are you serious?" Amy bounced on her toes lightly in place. "Mom, that sounds like so much fun. It'll be a first for us. We have never been on a cruise or to the Bahamas."

In an excited voice, Phoebe said, "I've never been on a cruise, and Mom hasn't either."

Jenna smiled warmly. "I can't wait for us to do this together."

Secretly, that was why Lindsay had thought of a cruise. She wanted them to all experience something they had never done before so it would be a special memory to share as a family.

"I'm going to take a shower and get ready." Lindsay didn't want to tell the girls, but she was also nervous about meeting Helen and John. *Probably more nervous than they are.* It was something that she'd never met them. Harris had said if they hadn't been in Europe, they would have visited her by now. They had sent her a get-well card and flowers. *What can go wrong? Helen and John might resent me for waiting so long to tell Harris the truth, but they have to share in the blame too.*

Phoebe's face was flushed from putting the cookies in the oven. She walked to her and gave her a hug. "It's going to be fine. I see you're concerned. It's going to be great to meet our grandparents. And we're going to impress them with our charm, and your triplets look gorgeous when we clean up."

"Yes, you are beautiful women. It's going to be an interesting evening."

Harris had reminded her in a recent text that it would go fine with going out to eat at a restaurant, and they would return to her house for coffee and dessert. Phoebe was like her dad trying to calm her nerves.

~

Instead of meeting them at the restaurant, they decided to meet at Lindsay's house first. Harris had managed to get off work earlier because of a patient's cancellation, so his parents followed him to Columbus. They hadn't wanted to travel together because Helen and John wanted to stay a couple of days longer to get more acquainted with their granddaughters.

Lindsay wore a black paisley midi dress with chic matching sandals that made her feel presentable to meet Helen and John. Amy and Jenna looked pretty in their Plain clothing. After the cookies were done, Amy had changed to a neatly pressed blue dress while Jenna wore a lavender dress. Their pure white *kapps* looked perfect too. Phoebe had curled her black hair and it brushed against her shoulders A white blouse and a black skirt graced her slender body.

At the sound of the doorbell, Lindsay walked quickly to open the front door.

Harris entered the living room. "Mom and Dad are here."

Lindsay put a hand on his arm. "Don't our daughters look wonderful?"

As Amy pushed her *kapp* strings past her shoulders, Jenna smoothed her apron while Phoebe just grinned. Lindsay was surprised Phoebe wasn't twisting her birthstone ring around her finger. *I guess one of us is relaxed*, Lindsay thought.

Harris blinked his brown eyes. "I'm the luckiest man in the world to have three gorgeous, smart daughters who take after their mother."

"Hello," Helen Manning said as she stood in the open doorway.

"Hello, it's nice to meet you. I'm Lindsay, and welcome." She smiled at Harris's mother, noticing she was a petite woman with big, gray eyes and glossy, brown hair that touched her chin. Helen colored her hair since she was in her seventies. She wore a subdued gray dress with a matching tailored jacket and red glasses, which added a nice spot of color.

"I'm happy to meet you too." Helen extended her hand to Lindsay. "And to see your daughters is a blessing for me and John."

"Where is Dad?" Harris asked with an annoyed look.

Helen shrugged. "He received a call and said he had to take it. Now, I want to meet my granddaughters in person."

As she walked to them, the triplets stood and greeted her.

Immediately, Phoebe hugged her grandmother. "Thank you for chatting with us yesterday. We thought it was nice to break the ice before you arrived."

Lindsay laughed. "My sneaky daughters. I didn't even know you three talked with Helen. I love it."

Helen continued speaking with the girls, and she asked Amy and Jenna about their injuries.

John appeared by her side, smiling. "You must be the woman who stole my son's heart. I can see why he's taken with you."

Lindsay smiled back. "And I see where Harris gets his charming personality from. It's nice to finally meet you. I hope you had a nice drive here."

"We did, except it took too long to get here in my opinion." John turned his face away from Lindsay to look at his wife. "Helen thought I drove too fast."

"I heard that," Helen said. "And you did."

Lindsay noticed that even though she wore wedge platform sandals, John towered over her. His smile and brown eyes reminded her of Harris.

John grasped her hand, his eyes filling with remorse. "I'm sorry we didn't listen to Harris when he told us about you. I wish we'd taken the time to meet you years ago. We missed out on having you as a daughter-in-law and spoiling our granddaughters."

Helen remained in the house with Lindsay while the others went outside to see Phoebe's small vegetable garden. She had a feeling Helen wanted to tell her something in private.

Helen offered her an apologetic smile and exhaled a deep breath. "When Harris told me you had given birth to our granddaughters, I cried for a long time. Well, I cried after the shock wore off. I'm sorry for all the lost years. John and I should've taken the time to meet you before even insisting Harris mustn't marry you. I know I can't make it up to you and your daughters, but for whatever life I have left, I'll try my best to be a good grandmother."

"It's not entirely your fault what happened. Harris is to blame too." Lindsay softened at Helen's explanation. "I also made mistakes."

The tension on Helen's face eased slightly as she looked at Lindsay. "John and I loved Callie like she was our own daughter. When she was unfaithful to him during their marriage, it broke our hearts."

Briefly, Lindsay reflected on how Harris had been unfaithful to her. Sure, they hadn't been married, but he'd confessed his love to her on the beach. "I'll show you Phoebe's bedroom first. I'm especially glad I have a guest bedroom now. Jenna's been sleeping in there and Amy's been sleeping with Phoebe, but next week Amy is going to switch with Jenna. It's been great having them here."

⌒

Phoebe giggled. "Did you see Dad's face when we told him to leave, so we could have a girls' night?"

Jenna nodded. "He looked indignant at us."

Amy took a handful of popcorn out of the huge bowl. "I love popcorn."

Jenna looked up from putting the Scrabble pieces back into its box. "How in the world can you eat popcorn after we had a huge steak dinner at the restaurant? Plus, I saw you eat a piece of chocolate cake and whoopie pies when we got home."

"Oh my gosh, that was the best steak I've ever had," Amy said.

"It was good." Phoebe leaned back against her fabric blue headboard.

After Jenna put the lid on the box, she started walking toward the closet. Phoebe hopped off her bed and said, "Jenna don't try to put the board game away. I'll do it. You're doing too much with your one good arm."

"It is hard to use one arm, but at least it's my left wrist that got broken."

Lindsay sat in one corner on an armchair covered in a white-and-gray geometric pattern. Happiness filled her soul as she gazed at her triplets. They wore the matching pink pajamas she'd given them. When she saw the sleepwear in Kohl's, she had to buy three of them. After Helen and the men had left the house, Amy and Jenna had taken off their prayer coverings and removed their hairpins out of their waist-length hair. Phoebe's hair was pulled back in a messy ponytail. It was sad Amy and Jenna were injured in the buggy accident, but it was also a blessing that gave them an excuse to stay with her and Phoebe.

Amy picked up her glass of water from the nightstand. "You have a pretty bedroom. I like the blue and lavender colors. I never saw a fabric headboard before, and the blue lamps are nice."

Lindsay tucked a lock of hair behind her ear. "Helen was impressed with the shower curtain. She never saw one with the periodic table of the elements on it. I told her Phoebe chose it."

"Chemistry is something I need to learn. I want to memorize the elements." Amy frowned. "We were never taught any science in our Amish school."

Jenna sat on the edge of the bed. "We only had history, writing, reading, and English."

"I remember you saying you learned English in the first grade." Phoebe returned to her spot on the bed.

"Some *kinner* learned to speak English earlier if their parents have contact in their jobs with non-Amish customers. We learned some English before starting school because we had a vegetable stand in the front yard," Amy said.

Lindsay nodded. "I remember that. Katie grew a lot of vegetables." She paused for a moment, then decided to go to bed. Standing, she said, "I'll see you in the morning. Have pleasant dreams."

"Mom, I'll get up early to make the coffee cake," Phoebe said. "You can sleep in."

Lindsay shook her head. "I can make it. The brunch isn't until eleven o'clock."

As she left Phoebe's bedroom, Lindsay hoped she would survive her lymphoma cancer. Life was too precious to leave her loved ones. *What if I don't go into remission or it returns later? I need to focus on my chemo treatment and take it one day at a time. God is watching over me. Even though I gave Amy and Jenna away, He made sure I have a relationship with them after all those years I couldn't be with them. I can't die now.*

Opening her drawer to get her pajamas, she thought about how nice it was of Helen to offer to take her to the chemo treatments. However, had it been out of guilt? She might only want to make amends because they'd demanded Harris marry Callie.

As she'd showed Phoebe's bedroom, Helen had said, "After Harris explained to us why you gave two babies up for adoption to an Amish couple, we got over our shock. I can see why you thought it was wise to give them to Katie and Roman. It's fun, though, to hear Amy and Jenna speak with their accents. They're sweet young women, and Phoebe is too. And the fact they haven't joined their Plain church makes me wonder if they will later."

Whether they decide to take their kneeling vows or immerse themselves into my world, I pray they'll be happy with their choices. I'll encourage my daughters in whatever they decide to do as it says in I Thessalonians 5:11: "Therefore encourage one another and build each other up, just as in fact you are doing."

Chapter Twenty-Five

Lindsay sat outside by her patio table sipping her morning coffee. The humidity and temperature were low enough that it was comfortable enough to enjoy the fresh air. She loved the early hours when it was quiet and peaceful. It was a time to read the Bible, to pray for her family and friends, to give thanks for her blessings, and to listen to God's voice. Feeling His love enter her soul started her day off the right way. She'd just finished reading out of her devotional book and Bible when she heard footsteps. Turning, she saw her daughter Amy. At the sight of Amy in her pink pajamas, Lindsay smiled.

"Good morning. We seem to be alike. Early risers and still in our pj's. I'm glad you came out here. It's nice to spend time with my firstborn while the other two are sleeping."

"I'm amazed how you can always tell Jenna and I apart."

"Your eyes are a bit larger than Jenna's, and you have a tiny scar above your mouth."

"You're very observant." Amy smiled. "Did *Mamm* tell you how I got it?"

Lindsay shook her head.

Amy shrugged. "I wasn't paying attention because I was looking at the beautiful butterflies while the men were playing horseshoes. I ran in front of them and got hit with a horseshoe."

"That had to hurt. How old were you?"

"I was four years old." Amy ran her finger around the rim of her coffee cup. "*Danki* for making a pot of coffee. *Ach*, Mom, I need to talk to you about something, and it's bothering me a lot."

Lindsay reached over and picked up Amy's hand. "What is it?"

"This might shock you, but before Jenna and I came here, *Mamm* told me it'll break her heart if I don't join the Amish church. She also said it would cause a concern about my salvation if I left our faith. I don't believe that. I know she isn't the only one who believes that. It's something Amish parents tell their *kinner*."

"I've heard the Amish only consider themselves good parents if their children join the church. If you don't take the baptism instructions and join, Katie will feel like she's failed as a mother. Katie likes to be successful in whatever she does." Lindsay gave a little laugh. "Of course, she'd never admit it because that would be prideful."

Amy nodded. "I have to admit that I wish, at times, you had kept all of us together, but it wasn't meant to be. You had so many things against you. I love many things in the Amish faith, and I love my parents, but I've never been happy about only being educated to the eighth grade."

"I wish with my whole heart that I could've kept you too. I know Helen and John wish I had, but I wonder if it would've made a difference if they had known the truth. They were determined for Harris to have a perfect wife and career. It's hard to say what would've happened if the truth had been known." Lindsay squeezed Amy's hand and released her grasp. "I believe in you, and I'll continue to pray for you as you make your decision. A verse in Isaiah 58 says, *'And the Lord shall guide thee continually.'* I'm sure God will guide you to make the right choice for your life."

Amy chuckled. "I told *Mamm* the same thing, that God would help me along the path I'm meant to follow. I've felt, before I met you, that I shouldn't join the church until after I went to college to become a nurse, but now I'm unsure. I'm looking forward to being an EMT. That might be enough for me. I love our classes, and I'm glad the instructors gave us assignments to continue working on while I'm here."

"And you're getting your GED soon. It's great your bishop has been understanding about your desire to get it."

"I can't believe Seth will be here today and we'll go home tomorrow. It's been wonderful spending time with you. Jenna and I want to go to your church tomorrow morning. Unless you don't want us to go."

"Are you kidding? I'd love for you to attend my church and meet my friends there. They've been a wonderful support for me during my cancer treatments. Our church has a wonderful prayer chain, and they have continued to pray for me."

"It seems to me it should be okay for me to join a Protestant church. I wasn't born into a Plain family. So if I don't take my Amish vows, I'm sure *Daed* would understand if I became Protestant. *Mamm* might ban me from our house."

"I don't think Katie would do that. She loves you and wants the best for you, but she obviously has strong feelings on the subject."

Amy sipped her coffee and grinned. "There's one thing I'm sure about. I love your coffee. I like how you use whole beans and your coffeemaker grinds them. I wonder if I could get an Amish version of your coffeemaker that runs on batteries."

Lindsay laughed. "The Amish are very resourceful, so it might be a possibility."

～

Phoebe could easily fall completely in love with Seth Yoder, but she knew she shouldn't. It was risky to date her sisters' brother. *I need to stay focused on my goal of becoming a physician. But he's too cute for his own good*, Phoebe thought as she stared at him. When her eyes met his green eyes, her heart fluttered. His smile touched a chord in her with its mixture of sweetness and mischief. Seth was the only guy who could pull this off with ease. His appeal was devastating. *Maybe suggesting we go swimming after our bike ride was a huge mistake.* She leaned back in her chair to relax and soak in the sun.

"It's cool Harris picked a hotel with an outdoor pool."

"I wish we had a pool. I love going swimming. After we dry off some, we better head back to the house. Mom said they'd take care of supper so I don't have to cook. But she doesn't want to eat late since you're leaving this evening for home."

Seth grinned. "I think your mom likes me and wants us to have time together."

"Or she wanted to get rid of you."

He rolled his eyes at her. "You're such a tease."

Seth's pool chair was too close to hers because he was a major distraction. She could see he had a stubble on his jaw which surprised her. Could he be trying to look more manly and older? She knew it bothered him that he was younger than her. *That isn't an issue for me, but the whole Amish thing is a problem for me. I'm attracted to Seth because he's different from guys I've dated in the past.*

"You're staring at me," she said, licking her suddenly dry lips. She paused to catch her breath.

"That's because you're beautiful, and I like you a lot."

Phoebe ignored the compliment. "I've had fun today. I'm glad you came."

He frowned. "I wish we weren't going back tonight, but I have to go to work tomorrow."

"What did you think of our church?" Phoebe had gotten the impression that Seth only went to church because they were all going. She'd been pleased her sisters, especially Amy, had wanted to go to their Protestant church.

"It was nice but a lot shorter than our church service. Your minister had a great sermon." He raised his eyebrows. "You can go to ours the next time you visit."

She shrugged. "I'm not sure when I can visit. I'll be starting school soon, and I'll have a demanding schedule with classes and studying a lot. I want to do well. And the little free time I have will need to be set aside for my mom."

"You aren't planning on ever attending one of our church days, are you?" His jaw clenched, and his green eyes slightly narrowed.

"I don't know. I might if I happen to be there on one of the days you have it. It's funny how you only have it every other Sunday." She let out a sigh. "Okay, I'll be honest. I think you want me to fall in love with your Plain life, and there are so many wonderful things I like about your faith. But there are some things I dislike. I don't like the limitation on education for one thing."

"I see why you would think that, but we never stop educating ourselves. Many Amish aren't able to purchase enough acres of farmland because it's too expensive, so they start various businesses. That has caused changes with using some technical things for business. We're allowed to take bookkeeping classes and some have computers in their stores to keep track of their inventory and ordering. Our bishop and ministers pray before they approve of something new that can be useful. Sure, it seems like we never change because we drive buggies and wear the same clothing, but certain things are allowed when it becomes necessary to family life. I don't have a high school diploma, but I'm considering taking some classes at a vocational school."

"That sounds good about the vocational school." Phoebe grabbed her blue-and-white cover-up and slid it over her swimsuit. "Would you ever want to drive a car instead of a buggy? You could do it now while you're in your *rumspringa*."

He grinned. "Are you getting tired of driving me around?"

"No. I love to drive."

"I did drive a friend's car once, which was stupid because I didn't have a driver's license. We just went on a few rural roads. It was okay, but I prefer traveling by buggy." As he gazed at her, his eyes remained unwavering. "So you can't become serious about me because I'm Amish?"

Her stomach turned over. *I don't want to hurt Seth, but I have to be honest.* "I can always be friends with you, but nothing more. It's hard because I do like you a lot and I have a great time whenever we're together." She noticed he was watching her intently. Her heart turned over at the longing in his eyes.

"How about I give you a kiss? Then you might change your mind about us just being friends."

As much as she wanted him to kiss her, Phoebe shook her head. "Save your kiss for a nice Amish girl."

Chapter Twenty-Six

Harris ran into Lindsay's bedroom at the sound of her moaning. Tears ran down her cheeks as she cried out in pain to him. "It hurts so much in my left leg and hip. The pain feels like it's in my bones *and* muscles."

Quickly, he sat on the edge of the bed, pulling her against his body. "I'm so sorry. The pain medicine should kick in soon." He'd given it to her twenty minutes ago. *Why does Lindsay have to suffer so much? Lord, please take away her pain.* Harris realized the shots were needed to stimulate her white blood cells so her number would raise high enough to have chemo. "I'll get you an ice pack to put on your left side."

"If it doesn't lessen soon, I will try ice. I know they warned us there might be pain, but I didn't have any idea it would be this severe. I didn't have any pain yesterday from the first shot of Zarxio." She sobbed. "Why did my white blood counts have to remain low for so long? I wanted to get my August treatment in before school started."

He rubbed her back and shoulders. "I'm not happy they made you wait. I told your nurse **practitioner** not to wait on the insurance's approval to pay for the shots. I didn't want your chemo delayed by weeks. I insisted I'd pay for your shots." Harris remembered how unhappy he was that Dr.

Richardson didn't see Lindsay at her last appointments when her blood counts were too low for treatment. He was too busy, and the insurance wouldn't approve the injection shots until after Lindsay's white blood count increased on its own.

"Harris, she said the cost is over five thousand a shot. I've already had two, and I'll have two more this weekend. I'm glad you didn't pay for my shots."

"If you'd gotten a shot two weeks ago, you might not have had this pain. I understood not having a shot the first week with you having low platelets and low white blood count. I know they assumed your count would improve by the next week. When it was only your low white blood count the second week, they should've given you a shot instead of continually playing this waiting game."

"And I didn't like that the nurse practitioner said I'd get an injection the second week. Then I didn't." Lindsay moved slightly away from him. "As much as I love leaning against you, I'm going to try resting on my side."

"I can't believe it's your third week of not having chemo treatments and you're finally getting your shots." Harris felt like he'd failed her when he hadn't been able to help her keep her white blood count high enough for chemo. It was unbelievable how low it had dropped. The truth was there wasn't anything you could eat to increase a white blood count. Chemo was definitely hard on the body.

As her eyes closed, Lindsay murmured, "The pain is a little less now but still bad."

"I'm going to get you an ice pack." He kissed her forehead. "I'll be right back."

"Thank you. You're too good to me."

"I wish I could take your discomfort away completely."

While he was getting the ice pack, Phoebe walked into the kitchen. "How's Mom?"

He glanced at the clock. "Did you get out early?"

"Friday is a short day for classes."

Although Phoebe had talked about living on campus for her first semester of graduate school, she decided to stay home. Harris knew Lindsay never encouraged her either way, but she'd told him she was secretly happy to have Phoebe home. He'd teased Lindsay, telling her she was a little like an Amish parent. They liked to keep their adult children at home until they married, and sometimes the young married couple lived with the Amish bride's parents.

Well, Phoebe won't be getting married anytime soon. She's focused on her studies. Amy isn't serious about anyone, but Jenna could be the first bride out of our triplets. She's enjoying dating Eli.

An hour later, Lindsay was asleep, so Harris and Phoebe went outside on the patio, carrying glasses of iced tea. "I have a favor to ask of you."

"Dad, I told you I'm fine with taking your name." She grinned. "Although, Phoebe Prescott might be a tad better sounding than Phoebe Manning."

Harris laughed. "Hey, there's no negotiation on this. I want you to have my last name. Your mom is all for it too."

"What is the favor then?"

"I want to propose to Lindsay, and I'd like your help in picking out the engagement ring."

Her mouth broke into a broad smile. "That's wonderful. You have to do this right and do a big gesture, like take her somewhere extra special when you propose. She's been through so much with having cancer."

"I don't have any place in mind, but I've thought about waiting until after her last chemo treatment is finished. With her delay in treatments, she might not be done until November." He rubbed his forehead. "I hate waiting until then. I love her, and we've wasted a lot of time already."

"Yikes, are you hoping for a short engagement? Do you think Mom will want to move to Cincinnati? You can't move here because of your practice."

He shrugged. "I don't know. I can move here and start a practice. We'll be engaged for several months. We can work everything out." He took a sip of his tea and wondered where he should propose to her. His mind was a blank until he remembered Lindsay saying how much she missed going to the beach this summer. He could plan a weekend over Labor Day, and they could fly to a beach.

Not the beach where they met, but a new spot. He grinned at Phoebe. "What do you think of me proposing to her on the beach?"

Phoebe's brown eyes widened. "That's perfect. We didn't get to go on our beach vacation this summer. She loves the ocean." She paused for a moment. "Just be sure to keep her safe, though. Her immune system is weakened from the cancer. I mentioned it once to Mom that it'd been a blessing we hadn't gone to the beach this summer."

"A beach setting might not be the best spot. I don't want Lindsay to become ill. You're probably thinking of the few people who have gotten flesh-eating bacteria while on the beach." He knew these unfortunate individuals had gotten small cuts and scrapes while enjoying the beach, and bacteria had entered the openings.

Phoebe stood. "I better go inside. Haley's coming over. I don't want her to wake up Mom. The beach is a good setting for you to propose. I'm sure you'll keep a good eye on her."

She went inside while Harris resigned to his thoughts. *The sunrise peeking over the ocean will be a fantastic time to propose. There will be fewer people awake when the sun is rising, so the beach will be more secluded and private. First, we'll have a cup of coffee on the deck or balcony. Lindsay loves her morning coffee. Then we'll head to the beach for a walk. I'll check out the beaches along Lake Michigan. Water is cooler there, so should be a safer spot for Lindsay. It won't be as far, and we can take a road trip instead of flying.*

~

Lindsay stared at Harris on his knees as he held a beautiful diamond ring. As much as she wanted to say yes, she couldn't ruin his life. She dug her toes deeper into the sand and tried to calm her nerves. "I love you, Harris, but I've seen what my cancer has done to you. I'm surprised you still have a practice. I can't marry you. What if I get cancer again? I can't put you through that."

He slowly stood. "Dr. Richardson said you might not get it again for years. It looks like you're going to be in complete remission. If it comes back, we'll deal with it."

Lindsay glanced away from Harris and saw how gorgeous the sunrise looked. He'd picked the perfect time and place to propose to her. She was touched he knew her so well. As she turned away toward him again, she noticed a photographer off in the distance. "Did you pay someone to take photos of us?"

He grinned. "Yes, I did."

"I'm impressed. You did a lot of planning. I thought it was sweet you wanted to come here for Labor Day weekend, but I didn't expect you to propose."

"How about I kneel again and you nod your head and say yes? We can have a long engagement to get you used to the idea that I'm committed to you for life. We'll have faith in God that you won't get cancer again. If you get it, I'll be next to your side anyhow, so it might as well be as your husband."

She stared for a moment at Harris. Lindsay saw how his brown eyes studied her with a hopeful look. He looked incredibly handsome in a white shirt and beige shorts. *I should put my trust in God… and in Harris.*

After a quick wave to the photographer, she gave the young man a thumbs up. Then she turned back to the guy she loved with her whole heart. "Okay, let's do this again."

Quickly, Harris kneeled. "I love you, Lindsay. Will you marry me?"

On Labor Day, Phoebe did the finishing touches on the food for the surprise engagement party. She expected her parents sometime in the afternoon. She glanced at everything on the counter to see if she'd forgotten anything. Paper plates, plastic silverware, cups, and napkins were at one end of the counter. Amy and Jenna had prepared the desserts while Phoebe had made the appetizers and finger sandwiches. Grandma Helen offered to bring a decorated cake to celebrate their engagement.

Amy smiled. "Everything looks festive. I love the blue-and-white balloons and streamers outside and the flower arrangements here in the house."

"I hope having the party already will be fine with Mom. Dad thought it was a good idea to have it now instead of waiting. If we'd mentioned it to her that we wanted to give them an engagement party, she'd tell us not to and that it was too much work for us." Phoebe had invited their friends a couple of weeks ago, feeling sure her mom would say yes to the proposal.

"Can you imagine if we had been raised together?" Amy stopped arranging oatmeal raisin cookies on a plate to look at Phoebe. "I'd probably be in college instead of studying for the GED. It's unfair we were separated, but I love Mom, and I know she did what was for the best at the time."

Phoebe continued putting crackers around a cheese ball. "You'll have your diploma soon. It hurt me that she kept you and Jenna a secret from me, but I understand why she did it. It had to be such a burden that she carried for years with missing you and Jenna."

Jenna put a plate of brownies on the counter. "I can't imagine not being raised in an Amish home. Amy, I wish you wouldn't keep thinking how better your life would've been if you'd been raised with Phoebe. I wish things could've been different, but we're together now. We're blessed with two sets of parents."

Amy frowned. "I'm sorry. I didn't mean to sound ungrateful about the life I had. I loved being raised by *Mamm* and *Daed*."

Jenna continued. "And I don't think Seth would've have been born if we hadn't been adopted. Look how *Mamm* and *Daed* were childless, then a pregnancy occurred after our adoption. That seems to happen with couples. They adopt, then they are blessed with their own biological child."

I wish Jenna hadn't mentioned Seth. I thought he might come to the party, but apparently, he's moved on with Veronica. That's for the best, Phoebe thought. "Well, it is what it is. We're here to celebrate a special time for our parents. I hope our guests will remember to park down the street so Mom doesn't see their cars."

Amy laughed. "I'm sure they will. You reminded everyone several times. You thought of everything. The party should definitely be a surprise for her."

At the sound of the doorbell, Phoebe went to the front door. She was pleased to see Michelle, Vickie, and their husbands. Haley and her family were behind them. Within minutes, the house was full of Harris's partners and church friends from Cincinnati. When their grandparents arrived, the girls realized all the guests were present for the party.

"This is exciting." Haley glanced at the food. "Oh my gosh, you have so much food, and it looks delicious."

Phoebe sipped her Coke. "You can go ahead and get a plateful of food. You better since you're taking pictures." Haley was a great photographer, so it was an easy decision to ask her to be in charge of taking photos. "I can't wait to see Mom's face when she gets here. She deserves happiness. And Dad does too."

Haley hugged her. "It doesn't get any better than this."

Chapter Twenty-Seven

As she stood in one of the church rooms, Lindsay couldn't believe it was her wedding day. She glanced at Roberta, who was lining up her bridal bouquet and the bridesmaids' flowers on a long table. She'd already pinned the flowers onto the groomsmen. Roberta was her wedding planner. She'd helped with everything and with teaching and recovering from chemo effects, Lindsay was grateful. Roberta said it was great practice for Haley's wedding next February to Scott.

A flutter of excitement raced through her. *Marrying Harris is finally going to happen.*

It'd been a year since she'd found her daughters Amy and Jenna, so that was one of the reasons she planned her wedding date for this month. Last June had been the start of her cherished memories with Harris and their triplets. If she hadn't been hit with cancer, would she have continued to put off telling the truth? Maybe. Or she could've finally broken her secret. As it turned out, she was thankful to God and to all the wonderful people who had prayed for her for months to go into remission. Her prayers and theirs had been answered. She was cancer-free. Her oncologist would schedule CT scans to keep an eye on it recurring. If it did, the cancer would be caught earlier so it wouldn't get to stage four again.

"Mom, you look deep in thought. You aren't going to be a runaway bride, are you?" Phoebe asked.

"I'd never do that." She squeezed Phoebe's hand. "I admit I had doubts after we were engaged, but Harris dissipated them."

"That's good because Dad sold his house in Cincinnati."

"I know. It was a shock when he decided to leave his Cincinnati practice." When Harris dissolved his part in his group practice, she felt relief that he'd found a practice to join in Columbus. "I'm happy to have my daughters as bridesmaids." Lindsay had considered asking Phoebe to be her maid of honor but thought it better not to single her out to have this honor. It would seem she loved Phoebe more than Amy and Jenna. The truth was that she did have a closer bond with Phoebe. It'd been the two of them for years.

Michelle was her matron of honor, and her son was the ring bearer. Harris's best man was one of his doctor partners, and his daughter was the flower girl.

"You're beautiful. I love your dress with the white lace and beading sequins. It looks so cool. It's a dress I'd love to wear on my wedding day if I ever get married," Phoebe said, shrugging her shoulders. "Even though Seth and I are back together, we don't see us getting married for a long time."

"You and Seth will figure it out. Keep praying for guidance about your lives." She touched a sequin on her dress, and said, "I'd love for you to wear my wedding gown. It was fun trying on dresses." It'd been a production full of laughter at the bridal shop with all her bridesmaids, Vickie, and Helen. Lindsay remembered how different her wedding to Paul was. Sure, she'd worn a white dress, but it had been her high school graduation dress. They'd gone to the courthouse and been married by a Justice of the Peace. Instead of a civil ceremony, she would marry Harris in her Protestant church with over two hundred guests in attendance.

Phoebe waved her hand at her sisters in the corner. "Jenna will be the next bride. She adores Eli. I wish I could be in their wedding, but I'll do something else to help."

Lindsay nodded. "I'm glad Katie agreed to allow Jenna and Amy to be in our wedding. Harris and his parents are thrilled too." She turned her head to look at Amy and Jenna. They wore the same light blue dresses as Phoebe and Michelle. The chiffon lace dresses were all floor-length with short sleeves. They wore simple white flats underneath the dresses. Jenna and Amy didn't wear prayer headings, but their hair was pulled back in buns. Phoebe wore hers the same way, but Michelle's hair was too short for this hairstyle.

Phoebe nodded. "I was surprised, but Amy reminded her mom they aren't baptized yet. Even though our dresses aren't plain, they are super conservative." She grinned. "And we're all dressed alike so none of us should stand out."

Lindsay had been tempted to buy earrings and necklaces for her attendants to wear with their dresses. The Amish never wore jewelry, so she decided to keep it simple and not purchase them. "I'm relieved Jenna's baptism classes don't start until after our wedding." Jenna and Eli planned on getting married in a year in an Amish wedding, so they needed to start taking their instructions. Jenna was disappointed her siblings were not joining her. Amy needed more time to take this step in their faith. Seth wanted to be with Phoebe, so he wasn't going to join until they both figured out what to do about their differences.

Roberta appeared by her side. She gently waved the veil at her. "Hey, girl, we better get your veil on your head. It's getting to be that time. Your future father-in-law is waiting right outside the door."

As Roberta attached the veil to her head, a flash of sadness entered her heart. For a moment, she yearned to have her own father walking her down the aisle. As a young child, her dad had been the center of her universe and the anchor holding their small family together. When he'd died from a heart attack, her mother hadn't been able to adapt to life without him. *I hadn't been enough for my mom. I was never important to her. Without my dad, Mom couldn't love me.*

She bit her lower lip.

Roberta frowned at her. "Don't chew on your lip. You don't need to be nervous. You look gorgeous. I hope Harris won't pass out when he sees you."

Katie stood beside Roberta and smiled. "I agree with Roberta. You look so *schee.* I'm happy for you and Harris."

"Thank you. And thanks again for the beautiful quilt you made for us. It's going to be perfect in our bedroom." Lindsay hugged Katie. She'd given them a quilt for a wedding gift. It was a double wedding ring design done in light and dark blues. Lindsay appreciated her recent kindness but felt Katie's heart had only softened toward her due to Jenna's news that she'd join the church.

"Amy and Jenna helped me with it, but I'm glad you like it. I think they'll be escorting Helen to her seat soon. I need to be seated before that happens, so I better leave."

After Katie quickly left the room, Amy came to her and hugged her gently. "I love you. I can't believe I'm going to be in an English wedding. I'm blessed to share your and dad's joy today."

"I love you too. It means so much to me you're in the wedding party."

"Amy, you're making Mom cry." Jenna stepped closer to her. "I feel like crying. I'm *froh,* too, that you and Dad are getting married."

Roberta handed bouquets to the triplets, then pulled a tissue out of her pocket and handed it to Lindsay. "I'm glad your makeup is waterproof. We better head out to the hallway. You all look beautiful."

Once the wedding party was lined up, Michelle turned around and said, "Here we go. You'll soon be Mrs. Harris Manning."

Lindsay nodded at her friend. "I'm definitely ready."

As she looped her arm through John's arm, he said, "I'm very honored to walk you down the aisle. I'm glad you asked me. I already think of you as my daughter. Helen and I wanted another child, preferably a girl, but it never happened." John kissed her on the cheek. "You and your daughters have enriched our lives so much. Seeing Harris happier than he ever has been is truly a blessing. We owe it all to you."

Lindsay wanted to say many things, but there wasn't time. The bridesmaids were already at the front of the church with Michelle taking her first steps down the aisle. "John, I'll always love Harris and you and Helen."

Roberta gave the ring bearer and flower girl a little nudge. "Okay, you two cuties. It's your turn. Don't forget to smile."

Before Lindsay and John took their steps, she stared at Harris, waiting at the altar for her. He looked handsome in a tailored gray suit, gray shirt, and a pale blue tie to match the bridesmaid's blue dresses. She hadn't wanted Harris, his father, and groomsmen to wear tuxes.

"Okay, Lindsay and John, you better start moving, or Harris will be meeting you halfway." Roberta chuckled.

Lindsay smiled. "I'm ready."

John said, "Let's do it."

Delicious Amish Cinnamon Bread

Ingredients

1 cup butter, softened

2 cups sugar

2 eggs

2 cups buttermilk or 2 cups milk plus 2 tablespoons vinegar
or lemon juice

4 cups flour

2 teaspoons baking soda

Cinnamon/sugar mixture:

2/3 cups sugar

2 teaspoons cinnamon

Directions

1. Preheat oven to 350 degrees.
2. Cream together butter, 2 cups of sugar and 2 eggs. Add
   milk, flour, and baking soda. Blend until completely com-
   bined.
3. Put 1/2 of the batter into two greased loaf pans (Basically
   pour 1/4 of the total batter into each pan.)
4. Mix in a small bowl the 2/3 cup of sugar and cinnamon.
   Sprinkle 3/4 of cinnamon mixture on the top of the batter in each pan.
5. Pour (or scoop) remaining batter to pans. Sprinkle with
   the remaining cinnamon mixture. Swirl with knife.
6. Bake for 45-50 minutes or until toothpick comes out
   clean.
7. Cool in pans for 20 minutes before removing from the
   pans.

Dear Reader

Thank you for reading *The Amish Mother's Secret*. When I started writing my character Lindsay, my inspiration came from a friend with lymphoma. I used many of the details of his illness for my character's cancer. Then an unbelievable thing happened to me. I was diagnosed with non-Hodgkin's lymphoma. I never expected to get cancer as it was not in my family history. I had severe pain from an enlarged spleen and made several trips to the ER and to an oncologist. No cancer was evident in the bloodwork. I think that was the beginning of my cancer. Though it hadn't appeared in my early blood tests.

It was hard telling my children I was diagnosed with stage four cancer. I rewrote the details in my manuscript so that my character reflected the type of lymphoma I had. I'm thankful to God I have been in remission.

When doing months of chemo treatments, I received thoughtful gifts, devotional books, and cards with wonderful Bible verses from friends and relatives. It helped me get through a difficult time in my life. I have the greatest readers and have appreciated all the prayers said for me to recover from cancer.

I enjoyed writing about the two mothers, Lindsay and Katie, in *The Amish Mother's Secret*. Both were from two different worlds, but their love never wavered for their children. God continued to work in their lives as they raised their daughters. Although giving two daughters to Katie and Roman broke Lindsay's heart, she knew adoption was the best choice for them. Writing about adoption was something I wanted to share in Lindsay's story. I hope the adoption aspect in the story line touched your heart.

Blessings,
Diane

Other Books by Diane Craver

Amish Fiction

Dreams of Plain Daughters Series
A Joyful Break, Book One
Judith's Place, Book Two
Fleeting Hope, Book Three
A Decision of Faith, Book Four

The Bishop's Daughters Series
Amish Baby Snatched, Book One ·
A Plain Widow, Book Two
Priscilla's Escape, Book Three
Christmas of Hope, Book Four
Anna In Love, Book Five ·

Amish Short Romances
An Amish Starry Christmas Night
An Amish Starry Summer Night

Christian Romance
Marrying Mallory
When Love Happens Again

Chick-Lit Mystery
A Fiery Secret

Contemporary Romance
Because of Whitney
Never the Same
The Proposal

Historical and Christian Fiction
A Gift Forever

About the Author

Diane graduated from The Ohio State University with a bachelor's degree. She met her husband, Tom, while teaching at an orphanage. They enjoy their life in Ohio and have been blessed with six children and several grandchildren. Diane started writing nonfiction and was published in *Woman's World* and *The Catholic Telegraph*. Later, she decided it would be a nice escape to write fiction. She wanted to keep her sanity in the midst of a large family. Two daughters, who were born with Down syndrome, live with them. Diane's favorite vacation is going to the beach with her family. She gives thanks for all her blessings, including being in remission from non-Hodgkin's lymphoma.

Diane is the author of Amish fiction, historical Christian fiction, inspirational contemporary romance, and chick-lit mystery. She is represented by literary agent Lesley Sabga of The Seymour Agency.

To connect with Diane, please visit www.dianecraver.com and www.facebook.com/Diane-Craver-153906208887

Diane loves to hear from her readers!

Acknowledgments

Thank you to my wonderful agent, Lesley Sabga, for believing in me. When she called and asked to represent me because she loved my voice, I felt like I had won the lottery. Lesley's work on my behalf has been a huge blessing.

Thank you to Dawn Carrington and the entire staff at Vinspire Publishing. I am thankful my book is with such an awesome publisher and look forward to continuing my writing career as a Vinspire author.

I am grateful to my family and friends for their prayers and continued support for my writing.

Thank you to my sweet husband, Tom, for all his love and belief in me through our many years together.

God has answered my prayers in too many ways to list, but I feel blessed by His unending and unconditional love for me.

Plan Your Next Escape!

What's Your Reading Pleasure?

Whether it's captivating historical romance, intriguing mysteries, young adult romance, illustrated children's books, or uplifting love stories, Vinspire Publishing has the adventure for you!

For a complete listing of books available, visit our website at www.vinspirepublishing.com.

Like us on Facebook at
www.facebook.com/VinspirePublishing

Follow us on Twitter at
www.twitter.com/vinspire2004

Follow us on Instagram at
www.instagram.com/vinspirepublishing

We are your travel guide to your next adventure.

CPSIA information can be obtained
at www.ICGtesting.com
Printed in the USA
BVHW030818150223
658491BV00002B/319